BLOOD
An Evil Dead MC Story

NICOLE JAMES

BLOOD
AN EVIL DEAD MC STORY

NICOLE JAMES

Published by Nicole James
Copyright 2017 Nicole James
All Rights Reserved
Cover Art by Viola Estrella
Cover Photography: Reggie Deanching / R+M Photography
Cover Model: Connor Smith
Back Photography: Egmont Strigl / Tradebit
Editing by CookieLynn Publishing

PROLOGUE

Blood lay chained to the filthy iron cot, his wounds
burning like fire. The room was like an oven in the heat of
the humid New Orleans afternoon. He knew it had to be late
afternoon by the angle of the sunlight coming through the
slats of the louvered shutters covering the windows. But that
wasn't the only reason the sweat was pouring off him; his
fever was spiking as the infection took hold.

He heard the lock on the door rattle, and looked toward
the sound, trying to focus. A man shoved a woman into the
room ahead of him. He remembered the man—a sadistic son
of a bitch—but they'd never brought a woman in before.

He tried hard to make sense of what he was seeing, but
she was just a pale green blur. Were those hospital scrubs?
He knew the fever was starting to mess with his mind. It had
to be, because when she hesitantly approached him, her
blessedly cool hand pressed to his forehead, and he looked up
into the face of an angel.

Was she coming to take him to heaven?

A laugh bubbled up inside him. Heaven? More likely hell is where he'd be going.

CHAPTER ONE

"Heard a rumor the other day."

Blood straightened from his shot at the pool table to look over at Undertaker. "Yeah, what's that?"

The President of the Evil Dead MC's New Orleans Chapter clutched the pool cue in his hands and studied the table. "There's word circulating around that the Death Heads are looking to patch over one of the smaller clubs near the Texas State Line."

"Ain't one of 'em worth a shit. All they'll be patching over is a bunch of pussies." Blood moved to the small high-top table and grabbed his beer. After finishing it off, he looked across the clubhouse to the bar and signaled the Prospect to bring them another round.

Undertaker grinned at Blood's blunt description, but held back his remark.

Blood pointed at him with the mouth of his empty bottle. "Fuck those Texas bastards. What's the bug up their ass this time?"

"We'll deal with them once we have all the information. I don't like to go off half-cocked." Undertaker sank the last ball on the table and moved to stand with Blood. He picked up the cigarette in the ashtray and took a drag, his eyes focusing on Blood through the smoke. "The trouble between our clubs goes back a long way. Back twenty years ago when Skeeter ran this club, and a guy named Buckeye ran the Death Heads in Texas.

"A couple of our guys were riding down I-10 with their old ladies on the back. A vehicle pulled alongside and fired a shotgun at them. The bikes went down. One of the girls was killed. We retaliated. They claimed it wasn't them."

"I've heard the story."

"Let me make my point. I was the one who handled the retaliation, and I did time for it. Come to find out, it wasn't the Death Heads that day; it was some hippie-hating rednecks in a pickup truck out for a joyride. I did what I did and paid the price for it. I've had to get right with that in my head. Choices I made, they changed everything. I let it eat at me for a long time; it affected everything I did, every decision I made. My point is, if we don't deal with the past, we can't move forward."

Blood nodded, still not sure what Undertaker was getting at, unless he was trying to tell Blood there were things he needed to deal with in his own past.

"You're a smart man, Blood. The smartest on my crew. You're quick to pick up on shit, always cut through the bullshit to see the heart of the problem. You can read people like a book. But sometimes its ourselves we have the hardest time seeing clearly."

"You about to bust my balls for something?"

"Not at all."

"What then?"

Undertaker shook his head like he wasn't going to answer... or had decided better of it. "You know you're like a son to me, right? Have been since the day I pulled you out from under the thumb of that piece-of-shit old man of yours."

His old man. Most days Blood tried not to think about him. He nodded, his eyes on the green felt of the pool table a long moment before they swung to the man who was so much more than his father had ever been. "You know I know that. You. This club. They're everything to me. The man I am today—that's got fuck to do with my shitty childhood. I'm a man because you made me one."

The corner of Undertaker's mouth pulled up, his eyes filling with what Blood knew was the love of a father for a son. Maybe Blood wasn't really his, but it sure felt like it. The man had always treated him like he was, and if he didn't quite buy Blood's denial of the effects his childhood had on him, the man let it go.

Undertaker took his right fist and tapped his chest, just over his heart and held out his knuckles to Blood.

Blood did the same, tapping his fist to his heart and bumping fists with his President. It was a sign of love, loyalty, and respect—something every brother in this chapter felt for each other.

"Evil Dead. First, last, and always," Blood spoke the club's motto.

"First, last, and always," Undertaker repeated back in a gravely voice then pulled Blood in for a hug and several pounding back slaps. He said in his ear, "Till I go to my grave, Brother."

***

Two beers later, Blood wandered outside the clubhouse where a group of his brothers stood. The air reeked of weed.

Sandman was saying, "Guys, I told you this story…"

Blood grinned as he lit up a cigarette, blew the smoke up toward the starry night sky, and said, "Guys this is your chance to say 'yes, you *did* tell us this story.'"

The men all chuckled.

"Fuck off," Sandman said, giving him a dirty look.

Blood blew him a kiss and asked, "What are we up to boys?"

"Talkin' about pussy," Bam-Bam said with a chuckle. "And who was the youngest when they lost their virginity."

Blood laughed at the joke, knowing full well they weren't talking about either of those things.

Sandman lit up a joint and took a long toke, then blew the smoke in the air and passed the joint to Easy. "I need to get me a woman."

"Get hitched," Easy suggested.

"Tried that. Twice. Bad idea, both times."

Bam-Bam asked, "What ever happened to that last broad you were with, Sandman?"

"I dumped her ass. She was creepin' me out."

"How so?"

"Let's just say she lives on the corner of Hoodoo and Voodoo."

Easy choked on the toke he was taking, his eyes watering with laughter. "Well, *she* sounds like a keeper."

Blood snorted. "You sure can pick 'em."

Sandman continued, "I'm talkin' potions, voodoo dolls, the whole freakin' shebang."

"Bet she's got a doll with your name on it." Easy passed the joint on.

Mud took it and observed, "Maybe that's why your knee's been bothering you, Sandman. She stuck a pin in it."

Blood replied with a grin, "Nah, if she stuck a pin, it'd be higher and to the left."

Sandman looked down at his crotch and paled. "Shit, man, don't fuckin' joke about that. *Fuck.*"

They all burst out laughing at Sandman's sudden unease.

"Remember that time Sandman brought that chick from Mississippi around?"

"The one he caught Bam-Bam with behind the shed?"

Easy chuckled. "Beat the shit out of him that night."

"Hey, in my defense, he hadn't claimed her."

The men laughed. "Only cost you a broken finger and two front teeth. Was she worth it?"

"Fuck no," both men said in unison.

Blood shook his head, trying to hide his smile while the rest guffawed.

"Here's to sweaty sex and bloody brawls!" Bam-Bam held his beer in the air.

"Here, here." Blood clinked his bottle with his brothers. That's what this club meant to him. No—it was more than that. Much more. It was brotherhood and family and *home*.

His gaze strayed over the compound and past the line of bikes parked along the side of the building.

Speaking of sweaty sex, Blood thought as he took a deep drag off his smoke and eyed the dark haired beauty standing over with the girls. Her eyes connected with his as he assessed her. She had thick long hair—perfect for wrapping around his hand—and long legs—perfect for wrapping around his hips. She was dressed in a tank top and shorts that barely covered her ass. He'd seen her at clubhouse parties once or twice—caught her checking him out before, too. Didn't think she had hooked up with anyone in the club yet. Maybe she was holding out for one brother in particular. Maybe, by the look in her eyes, that brother was him. He slowly blew the smoke toward the sky, his gaze still on her. Hell, he needed a good fuck. Why not take what she was offering? He flung what was left of his smoke into the night and stalked toward her. He didn't pause to chitchat or return the greetings some of the women gave him.

"Hey, Blood."

"How's it goin', Blood?"

He didn't say a single word, just clamped his hand around her wrist and tugged her through the parking lot and around the building. She had the good sense not to question him as she quick-stepped behind him. Perhaps she'd been paying attention, perhaps she'd studied him, knew he didn't like a lot of talk, knew just what she could expect from him.

Blood took what he wanted; he didn't debate it, didn't negotiate it, and didn't waste time seducing it.

He kept going, leading her straight to the shed in back where the brothers all did repair work on their bikes. It was a wood building with a concrete floor. He yanked open the door, flicked on the lights, and pulled her inside. Kicking the door shut, his eyes glanced over the interior. There was one bike up on the bike lift, half torn apart. The surrounding walls held several workbenches. There were two bikes waiting for repairs. His gaze locked on the last bike. The Street Bob on the end would suit his needs.

He pulled the girl to him, catching her face in his hands and bringing her mouth up to his. As he drove his tongue inside, he walked her backward toward the bike. When she bumped against it, his hands went to the hem of the Harley tank she wore and, in one smooth movement, pulled it over her head and tossed it aside. It landed on the side mirror, where it dangled. His eyes hit her pushup bra—pretty little rhinestones set in lace. *Nice*. He appreciated the effort and wondered if she'd dressed with him in mind, but he didn't waste too much time admiring it, and he didn't spew any flowery compliments either. With a flick of his fingers the fastening popped free, and he tossed it aside as well. It landed over the handlebars of the Fat Boy one bike over.

Nice rack, pale skin, and pretty pink nipples. He bent, his mouth latching onto one while he took the other between his thumb and fingers and pinched until she moaned and her fingers threaded through his hair to pull his face closer. His mouth moved to the other side, giving it equal attention.

Her tits were nice, but what he really wanted was to sink his dick in her pussy. Wasting little time, his hands went to the waistband of her shorts, and a moment later he was yanking them down her thighs. Then he spun her, sunk his fist into her silky hair, and shoved her down over the seat of the bike.

He undid his pants and pulled out his dick. His fingers found her pussy, sliding inside to find her wet.

"You ready?" he growled. Two short words. That's all he gave her. He hadn't come in here to talk, and if she'd come with him for more than a quick fuck, she'd misjudged him.

She nodded under the fist that was still tight in her hair.

He lined up and drove into her with a thrust that had her going up on her toes. Her back arched, but he held her down, keeping her chest pinned to the seat. He smacked one cheek. "Keep that pretty ass in the air."

He thrust into her, over and over again.

She clung to the bike and melted against it.

He smacked her ass again, harder this time. "Up on your toes. Show me how bad you want me to fuck you."

She complied, and he felt a tremor in her legs.

"You're gonna take it as hard as I want to give it, right?" he growled as he released her hair and gripped his big hands around her hipbones. She nodded as his eyes moved over her body. She was thin, but she had a round ass—a *spank-able* ass—the kind he liked. He could see his handprint standing out in red against her pale skin, and the sight of it spurred him on.

He plowed into her, smacking her ass again, and felt her clench down around him, moaning. The girl liked it a little rough. Good, because that's how he liked to give it. But it wasn't enough. He wanted her to come apart, he wanted to feel her come all over his dick as she exploded in orgasm.

His hand dipped between her legs, his fingers searching out that little trigger while his other palm pressed the small of her back down, holding her pinned like a butterfly for him. He played with her, toying until she was bucking like a wild thing, begging him for more.

He adjusted his stroke until he knew by her reaction he was driving into her g-spot. He clenched his jaw, holding himself in tight control, not about to come before the lady. That was one thing he never did, no matter how little the girl meant to him. He always made sure they got theirs.

Slowly, she began to pant. He grinned. He loved hearing that sound—the one a woman made right before she came. He kept at her, driving that spot and stroking that little trigger until she exploded into orgasm, moaning her pleasure.

He let up then, but only to clamp his hands around her hips and drive into her in a frenzy until he felt his own release coming on like a freight train. Just before he spilled into her, he pulled out, took his dick in one hand and came all over her ass and the small of her back, milking it until the very last drop.

His breathing was labored, and his legs were weak as he tucked himself back inside his jeans. He grabbed a red shop rag and wiped the mess from her skin. There would be no little accidents for him. No unwanted babies some bitch could try to pin on him like he'd seen happen to so many of his brothers. He tossed the rag in an old oil drum and stepped back.

The girl stood and turned, pulling her lace panties and shorts up as he tossed her tank back at her.

"Leave the bra here," he ordered.

She frowned. "What?"

He stared until she slipped her tank on over her naked breasts. He grabbed the bra off the handlebars and, with a swing of his arm, sent it into the rafters of the shed. He watched her eyes lift to the collection already hanging haphazardly up there like leftover Mardi Gras beads.

She was nothing special—just one in a long line. He'd just made that clear to her and hadn't needed to say a harsh word to do it. That's the way he liked it. He didn't need any of these bitches thinking just because he fucked them they owned a piece of him. Not gonna happen, sweetheart. But he didn't need to be unnecessarily cruel, either.

He led her outside the shed, flicking the light off and closing the door. Then he pulled her close, kissing her. Pulling back, he looked down into her face. "You've got a real sweet ass, babe, and I liked playing with you. You want to play with me again, I'm all about it, but that's all I'm offering. Don't go setting your sights on me for anything more, understand?"

He studied her eyes as she looked up into his face, and he could tell she didn't like the boundaries he'd just laid out but nodded anyway, apparently willing to take what she could get.

"Good. Glad we got that cleared up. You want a beer?"

She smiled. "Okay."

"Okay." He looped an arm around her shoulders and led her toward the clubhouse.

***

The moon was high in the sky when Blood lifted his big black Harley off its kickstand and fired it up. He twisted the throttle, and his tires crunched on the gravel as he rolled slowly across the lot. With a nod to the Prospect standing guard, he pulled out through the wooden gate and headed home.

The clubhouse was located in Slidell, across Lake Pontchartrain from New Orleans. He headed down Hwy 11 to cross the lake at the old Maestri Bridge or Five Mile Bridge, as most called it. He preferred it to the newer I-10 Twin Span Bridge built just to the east which had been virtually destroyed in 2005 by Hurricane Katrina. The Five Mile Bridge, built back in 1928 was concrete, and its sturdy construction had stood up to the onslaught, leaving it largely undamaged and the only route to New Orleans after the storm until repairs were finally completed on the other.

The cool night air felt good on his face as he crossed over the Pontchartrain. It was peaceful with just the calm water below him and a sky full of stars above. He loved making the trip across this bridge on beautiful nights like this. Just him and his bike rumbling under him as the wind rolled over him. It gave him a few minutes of peace, and his mind wandered back to what Undertaker had said tonight.

Death Heads poaching across the state line was trouble they didn't need. But if trouble came, they'd handle it. *He'd* handle it. No one was going to fuck with his club.

Reaching the other side, he veered left, picking up Chef Hwy, which took him up through the neighborhoods on the east side. Little Saigon, the boys referred to it as, where thousands of Vietnamese refugees sponsored by the Catholic Church had settled after the fall of Saigon in 1974. They'd taken to the similar climate, many with fishing skills finding work on the shrimp boats.

Blood rolled up through Chalmette, past the refinery district on his left and on up where it bordered the lower ninth ward on his right. He followed it up through the seventh ward and Marigny. Making the final turn curving around onto N. Rampart Street, rolling into the Quarter at just past midnight.

A couple more turns and he was almost home.

Around the corner from his place, he spotted a girl standing on the street corner. She was young, scantily dressed, and obviously working the streets in this section where no tourist ventured. In this part of town, on the outskirts of the Quarter, if you went one block in the wrong direction, you were likely to get robbed, if not worse. The parking garage two blocks down had shootings on a weekly basis.

Blood was familiar with most of the girls who worked this area; he knew them all on sight. He never made use of their services—Blood had all the women he could want at the snap of his fingers.

This one was young—too young—and probably a runaway, naïve, and desperate. This city would chew her up and spit her out. A lot of girls like her ended up either strung out on drugs, dead in an alley of an overdose, or used up, their lifeless body dumped out in the swamp somewhere, never to be found.

Blood eyed the girl and wondered if John and the man he worked for already had their hooks in this one like they did every other girl in this part of town.

A girl didn't last long on the streets of this town without a pimp getting a hold of her, and in this part of town there was only one.

Blood coasted to the curb beside her and watched her eyes skate over him and his bike as she approached, obviously thinking him a customer. He watched her long legs and heels eat up the ten feet between them.

"You lonely, sugar?" she purred in a sexy voice designed to reel him in as one hand seductively twirled her auburn curls.

The corner of Blood's mouth lifted. "You new in town, kitten?"

She smiled. "Kitten. I like that."

"What's your name?"

"Anything you want it to be, Mister. I'll be your kitten, if that's what you want." Her head dipped, her eyes going over his bike, probably sizing up how much she thought he might be worth and adjusting her price accordingly.

He reached out and tilted her chin up, bringing her gaze

back to his. "Asked you a question. Didn't hear an answer."

She swallowed, her eyes getting big at his no-nonsense tone, and replied softly, "Ivy. It's Ivy.

"Ivy." His eyes moved over her face. "You got a last name, Ivy?"

"Reynolds."

"Where's home, Ivy Reynolds?"

"Ninth Street."

"No. Where's *home*?"

She sucked her lips in, her eyes searching his before apparently deciding it wouldn't be smart to lie to him. "Iowa."

"Iowa. That's a long way. What brought you to New Orleans, Ivy from Iowa?"

"I got sick of cornfields."

Blood grinned. "I can understand that. But this isn't Oz. If you're looking for over-the-rainbow, you won't find it in this town. Think you probably already figured that out, didn't you?"

She stayed mute, but nodded.

"This isn't a safe town for a young girl." He studied her eyes, then lifted his chin. "Black Jack get a hold of you yet?"

Black Jack Boudreaux was the local crime boss—he ran all the sex trade in this parish and ran a good portion of the drug trade pouring in through the port as well.

She shook her head and answered softly, "John."

"John." Blood nodded. Black Jack's right hand man. Blood knew him well. He kept the girls in line and did all Black Jack's dirty work. Blood glanced up the street. "He been around tonight?"

"Not yet."

"You should go back to Iowa, Ivy. This isn't a life you want. You won't survive it. None of you girls ever do. And I've seen a bunch."

"I can't."

He nodded. "You only think you can't." He paused, studying her. She looked thin, but she didn't look like she'd fallen into the drug trap yet. "He takin' all you make?"

She glanced down the street and then back to him, admitting, "Most of it."

"You got money to eat?"

She looked away, and he knew she didn't. He dug a twenty out of his hip pocket and held it out to her. "Get yourself some chow."

Taking it, she glanced around the street again fearfully.

Blood's eyes followed, then on impulse, he dug in his vest and pulled out a pen. Clicking it, he took her hand and yanked it toward him to scribble his number on her palm. He released her, saying, "You get in trouble or change your mind about that bus ticket, call me. I'll do what I can."

She looked at the scrawl, and then those too-innocent green eyes lifted to his as she nodded.

"Take care, Ivy." Blood twisted his throttle, gunning his engine before dropping the bike into gear and pulling away, roaring down the street. At the corner, he took a right and rolled down an alleyway barely wider than his handlebars. He turned into a quiet courtyard and climbed from his bike. Then he took the outside staircase to his second floor apartment.

He let himself in, tossing his helmet and shit on the couch. His place was small, but quaint. He kept it neat—a direct contrast to the homes of some of his brothers. There were no overflowing ashtrays or empty beer cans at Blood's place. He hated clutter.

His place was old, with a lot of French Quarter character, and he loved it.

He grabbed a beer and strode out onto the wrought-iron balcony that overlooked the courtyard, but also had a view through the alleyway to the corner across the street.

He sat on a metal chair and leaned back, putting his booted feet up on the railing. Then he reached over to the little glass-topped table where he kept a pack of cigarettes and a lighter, and he lit one up.

He blew the smoke toward the starry night sky.

The sounds of Bourbon Street blues and jazz carried through the streets of the Quarter to his ears. Bougainvillea vines climbed his neighbor's intricate ironwork, the fuchsia petals blowing in the warm night breeze, carrying with it an intoxicating combination of the pink blossoms as well as jasmine and honeysuckle.

Blood's thoughts soon drifted back to the dark haired girl he'd fucked earlier.

He thought about his life. In some ways he was more than satisfied. He loved his brothers, loved his club and the life it had given him. He ran the pads of his fingers absently over the embroidered patches of the letters that ran down the front of his vest. *DFFD*. It stood for, Dead Forever, Forever

Dead, as in the Evil Dead MC. It represented the commitment he and his brothers had to their club and to each other. That club meant everything to him. It had saved him in so many ways—taught him what it was to be a man. Not the kind his father was, but a man a brother would want to stand beside proudly. That kind of respect was earned; it wasn't given out of fear of a beating, like his father had always seemed to believe. Yes, he loved his club and the brothers it had given him.

He thought about Undertaker's words. Nothing was going to threaten his club, not while he drew breath. He'd defend it and his brothers with his dying breath. It had become his life's meaning, his only goal. And if new trouble was stirring, then he'd devote every ounce in him to seeing it was squashed like a bug. He owed Undertaker no less.

Yes, in many ways, he had everything he'd ever wanted. Brothers at his back, men he could depend on, men he'd die for, and knew, without a shadow of a doubt, they'd die for him.

His eyes moved around his home. He had a place he loved in a part of the city he loved and a motorcycle parked in the courtyard he'd built from the ground up. It was sleek, mean, and badass. And it was his baby.

Yes, he had a lot to be grateful for in his life, but something was still missing. He knew it when he saw what some of his brothers had. Shades with Undertaker's daughter, Skylar, Ghost with Jessie… They'd found that special one, that so-called soul mate, and he was happy for them, but he envied them, too. He wondered if maybe that kind of happiness just wasn't in the cards for him. A woman you could come home to, murmur in the dark about your day to, cuddle with as the dawn broke. One who'd have your back through the dark times when everything went to shit, laugh with you through the good times… Someone to bring you back to earth when your head got too big. Someone to share memories with, build a life with, start a family with. That had never interested him before.

He huffed out a laugh. *Hell, no.*

For a long time now, he'd thought of women as just things to be used, never trusted. His father had drilled that into him from an early age. Women couldn't be counted on. They bailed at the first sign of hard times. And one woman in particular from his past had emotionally scarred him so badly he didn't know if he could ever trust another. That had been his experience, and he'd lived by it all his adult life.

Until he began to see some truly good women come into the lives of some of his brothers and how those women had made them better men. They didn't make them weaker; they didn't tear them down, lie, cheat, and steal from them. No, they made them stronger. They shared a real relationship with some of his brothers; a bond that was rock solid and couldn't be shaken no matter what life threw at them.

Blood would never have believed that was possible, not in a fucking million years, until he'd witnessed it, seen it with his own eyes. That unicorn did exist.

But Blood had a hard time reconciling any of that with the way he'd been brought up. It flew in the face of everything he'd ever been taught by his old man. And yes, he knew the man was a son-of-a-bitch, but he'd been Blood's only male role model during his formative years. Whether it was right or not, those seeds had been planted, taken root, and grown like a choking vine that consumed everything, pushing out all the good. Blood fought them back daily, trying to contain them like some spreading Kudzu vine that couldn't be killed.

He'd watched his brothers closely, seen the way some of them truly had partners in the women they'd found.

Now that he'd seen it, he realized that as uncharacteristic as it may be, he couldn't help but admit to himself, if no one else, he wanted it, too.

But hell, the women he met, the women who hung around his club? While there were some good women, none of them were that special one. Not for him. None of them were anyone he couldn't live without or who had that something extra that could turn around his way of thinking and make a lie of everything his father had drilled into him. So he took what he needed from them and never looked back.

Gazing up at the stars now, he wondered if any of it would ever be in the cards for him.

A sound caught his attention: a woman's scream. It echoed off the buildings and had him dropping his booted feet from the rail and peering to look between the brick walls framing the alleyway.

Across the street, on the corner, he spotted two girls— one was Ivy, the other a girl he recognized as Cherry. She'd worked that street for six months now—just another runaway Blood had tried to convince to go home. He was always trying to run them off from the clutches of Black Jack and his men. Because watching that son-of-a-bitch get his hooks in them, use them up, and throw them away like yesterday's garbage, had eaten at him. It got under his skin like nothing ever had. He'd been unable to sit still for that shit, so he'd made up his mind to do something about it. More times than not he failed, but once in a while he succeeded, and it drove the man crazy.

Blood enjoyed nothing more. Anything he could do to thwart that bastard was well worth it. He only wished they'd all get on buses back to places like Iowa, Indiana, and Illinois.

His eyes zeroed in on the commotion taking place on the street corner. A guy was hassling them, twisting Ivy's arm. When Cherry tried to intercede, the guy pulled a knife.

Blood stood, flinging his cigarette into the night. Where the hell was their damn pimp, John? He usually watched them like a hawk, especially when he was turning out a fresh one.

The punk slashed his blade in the air toward Cherry in an effort to keep her back while he tried to drag Ivy to a car. When Ivy tried to fight him off, he slammed the butt of the knife into the side of her face, stunning her into submission, and continued dragging her toward the waiting vehicle.

Poaching new talent—that's what this guy was doing. Grabbing girls off the street to work the Ninth Ward or down by the docks or out by the oil refinery. Black Jack and John might not be a girl's dream boss but they were head and shoulders above what was in store for these girls in the low-income sections this guy probably intended to take them.

Blood vaulted over his balcony railing to the staircase landing, taking the remaining stairs three at a time. Then he sprinted across the courtyard and down the alleyway. He had his gun drawn as he darted across the street, coming up behind the girl's attacker.

Blood brought the butt of his gun down on the guy's head, dropping him like a ton of bricks. Before the guy realized what was happening, his knife clattered across the sidewalk.

The girls screamed as a shot rang out from the driver of the vehicle.

Blood spun and fired back.

Bam! Bam! Bam! Bam!

The red Cadillac, with its twenty inch chrome rims, squealed off from the curb with four new bullet holes in the side, compliments of Blood.

He looked down at the piece of garbage sprawled at his feet, out cold, then his eyes lifted to the girls. Ivy was a trembling wreck, her hand holding her battered face. Cherry was calmer, having been on the streets longer.

Blood moved to Ivy, brushing the hair off her cheek to reveal the knot already swelling and turning purple, a gash in the center.

"I'm okay." Her glassy eyes met his.

"Where is he?" Blood snapped at Cherry, the tick in his jaw betraying the fury vibrating through him.

She shrugged nonchalantly, but she knew what he was asking. "John's been busy with other stuff."

"Maybe you need to find yourself a new pimp," he suggested with a glare.

"You know Black Jack owns the Quarter." She moved to Ivy, putting her arm around the shaking girl.

Blood stepped back and lifted his chin, ordering Cherry, "Take her and get out of here before that Caddy circles back around for this asshole." He kicked the man at his feet and then looked up at Ivy. "Think about what I said, kitten."

He watched them hustle down the street and around the corner, disappearing into the darkness. Then his eyes slid to the right, down the street two blocks over where Black Jack's compound was located.

Cherry's words came back to him. *John's been busy.* Blood wondered what he was busy with. What could be more important than taking care of his inventory? Whatever it was, it had something to do with Black Jack. Blood had no doubt about that, and he suddenly felt the need to find out what that could be, because keeping tabs on what Black Jack was up to was never a bad idea.

Blood strode up the street.

Two blocks down, he turned and headed down a dark alley that ran along the back of Black Jack's compound. Rounding the corner, the sight that met his eyes had him stopping dead in his tracks. There, looking just as surprised to see him as he was to see them, were four members of the Death Heads MC standing next to their bikes.

What the ever-loving fuck?

Death Heads ran out of Texas. They rarely ever crossed into Louisiana, let alone all the way east to New Orleans.

This was Evil Dead territory, and they knew it.

The four men glanced over at him. Everyone stood frozen in shock for a split second. And then, before he could pull his gun, a shot rang out, and he felt a bullet tear through his side. A split second later, something slammed into his head from behind and everything went dark as he sank to the ground.

CHAPTER TWO

The four men stood over the slumped body of the Evil Dead MC patch holder.

"Holy shit. Greasy, what the fuck is he doing here?" one of them asked, stunned.

"Stoner, check the street. Maybe he isn't alone." Greasy jerked his head toward the corner the man had come around.

"Didn't hear no bike," Stoner replied.

"That don't mean shit," Greasy snapped back, his irritation showing. "Move."

Stoner moved off to check.

"Ratchet, pull his wallet," Greasy ordered another one of his men.

The man squatted down and dug through his pockets, coming up with a wallet. He flipped it open, snagging the bills.

"Who is he?" Greasy growled from where he stood over the prone body.

Ratchet pulled his license and studied it in the

moonlight. Then he passed it to Greasy.

"Fucking hell," Greasy bit out as he examined it. His eyes flicked up to Ratchet. "Who the hell told you to shoot him? Did you kill him?"

Ratchet put two fingers to the carotid artery in the man's neck. "Don't think so."

"You better fucking hope not. Snake will kill you if you fuck up this deal he's trying to make, at least until it's locked down."

"What are we gonna do with him?"

Greasy jerked his chin. "You and Critter pick him up and throw him in the van. Take him to the stash house 'til we figure it out."

"Why don't we just dump him? Or better yet, leave him here?" Critter suggested, staring down at the man.

"No way. He may be useful."

***

Greasy tossed his cards on the scarred wooden table, not about to bet another dime on his piece-of-shit hand. He glanced around the dingy two-story shotgun row house they'd been holed up in with their captive for the last two days. Place didn't even have a goddamn television.

"You're folding?" asked Stoner.

"Yeah, dimwit, I'm folding. What was your first clue?"

Stoner grinned over at the man across the table. "Guess that just leaves you and me, bro."

Greasy stood, grabbed the bottle of Jack off the table,

and headed toward the aging window AC unit—the only one in this rattrap. He'd be glad when their business in New Orleans was finished, and he could head back to Texas.

At least there you could catch a breeze once in a while, and you didn't have all this stifling humidity that could suck the breath from a man's lungs. Yeah, he couldn't wait to scrape the mildew of this town off of his boots.

Ratchet tromped down the stairs. "We got problems, boss."

Christ. What now? This whole trip had been one clusterfuck after another. "Well, what?" he snapped. "You gonna tell me or am I supposed to guess?"

"He's worse, burning with fever. I think infection is setting in. If you got plans, better do something about it quick; his usefulness isn't gonna last much longer."

"Well, maybe if you hadn't shot him that wouldn't be the case, you moron."

Ratchet stared at him, stone-faced. Hell, the man probably felt no remorse—not even for causing his club this problem—but what did he expect from a known sociopath.

"Just stay the fuck away from him. Hear me?"

"Sure."

The man had agreed readily enough, but Greasy knew Ratchet had been up there tormenting the man like he'd caught him doing repeatedly since they'd brought him here. The man took pleasure in it, too. Greasy didn't give a damn, other than it was probably making the situation worse, and now he had to deal with it, goddamn it. He pulled his phone out and made the call he dreaded.

***

Snake pulled his phone out and put it on speaker. He barked, "Yeah?"

"We got a problem."

Snake glanced around the empty lot behind an abandoned manufacturing building on Bienvenue Street. "Swear to God, Greasy, you better not tell me that fucker escaped."

"Nope, but he's getting worse. Fast."

"Fucking hell."

"Needs medical attention. Like now."

"And what the fuck do you want me to do—pull a doctor out of my ass? Hijack a paramedic wagon? Kidnap a goddamn nurse?"

"We could dump him off at a hospital. We'd have to give him up, but at least we wouldn't have killed him. What with the deal you're trying to make, don't figure that would go over too well."

"Motherfucker, I'm not dumping him anywhere! He stays where he's at."

"He's gonna slip into convulsions… and then a coma."

"Oh, so now you're a fucking expert?"

"Just seen it before. My kid sister."

Fuck. Snake felt like shit. He'd forgotten that when Greasy was a kid, his piece-of-shit parents had been too strung out on drugs to get their six-year-old daughter to a doctor. Greasy had watched her die from fever when he was just ten years old.

"Sorry, man. I'll figure something out." Snake slid his phone into his pocket and glanced up at his two Brothers and the lowlife drug dealer who owed the club a grand. "Where were we?"

"We were about to beat this asshole to death with a lead pipe," his Brother reminded him with a grin.

Snake grinned back at Bagger's exaggeration. "Oh, right."

"Wait. You need a nurse? I know one," the man pleaded, his hands up.

Snake cocked his head to the side. This wouldn't be the first time some loser facing a beating—or worse—had offered up something in trade for sparing his life. "Do you now?"

Bagger crossed his arms. "This ought a be good."

"Swear to God. My sister-in-law."

"Your sister-in-law."

"Well, used to be."

"You live in Texas. We don't have time to drive back and get her."

"She's here in New Orleans. Not far."

That got his attention. "And she'd help us?"

"She'll do whatever I fucking tell her."

Snake grinned. "Good answer. Maybe you have your uses still."

CHAPTER THREE

Catherine Randall stood at the nurse's station, shuffling through the charts. Her long tawny hair was pulled back in a ponytail that hung like corn silk all the way to her waist. Her delicate features held very little makeup, but her big blue eyes with their long lashes needed no more than just a bit of mascara, and that was usually all she wore.

"Aren't you supposed to be gone, Cat?" Deloris asked from her seat at the computer.

Catherine flipped the chart she'd been studying closed and looked at the watch on her wrist. She hadn't realized it was already four o'clock. "God, yes."

"So what are you going to do with your vacation?"

Cat looked over at the black woman in her late fifties who had become a good friend ever since Cat came to town a year ago. "Not a blessed thing. Sleep late, lie around, and do nothing. Maybe finish that book I started."

"Sounds heavenly."

Cat moved behind the woman's rotund body and hugged her neck. "Love you, Del."

The woman patted her arms. "Oh, hush with you. Go on and get out of here, now, before Dr. Reinhardt comes around the corner and finds something for you to do."

Cat's eyes got big. "Oh hell no. I'm out of here."

Deloris chuckled. "You better hustle your butt quick, gal."

Cat waved and headed to the nurse's break room. There was a small set of lockers against one wall. She opened hers and grabbed her purse. Her gym bag sat at the bottom of her locker. Usually, she stopped at the gym after work, but tonight she was exhausted. She slammed the locker closed then headed to the elevator and punched the button for the first floor. When it arrived, she stepped in, pulled her cell phone out, and checked for messages. The doors were just about to close when a hand slid in between, stopping them.

Crap. She'd almost made it. The doors slid back open and who of all people stepped inside but Dr. Reinhardt. *Double crap.*

He smiled.

Cat slunk back against the corner as he pressed the button for the second floor. The man was an obnoxious jerk who tried to corner Cat any chance he got and hit on her. She'd thought about reporting him on more than one instance, but she didn't want to risk her job. Instead, she tried to avoid him as much as possible, which wasn't always easy. The last thing she wanted was to be caught in an elevator—of all places—with him.

Her eyes swept over him as he eyed her. She supposed
he was attractive enough for a middle-aged man. He was tall,
trim, with light brown hair that was just beginning to gray at
the temples.

"How have you been, Catherine?"

"Just fine, Dr. Reinhardt. Thank you."

"That offer for dinner still stands."

She glanced away and chose her words carefully. "I'm
flattered. Really I am, but I don't think it would be a good
idea. Considering we work together."

He stepped closer, crowding her against the wall.
"Nothing wrong with a little workplace romance. I
understand you're up for your annual review next month.
Maybe you should reconsider."

The bell dinged, and the doors began to slide open.

He had no choice but to step away quickly before the
people waiting to get on saw his inappropriate behavior. He
gave her one last look as he moved to step out. "Have a nice
night, Ms. Randall."

Two hospital administrators got on, nodding to the
doctor as they did.

As the doors slid closed, she blew out a sigh of relief.
Thank God she didn't have to see him again for two weeks.
Two *heavenly* weeks. She grinned. She was going to take a
long, hot bath, drink a beer and curl up on the couch, and
watch television. For once she could stay up all night and
sleep in late.

Exiting the elevator on the main floor, she crossed the
lobby to the entrance to the employee-parking garage. She

hastened her steps, the cool, dimly lit structure always giving her the creeps. She made it to her car, beeped the door unlocked, and jumped inside, tossing her purse on the passenger seat.

Fifteen minutes later, she pulled into her apartment complex and parked in front of the second building. Her unit was on the second floor. She grabbed her bag and headed up the stairs to the apartment she shared with her younger sister. Holly should be home by now. She was enrolled in a local community college.

Cat inserted her key in the lock and pushed the door open, calling, "Holly, you home?" She slung her bag down on the couch and picked up the stack of mail on the side table. "I'm ready for a beer. And a bath. That jerk, Reinhardt asked me out again, can you believe it?" She flipped through the stack as she absently wandered into the kitchen, her eyes on the mail. "He cornered me in the elevator…"

Her words trailed off, and the envelopes fell from her hands as she took in the sight that waited for her in the kitchen. There were two scary leather-clad bikers, one leaning against the sink with his arms folded, the other kicked back in one of the tiny dining chairs. But the scariest part was the man standing across the room, holding a knife to her terrified sister's throat, his other hand clamped over her mouth.

"Glad you could join us, Cat," he said with a grin.

Dax! Cat knew him well. He wasn't a biker, but he wanted to be. No, Dax was a low-life drug dealer. The man had seduced Cat's older sister and talked her into marrying him. What a mistake that had been. Cat had begged and pleaded with her, but all the pleading in the world hadn't stopped Stacey from running off with him. She'd been blindly in love.

Cat understood Stacey's first attraction to the man. He was a good looking guy with his dark hair and piercing blue eyes, but Cat always thought they were cold eyes that held no real feelings for her sister, other than his desire for her body. He'd used her up, and when he'd gotten into trouble with a customer—a biker customer at that—she'd been the one to pay the price. A year after they were married, she'd died in a suspicious car explosion Cat was sure had been meant for Dax.

After her sister's death, Cat had taken her younger sister and moved them both out of the trailer they'd lived in with their alcoholic mother, determined that the same fate wouldn't befall her younger sister.

It had been a hard childhood for all of them, and Cat understood Stacey's desire to escape life in the trailer park in the east Texas town of Beaumont. She herself had worked and planned to make it out. It was why she'd studied so hard in school, and then worked harder to put herself through a nursing program her high school guidance counselor had helped her get into.

She'd done so much to escape this crap and now, here it was, standing in her kitchen, threatening the one thing she held most dear.

"Dax. What are you doing here?" She could barely get the words out as her stomach dropped.

He grinned, and her eyes slid to the bikers. Everything in her told her to step back, to make a dash for the door, but her gaze locked onto the fear in her little sister's wide eyes, and she knew she could never leave her.

"Just waitin' on you, Kitty-Cat." Dax grinned as he called her that sickening nickname he'd always used.

"She the one?" the biker at the table asked, his eyes sweeping down over her pale green scrubs.

"She's the one," Dax confirmed for him.

The biker stood. "Then let's go. We've wasted enough time waiting for her sweet ass to show up."

The one leaning against the sink interrupted with a wicked grin. "She said something about a hot bath. Maybe we could give her some time for that. I'll scrub your back, angel."

Cat's eyes darted to Dax. "What do you want?"

"You, Cat. Need you to come with us. We need you to put your nursing skills to use. Got a man who needs your help."

"I'm not going anywhere with you. And I sure as hell am not treating any dirty, drug-dealing biker."

At that, the one with his arms folded, straightened. "I've heard enough out of this bitch. We goin' or what?"

Dax jerked on Holly, causing her to scream behind his hand as he put the knife near her eye. "You'll do exactly what you're told. Or I'll kill your sister."

"Okay! Dax, let her go. Please. I'll do whatever you want. Just don't hurt her."

He lifted his chin toward the men. "You take her. I'll

stay here with little sister as insurance Cat complies and gives it her best effort."

With that, the man by the sink grabbed her arm and hustled her out of the kitchen.

She twisted, calling back, "Holly! Everything's going to be all right! I love you, Holly!"

The man jerked her to a stop, pulling her around to face him. "Shut up, bitch! You make one sound once we leave this apartment, you try to alert *anyone* and your sister is dead. You understand, *Kitty-Cat*?"

She looked up into his taunting face and read the cold truth in his eyes. He'd do it in a heartbeat and not think twice. She nodded. "Yes. I promise. No trouble. I swear. Just don't hurt her."

"Keep your mouth shut, do what you're told and maybe you'll both live. You don't, I'll kill you both myself and dump your bodies out in the swamp where nobody will ever find you. Got it?"

She nodded frantically.

He shoved her out the door, and they dragged her to some bikes parked at the end of the row. She was ordered onto the back of one, and a moment later they roared out of the parking lot.

Fifteen minutes later, they surprised her by pulling into the parking garage of the hospital. They parked in a dark deserted area and shut the bikes off. She scrambled off the back and asked, "What are we doing here?"

The tall one with the ponytail yanked her close and spoke to her in a low stern voice. "Guy you're treating has a gunshot wound." He jerked his chin toward the entrance. "Get whatever supplies you'll need to treat him and get your sweet ass back here pronto. Remember, keep your mouth shut or your sister is dead. You've got twenty minutes. Move!"

He shoved her toward the entrance.

She dashed inside, thankful she still had her badge hanging from the lanyard around her neck. She quickly moved up to the third floor, grateful no one rode up with her. As the elevator slowly rose, her mind frantically searched for everything she would need to treat this man. Most items she would have no problem getting access to. She only hoped the man hadn't lost too much blood. There was no way she could get access to the hematology department. She would have to have special authorization for that.

The elevator doors slid open. She lucked out as Deloris, who was still on duty, faced the other way on a phone call. Cat darted down the hall to the break room, hearing the voices of other nursing staff in open doors as she passed room after room. Reaching the break room, she found it empty. She quickly opened her locker and grabbed her gym bag. It was big enough to hold all the supplies she'd made a list of in her head in the elevator: sterile packs, gloves, masks, gauze, suture kits, bags of fluid for intravenous administration, cannula set, forceps, antibiotics, analgesic, tourniquets, syringes, blood pressure cuff...

Her mind was spinning, hoping she wouldn't forget anything. She stood back up, and her eyes landed on the phone hanging on the wall. She paused, her hand on the locker. She could call the police, but what would happen to her sister? Would they be able to break in and save her from Dax before he hurt her? Oh God, was he hurting her even now? And what of the two bikers waiting for her in the parking garage as the precious minutes ticked by? And what if the police didn't get to Holly in time?

She couldn't risk it. She slammed the locker closed and moved down the hall to gather her supplies.

Seven minutes later, she had everything stuffed in her duffel bag and was headed to the elevator.

"Hey, girl. I thought you left earlier?" Deloris asked from the desk, stopping her dead in her tracks.

Damn.

She turned, pasting a bright smile on her face only to also find Dr. Reinhardt standing at the station. He glanced up from a chart, his eyes moving over her.

Cat looked over to Deloris. "I just forgot my gym bag. I decided I might want to pick up a spin class or maybe yoga over the week."

Deloris nodded blankly, her eyes falling to the duffel. "Okay. Well, have a great time."

"I will. Bye." She waved and dashed down to the elevator. She jabbed the button repeatedly, like that would make it arrive any faster, as she watched the numbers over the door blinking on and off as the elevator moved from the first to the second and paused.

Crap! Come on!

She checked her watch, debating whether to dash down the stairwell instead. She'd used up eighteen minutes of the twenty the bikers had given her. Glancing back up, she saw the number three finally light up. The doors slid open and just as she was getting on, Dr. Reinhardt walked around the corner.

"Going down?" he asked.

She nodded and stepped on, mentally cursing her luck. She punched the lobby button, praying he'd get off on the second floor, but he never pushed that button. He looked over at her.

"Going home?"

She nodded. "Yes. Just forgot my bag."

"I'll walk out with you. I'm headed home myself."

Her eyes slid closed. *No, no, no!* she silently screamed. They reached the lobby and crossed toward the parking garage entrance. "I'm parked in general parking. I'm sure you're parked in the Physician's lot."

"I am. I could walk you to your car, though, if you'd like."

"Oh, no need. I'll be fine."

She was saved when another doctor waved him down in the lobby. He turned, and Cat took that opportunity to dash out the door. She took off running through the parking garage to the bikes.

Both bikers straightened when they saw her running toward them at full speed.

"Hurry! Start the bikes!"

The men must have been accustomed to this type of quick exit because they fired their bikes up quickly with no questions asked, and she jumped on the back.

"Go! Go! Go!" She turned to look over her shoulder as they tore around the corner, and she spotted Dr. Reinhardt just coming through the door. She caught the stunned look on his face as he saw her roaring off on the back of the motorcycle, the sound echoing off the concrete.

She couldn't worry about that now. The only thing important to her was doing whatever she had to do to make sure Dax didn't hurt her sister.

Cat clung to the biker as the motorcycles rode through town. She watched the city zoom by in a blur and soon realized they were headed down toward the Quarter. In the year and a half she'd lived in New Orleans, she'd never once been down there. She'd been so busy getting settled at work and making sure Holly was settled in school that she had just never gotten around to it. Really, if she was being honest, she hadn't done any exploring at all in her new city. She pretty much went from home to work to the gym and back again.

The bikes turned down North Rampart and skirted along the edge of the Quarter until it curved to the right, and then they turned off on some side street. It was sundown, and she didn't catch the name of the street. The area looked pretty sketchy, though.

They pulled past a two-story rundown clapboard on the left that sat on the corner. It was a dirty gray, the color of driftwood. A second floor gallery surrounded the upper story. It was trimmed with peeling white paint. Half of the turned spindles were missing from the railing. A busted up metal folding chair lay on its side. Graffiti was sprayed all over the building across the street.

They rode to the edge of the building and pulled behind a six-foot wooden privacy fence. Several bikes were already back there. The two men parked next to them, and she scrambled off.

The tall one with the ponytail—who seemed to be in charge—led the way up a set of back stairs that clung to the exterior. The other man shoved her after him. The wooden stairs creaked under the men's weight, and she grabbed the handrail, half afraid the whole thing would pull from the building and crash to the ground, taking them along with it.

She tried to glance around her surroundings, wanting to remember landmarks in case she needed to run. She noticed a man she hadn't seen when they'd ridden in. He wore a leather vest with the same patches as the other two. She watched as he moved to the gate and secured it with a heavy chain. If she had to escape, she'd have to jump the fence or find another way out of the building.

They reached the top of the stairs, and the biker in front rapped twice on the door. A man opened it, and they all trouped inside. Cat found herself shoved into a second story hallway.

She whirled on the man behind her. "You don't have to shove me. I'm cooperating, aren't I?"

The man in front stopped and turned back, his eyes skating from her to the other man. He raised one brow at him. "She too much for you to handle, Bagger?"

Bagger grabbed her upper arm and yanked her to him. "Keep your mouth shut, bitch, or I'll shut it for you."

She did as he said, cursing herself for inciting him. Now

that they were off the bikes and inside a building, she realized her situation was just as precarious as her sister's. She'd now seen four bikers, counting the one down at the gate, and she could hear voices coming from more downstairs. And she was in this house with all of them. She prayed they only wanted her for her nursing skills.

Her hands tightened on the gym bag she had clutched in her arms.

"Snake!" someone shouted up from downstairs.

The one with the ponytail answered, "Yeah."

"You get some help?"

"Yeah." Then he grabbed her arm and shoved her toward the man who'd opened the door. "Take her in, Ratchet. We got business to discuss."

The one called Ratchet, a tall man with a shaved head and soulless eyes, led her down the hall as the other two clomped downstairs. Ratchet fiddled with a key in a lock and then pushed her in ahead of him.

CHAPTER FOUR

It was stifling hot in the room. The windows were shut, and there was no air. Louvered shutters let in the last of the sun. Cat noticed all that in a nanosecond.

Her eyes were drawn to the iron cot where a man lay chained, his wrists cuffed over his head. He didn't look good. He didn't look good at all.

She bit her lip, her eyes moving over him as he lay on the stain-covered, thin bare mattress. He had a dark beard and dark hair soaked with sweat. He wore no shirt over his tattooed body, but he had on a pair of jeans and biker boots. He must be a tall man, because he took up every inch of the length of the bed.

He looked like the incarnation of the word trouble: a biker. She had to be half mad to even consider helping him, but then she thought of Holly. She had to do whatever was necessary in order to get her back.

There was what appeared to be a torn sheet as a makeshift bandage wrapped and tied around his chest. It was stained with blood, but it did not look bright red, which was a good sign. Blood loss had been her biggest fear, but maybe he wasn't too bad off. The whole way over here she'd worried what they'd do to her if he was too far gone or his wounds were too severe for her to help.

She moved a step closer.

He may not be heavily bleeding, but he didn't look good. His skin tone was gray, and he was sweating profusely.

With the second sweep of her eyes she noted the man, not the patient. She had an impression there would be raw power emanating from him if he hadn't been laid up with this injury. His shoulders were broad, and his biceps bulged. His bare chest, gleaming with a sheen of sweat, was hard muscled beneath taut, tanned skin. That muscle continued over a ripped stomach, a trail of dark hair disappearing beneath the low-riding waistband of his jeans. Her eyes again darted to his face, and she felt a strange shiver.

His eyes moved to her as she dropped her bag and approached him. They looked glassy and feverish, but they met hers from under heavy lids—dark fathomless eyes that seemed to look into her soul. She shook herself from the strange feeling and leaned over to press her cool hand to his forehead. He was indeed burning up.

No matter the fact that—in her snap judgment—he was just another dirty lowlife biker, she still couldn't bear to see someone suffering like this. She turned to the man standing just inside the door, the one called Ratchet. "Do you have any ice? And some towels?"

He just stood there.

"Please. I have to cool him down."

He rolled his eyes, but left, locking her in. She frantically dug through her duffel, pulling out her supplies and laying them out on a sterile pad she spread out on the mattress. She snapped on a pair of gloves and a mask, and then gently cut the dirty bandage off so she could examine the wound.

"What's your name?" she asked him softly as his eyes studied her, almost like he couldn't believe she was really there. He even let out what she thought was a huff of laughter. When he didn't answer, she assured him, "I'm a nurse. I'm here to help you."

"Help me?" He did laugh at that, and then winced in pain.

"That's funny?"

"Yeah. That's funny." His voice was hoarse, like he hadn't even been given water.

"What's your name?"

"Blood."

She frowned. Was he telling her he was bleeding? She again studied the wound. "The bleeding doesn't look too bad. You were shot?"

He nodded, gritting his teeth as she touched near the wound and examined the edges. Infection was definitely setting in. She needed to get an IV started so she could get some fluids and antibiotics in him. But first she needed to know if the bullet was still lodged inside She moved to the other side of the bed to get a better look at his far side. She leaned closer, bending over him and gently looking underneath him. On the edge of his back was another wound.

It actually was smaller and may have been the entrance wound, with the slightly larger hole in his front side being the exit wound. On closer examination, she determined that a rib, in all probability, deflected the bullet. It may have been what saved him. As gunshots went, this one wasn't too bad, having barely gone through the outer flesh of his side and affecting none of his organs.

The door opened, and Ratchet came in with a bowl of ice and a couple of towels. He set the ice down on the small side table and tossed the towels on the bed.

"I need you to un-cuff him," she said.

"Un-cuff him? No way." Then without another word, he slammed back out of the room.

She moved to the door and kicked it several times, yelling through the wood. "Come back here!"

Nothing.

"Damn it."

She moved back to the bed and ripped one of the thin towels in half. She dipped it in the ice water and wiped his face down.

He sighed at the cool touch.

"You have a fever, I know. I'll get an IV going in a minute, but I need to get them to un-cuff you." She wrapped a handful of ice in the torn piece of towel and pressed it to his forehead.

"My ring," he murmured in his hoarse voice.

She frowned. "What?"

"My ring. Take it off me. Please. If I die...see it gets to my club."

"Shh. Don't talk. I'm going to take care of you."

"Please." He pinned her with a frantic look. "Take it."

She saw the desperation in his feverish eyes, and she looked to his hands. A big silver ring with three skulls in a design sat on the third finger of his right hand.

"Take it," he snapped.

She reached up and pulled it off, studying it. It said *Evil* on one side and *Dead* on the other. Was that the name of his club? She met his eyes.

"Don't let them find it. They missed it. If I die, get it to my club. Promise me."

"I don't even know your name."

"Blood."

She frowned, glancing down at his wound again. "What?"

He shook his head impatiently and growled, "No, damn it! My name is Blood."

She looked at him questioningly. "Blood?"

He nodded.

"Well, Blood, you don't have to snap at me. I'm here to help you."

He grimaced. "Sorry, darlin'. It's just the pain talkin'." His eyes drilled into hers. "Promise me."

She couldn't find it in her to refuse him, so she nodded. "I promise."

He closed his eyes, apparently content with her answer.

She slipped the ring down into her bra, hoping it wouldn't be found there. She didn't have a clue how she would find this man's club, but she wasn't planning on letting him die, so hopefully it would never come to that. Looking up, she caught his eyes on her chest. He'd been watching her.

She pressed the ice pack to his forehead again and attempted to soothe him. "I'll see they get your ring, but I'm going to get you well. You're not circling the drain yet." When she saw the confused expression on his face, she clarified. "Sorry. Nursing humor. You're not going to die on me. You hear me, big guy?"

He attempted to laugh again. "Bossy little thing, aren't you?"

She could be if she had to be. She looked to the door. Dammit, she needed to get him un-cuffed so she could get his IV started. He needed fluids. Picking up a piece of ice, she brought it to his lips. "Here, suck on this. It'll soothe your throat till I can get you some water."

He opened his lips, and she slipped it in, noting his perfectly straight white teeth. She took in his face. He was handsome with warm brown eyes and slashing brows. Her eyes moved over his muscular tattooed arms stretched over his head, and then down his broad chest to his slim hips. He was well-built man.

She repositioned the ice pack on his forehead and rose from the bed. "I've got to get those cuffs off you."

She moved to the door, glancing back to see his eyes following her. They were still glassy with fever, but they tracked her movements. She banged on the door and kicked at it for a good five minutes before somebody finally stomped up the stairs.

It was Bagger this time. "What the hell do you want?"

"I need to give him an IV."

"So give him a fucking IV."

"I need you to un-cuff one of his hands."

"Not a chance."

She folded her arms in an obstinate stance. "Then what the hell did you drag me here for if it's just to let him die? Huh?"

The biker looked at her dumbfounded.

She gritted her teeth and snapped, "Un-cuff him! Now!"

Suddenly more boot steps pounded up the stairs, and Snake came in the room. "What the hell is she screaming about?"

"Says she needs him un-cuffed."

Snake turned on her and barked, "Not a chance. He stays cuffed."

"Like I told your friend here, I can't administer the IV with him like this!" She flung her arm out toward the bed and gave them a look that hopefully told them both what idiots she thought they were. "If you didn't want my help, why the hell did you bring me here?"

"He needs an IV?"

"*Yes*. That's what I've been trying to tell you!"

Snake stared her down then jerked his head at Bagger. "Go ahead. One hand. But stay here and watch him."

Bagger nodded at the orders, and Snake stomped out of the room.

Bagger looked over at her as he moved to the bed and dug the keys out of his hip pocket. "Nobody talks to Snake like that. You better watch your mouth from now on. You do it again, he's likely to put you through the wall."

"Then I guess you'll be out a nurse."

"Of all the nurses, we picked Nurse Nasty."

"Screw you, too."

Bagger actually chuckled as he stepped back. "There. Satisfied?"

"No. I need some water." Her hands landed on her hips as she glared at him.

Bagger rolled his eyes, but didn't bother arguing with her this time. "Christ, you're a lot of fucking trouble." He moved toward the door and hollered down the stairs. "Stoner, bring me some bottled water!"

Cat got busy preparing the IV. She ran her hands over his arm, rubbing vigorously to try to get the circulation back to get the needed vein. He groaned and flexed his hand, shaking it out.

His eyes met hers, and he whispered, "You're cute when you're being all fierce and shit."

She ignored him, moved to her supplies, and set them on the bed. She tore open the packaging for the IV fluid bag. She had no stand, so she improvised and rigged it up to the iron bedpost above his head, using a strip of the plastic packaging. Then she unrolled her IV pack on the bed next to him and tore open the tubing set. She readied some strips of tape. Now she just needed to insert the needle and cannula in his arm.

She put on a fresh pair of gloves, took his arm and tied a tourniquet around it, and searched the back of his hand for a suitable vein. Then she cleaned the site with an alcohol swab. As her hand rubbed over his skin in a circular motion, she glanced up at him. His eyes were watching what she was doing, but they looked glassy. "I'm going to get fluids in you. The needle may pinch, okay?"

He glanced up and nodded. Whether he understood or not, at least he wasn't going to fight her when she tried to stick him. She inserted the needle, setting the cannula in place, attached the line, and taped it off. She stood and slowly opened the line, filling it with fluid. It flowed in just like it was supposed to, and she released a breath, glad she didn't have to remove it and start over.

Once the IV fluids and antibiotics were flowing, she injected a pain medication into the catheter in his hand. Glancing up, she saw him watching. "It's pain medication. You'll feel better soon, which is good because I have to clean your wound. And I'm not going to lie to you, Blood, it's going to hurt."

He nodded, and the hand with the IV lifted, his fingers reaching out and clasping onto her pinky to give it a little shake. "Thanks, Doc. But you don't have to lie to me. I'm going to die, aren't I?"

She frowned as she disposed of the used syringe and pulled her gloves off. "I'm not lying to you. You're not going to die. And I'm not a doctor."

He looked at her, his eyes trying to focus, and she could see the fever was still affecting his mind. She brushed the hair back from his forehead, and his eyes slid closed like he relished the small gesture of kindness.

She turned to the biker who stood by the door with his arms folded. "Can we get these windows open and a fan in here? It's hot as hell."

He wiped his brow, the heat affecting him as well, and she could tell he didn't want to stay in here a minute longer than he had to, either. "Windows are nailed shut."

"You're kidding me, right?"

"Nope."

"It's stifling in here."

He opened the door, but that was it. At least it let a little air flow in.

She turned back to her patient, cracked open a bottle of the water, and lifted his head up to pour some in his mouth. "Here, drink this."

He guzzled it down until he had to quit to gasp in air. She set it down and dipped a cloth in the ice water wiping down his face again.

A little while later, she glanced up at the IV and then at her watch. She thought she'd given him enough time for the meds to kick in, and she needed to clean that wound.

She readied her supplies and grabbed one of the towels, tucking it under him as she prepared to irrigate the wound to clean it. Snapping on a new pair of sterile gloves, she quickly moved through the steps. Once the wound was clean, she had to pack it with some gauze soaked in saline solution.

He grimaced a couple of times, but he was mostly stoic.

Bagger moved out into the hall where it was cooler and sat against the wall.

She re-bandaged her patient, and he soon drifted off to

sleep.

She checked his blood pressure and temperature, swiping the instrument across his forehead. He was still hot, but his temperature had dropped a degree from one hundred and six to one-hundred and-five.

There was a wooden chair in the room, and she moved it next to the bed. Keeping an eye on the IV flow, she picked up an old magazine from the bedside table and fanned him. When her arm got tired, she tossed the magazine and dipped the towel in the water from the rapidly melting bowl of ice and wiped down his bare skin, trying to do everything she could to bring his fever down.

As her hand stroked his chest, she couldn't help but be affected by his muscles. She'd had a lot of patients, but never one built like this one. She stroked over his neck and face, brushing his sweaty hair back as she struggled with the conflicting emotions warring within her. On one hand she'd sworn to help people, but on the other hand, she hated bikers. It was men like him she held responsible for her older sister's death. And men like him who were responsible for her younger sister being held at knifepoint. She closed her eyes and said a prayer, hoping Holly was all right and that Dax hadn't hurt her.

Opening her eyes, she looked at the man she was expected to save.

As much as she wanted to hate him, she couldn't help but admit he was an attractive man. How could such a beautiful man be one of these filthy bikers? What a waste of one of God's greatest, most magnificent creations.

She sat with him for hours while the first bag of IV fluids slowly emptied, alternately fanning him and wiping down his sweating body with cool water. She glanced into the hall; the biker had fallen asleep against the door that led to the outside staircase and freedom. Unfortunately, she'd never be able to get past his sleeping body to those stairs. And she could hear the others downstairs arguing about a poker game. There would be no getting out that way.

She got up from the chair she'd pulled next to the bed, stretched her aching back, and moved to the window. She peered through the louvered slats and the grimy window beyond. It was night now, probably close to midnight. She could see the headlights of cars moving down Rampart Street at the end of the block.

She surveyed the gallery that surrounded the front of the building. Perhaps, if she could get the window open, she could sneak out onto it. But upon closer examination, she realized—like the biker had informed her—the window was indeed nailed shut.

Who does that for God's sake? Especially in a town that was incessantly hot and humid. She glanced toward the bed and her patient resting upon it, and she had her answer. Bikers who planned to keep someone locked up, that's who. Bikers who didn't want their captives crawling out the window.

Of course, she might be able to break the glass, but they'd probably hear. Who was she kidding? As long as Dax held Holly, she wouldn't do anything that would jeopardize her sister, and escaping would only get her sister killed.

Cat picked up the magazine and fanned herself. The heat was getting to her. She touched Blood's forehead again. He felt clammy and she could see him start to tremble with the onset of chills, tremors moving over his body.

She stepped to the end of the bed and pulled the light sheet over his body, tucking it around him. His body began to shake even harder, and his teeth clacked together. She smoothed the hair off his brow, murmuring to him, "You're going to be okay."

His glassy eyes opened and looked up at her. "Cold," he whispered.

"I know. The fever is breaking. Your body is fighting off the infection. I'm giving you medicine for that. You're going to get better soon."

His eyes drifted closed again, and the tremors subsided.

She looked up at the almost empty IV bag. Moving to her duffel, she took out another bag and began to switch them out, humming to herself as she did the work, trying to block out the yelling and cursing and increasingly drunken laughter coming from downstairs.

She said a quick prayer that none of them wandered up here looking for some fun with their new nurse.

When she was through with her task, she sat back in the uncomfortable chair. The only light source came from the dim light of the small table lamp. It was just as well—sitting in the subdued light seemed cooler, even if it was probably only wishful thinking.

Eventually, her head began to droop, and soon she nodded off in sleep.

CHAPTER FIVE

Blood awoke and glanced around at his surroundings. Judging by the faint gray light coming in from the windows, he figured it must be just after dawn. He kicked the covers off; they had been soaked with his sweat. The fever must have broken finally.

The room was a little cooler now, but he knew as soon as the sun rose and climbed in the sky, the room would heat up again. He saw the IV catheter sticking out of the top of his hand, taped down with clear medical tape. His eyes followed the tubing up to the bag rigged to the bedpost, and then his gaze fell to the woman dozing in the straight-backed chair at his bedside.

Well, goddamn. She was real. He thought he'd dreamed her up, but there she sat, his guardian angel, asleep in a chair. She was dressed in green scrubs, her long blonde hair tumbled in a ponytail over her shoulder, a cascade of silk he longed to run his fingers through. His eyes moved over her thin frame. It was hard to make out much about her figure in the baggy scrubs, but he made out the shape of breasts that would be at least a handful. *Christ, he's laying here half dead, and he was thinking about sex.*

His eyes climbed up her long graceful neck to her angel face. Beautiful cheekbones, full pale pink lips made for kissing—or something better—delicately arced brows over big slanted eyes… A fringe of long lashes lay against her cheekbones as she slumbered, just a touch of mascara darkening them. A smattering of the barest freckles covered her nose.

Blood grinned, not sure why that got to him.

He didn't know how long he'd been in this room. A few days? A week? It was all a fuzzy blur. But he remembered the girl and the way she'd bathed his skin with cool cloths, assuring him he would be okay. Promising him she'd…

His eyes darted to his hand still cuffed to the iron head rail. His ring was gone. She'd done as he'd asked and taken it, hadn't she? Or had he just dreamed that? Had the Death Heads taken it like they had his cut?

His eyes moved over her then fell to her chest again. He seemed to remember her tucking it into her bra. Or did he imagine that, too? It was all so fuzzy.

He moved, and the cuffs rattled. Her eyes opened, and she looked blankly over at him, their gazes locking. Blue. They were blue, just like in his dream, blue and beautiful. And they were staring wide-eyed and innocent into his.

"My angel," he murmured.

She licked her lips and frowned. "What?"

He just grinned back at her.

"You're awake," she said in a soft voice that melted over him like honey.

He nodded, kicking the covers farther off him.

She noticed and reached for his forehead. "You're clammy. That's good. It means the fever has broken." Her eyes moved to the IV above his head. "You still have about an hour's worth left of fluids. I gave you a second one during the night. Each last about six hours."

He nodded.

"Do you want some water?" she asked, standing.

"Please," he rasped out.

She helped him sit up, jamming a pillow behind him so he could sit against the headboard. Then she brought a bottle of water to his lips. With one hand still cuffed and the other with an IV he wasn't the most coordinated, but he was able to take the bottle.

"Thanks." His eyes stayed on her as he guzzled half the bottle.

"Do you…have to use the restroom?" she asked hesitantly.

He shook his head. "No."

"Probably because you were so dehydrated."

He nodded taking another long drink, his eyes on her. When he pulled the bottle back down, he said, "I thought I dreamed you."

Her smile lit up her face and took his breath.

"I'm real." Her eyes moved around the room. "Unfortunately."

He nodded, realizing she didn't want to be here anymore

than he did. He lifted his chin toward the man asleep on the hallway floor. "You with them?"

Her eyes got big. "Me? No. I'm definitely not *with them*."

"Then how'd you end up here?"

"It's a long story."

He rattled the cuff. "I've got time."

She cocked her head to the side, her eyes moving to the handcuff. "How'd *you* end up here?"

"Just in the wrong place at the wrong time." He glanced toward the hallway again, uncertain how much he should share. He still didn't know her relationship with these assholes, and he wasn't sure he could trust her. He studied her eyes. She'd taken his ring though and made that promise to him. Why would she do that if she was working with them?

Blood had lived most of his life knowing when to keep his mouth shut, being careful with giving his trust out. It was a hard lesson he'd learned very early in life—one he wasn't about to forget now. But she'd helped him, and in the position he was in she might be the only shot he had, the only person who might be able to get him out of here. Or, at the least, she might be able to get word out to his club.

Way he saw it, he didn't have much of a choice. He'd have to take a chance on her. "You're still in your scrubs. They kidnap you out of a hospital parking lot?"

She frowned. "Where did you come up with that?"

"It's what I'd do," he admitted and watched her chin lift. Hell, he was just being honest, but he could see she didn't care for his answer. She'd treated him, but she didn't like him, or maybe more specifically, men *like* him. "You don't like me much, do you?"

"You're a biker, like them. And I don't like bikers."

He shook his head slowly. "Not like them. My club and the Death Heads are sworn enemies."

"Well, I didn't think they had you cuffed to the bed because they liked you."

He gave her half a smile. *Sarcastic little wench.*

"So…you came on their turf and—"

He cut her off. "This isn't Death Heads turf. This is Evil Dead turf."

"Evil Dead. That was on your ring."

He nodded. *She was observant, too.* "Evil Dead MC. My club."

"So—" She looked toward the hallway. "If this isn't their territory, what are they doing here?"

"Hell if I know."

"And if you're enemies, why are they concerned enough to get you medical care? Weren't they the ones who shot you in the first place?"

He watched the pretty little frown on her face. She was sarcastic, observant, and *smart.*

"Been wonderin' that myself. Maybe they didn't mean to shoot me. Or maybe they decided I could be of better use if I'm kept alive."

"For what?"

He shrugged. "Haven't figured that out yet. Maybe for leverage with my club. A bargaining chip."

"To get what?"

She was sarcastic, observant, smart, *and curious*. Blood shook his head. "Doesn't concern you, Doc."

"I told you, I'm not a doctor."

"Fine, then I'll call you Scrubs."

Her brows arched. "Not if you want me to answer."

He fought back a smile. "What's your name?"

"Catherine. My friends call me Cat."

"Cat." He tried it out on his tongue and nodded. "Suits you."

"I said my friends call me that."

His brows shot up. "And I'm not included in that bunch, is that what you're sayin'? Honey, right now, right here, I'm the only friend you've got."

She looked toward the hallway. "I'm just here to get you well. That's all."

"You still got my ring?"

Her head swiveled back, and she put a hand to her breastbone. "Yes."

So, he hadn't dreamed that part. She *had* stuck it in her bra. He nodded and whispered, "Think you could get to a phone? Make a call?"

Her eyes were sharp when they met his, and she answered in an equally hushed tone. "You mean call the police?"

He shook his head with a grimace. "No. No police. MCs don't ever call the police."

She gave him a stunned look. "Even *now*?"

"Even now."

"Then who?"

"My club. You get word to them, they'll get us both out of here."

"Both of us? Why would they give a damn about me? "

"Listen to me, Cat. I give you my word, I'll take you with me."

She eyed him as if she were weighing his words and the strength of his promise. In the end, she shook her head. "It doesn't matter. I don't have my phone. I don't have anything but the supplies." She gestured toward the duffel on the floor.

His eyes fell to it, and then he looked toward the man in the hall. "Think you could get his?"

"If I tried and woke him," she broke off, shaking her head. "I'm not sure what he'd do."

"What about the rest? They all passed out downstairs?"

"I don't know." She moved to the window and peered out. "There's a guy out in the backyard by the bikes taking a piss."

Blood's eyes again fell to that duffel on the floor. "Where'd you get the supplies?"

"The hospital where I work."

"What if you needed more? Would they take you back to get them?"

She bit her lip and looked toward the hall. It was the cutest little gesture he'd ever seen. There was something about the way her perfect teeth bit into that plump bottom lip that really got to him. She turned back, and his eyes lifted.

"Babe? Would they take you?" he pressed when she didn't reply.

"Maybe," she admitted.

He nodded, suddenly feeling the strangest need to protect her. Feelings of protectiveness for women weren't completely foreign to him, but they were damn rare. There was something about this one that brought it out in him in spades. There was a worldliness about her, but there was an innocence, too—innocence he felt the need to protect. She was in way over her head here.

He lifted his chin toward the hallway. "Don't care how you do it, but you get them to take you to the hospital. You do, you'll be safe, away from them."

"You still need treatment."

"Don't worry about me. You make that call for me, and I'll take my chances with my club."

She shook her head. "I can't."

"Why not?"

"It's complicated."

Blood frowned and then his jaw clenched. "You *are* with one of them, aren't you?"

"No!" she hissed, trying not to be too loud. "I told you that. There's not a chance in hell I'd ever be with a fucking biker."

A fucking biker. Great, the only chance he had rested with a woman who couldn't stand the likes of him. Lovely. Well, he'd just have to change her mind about him then. "Sounds like there's a story there. They hurt you?"

She shook her head.

"They have something they're holding over you? Other than the threat of your own safety." She looked away, and he had his answer. He felt the need to set her straight. "You've seen too much, you know. If you're not with one of them—"

"I'm not!" she swore vehemently.

"Then they'll never just *let you go*. Death Heads aren't too keen on leaving loose ends. Witnesses being at the top of that list."

"They promised. If I helped them, they promised—"

"Their promises don't mean shit, little girl."

"And yours do?" she snapped at him.

"I don't make promises unless I mean them."

She huffed. "Right."

"Don't trust them," he warned.

"Look, if you die, maybe they'd kill me. But I'm not going to let you die."

"Babe, they won't let you live either way. You've seen too much. Once your usefulness is over, they'll get rid of you." He watched her face. Maybe he was getting through. Goddamn, he hated the fear his words put into her eyes. "I wish I could get you out of here."

"Well, you can't."

"If you get to the hospital, you can get away."

She stared at him.

"Look, all I'm asking is for you to make a phone call. I'm not asking you to let me go."

"I can't."

"Why not?"

"Because."

"Because why, angel?"

She looked down and plucked at the hem of her shirt,

and he knew she was struggling with telling him something.

"What is it?" he prodded. "What do they have on you?"

"They have my sister."

Blood's eyes slid closed. *Fuck.* If they were holding her sister as leverage, and he was betting they had her at another location, they could kill her before anyone could get to her. But there was one thing his pretty little blonde savior still didn't seem to grasp. He opened his eyes and pinned her with a look. "When this is over, when your usefulness is done, they'll kill you *both*. They aren't going to let either of you go."

Her eyes welled with tears. "But they promised. They said if I helped, they'd let her go."

Blood shook his head. "They won't. I guarantee it."

A tear rolled down her cheek.

"Hey." His hand moved over and took hers, giving it a squeeze. "I'm the only shot you've got of saving your sister."

"You? How can you save her? You're cuffed to the stupid bed." She sniffled.

"You get that call out to my club, they'll come busting in here and get us out. Then we'll get your sister. Do you know where they're keeping her?"

She wiped the wetness off her cheek. "Dax has her at my apartment."

"Dax? Who the fuck is Dax?"

At his harsh words, she looked toward the hallway and then to him. "*Shh...* they'll hear you."

"Tell me," he demanded in a softly spoken order.

"He used to be my brother-in-law."

"Used to be?"

"My older sister was married to him."

"They split up?"

"She was killed."

Blood clenched his jaw, hating to see the pain on her face. "I'm sorry."

She brushed it aside with a wave of her hand, like his apology was meaningless. And perhaps to her it was, but he'd meant it. This girl didn't deserve to have such pain in her life. She didn't deserve any of this shit. He'd only known her a day, but already he could decipher that much. "So, your brother-in-law is a Death Head, then?"

She shook her head. "No, but I think he wants to be. At least he wants to be on their good side. You see, Dax is a drug dealer. And when he gets on the wrong side of people like them, innocent people end up dead."

"Your sister?" Blood frowned, linking the parts of this story together.

She nodded. "My sister."

"What happened to her?" He was almost afraid to hear the answer.

She met his eyes with her clear blue ones. "Car bomb."

Blood's chin lifted, the pieces falling into place. "Meant for Dax."

"And my sister paid the price."

"But now he's back in good with them?"

"Apparently. Or trying to be. I don't know."

"And he was good with putting both you and your sister in danger like this?"

She nodded. "Dax is only concerned with himself."

"Dax is a dick."

She grinned at that. "I couldn't agree more."

"When we get out of here, I'm gonna kill him for you."

She looked at him with wide eyes. Obviously, no one had ever offered to solve the Dax problem for her before. He meant it. Every word, and he could see she saw that fact written on his face.

"I didn't ask for your help."

"No, cupcake. But you got it, just the same."

She lifted her chin, considering. "You're just saying that to get me to help you."

"First of all, I shouldn't have to talk you into helping me. I thought that's what nurses do—help people. Second, no, I'm not just saying that. I don't just say shit. Ever."

He could see she hadn't a clue how to take him. That was okay; she'd learn. He'd make sure she did—in more ways than one. In any other situation, Blood would already be all over her, would have backed her against the wall and shown her. He was the kind of man who took what he wanted where women were concerned. He didn't chitchat with them—never had to. Dealing with women in this way was new for him. Cuffed to the bed, he was in a situation where he actually had to talk to her, get to know her, seduce her verbally into doing what he wanted. This was all new territory for him.

"You find me hard to handle, don't you, babe?"

She scoffed and looked away. "I have no desire to 'handle' you at all, Blood."

"Bet I could prove you wrong."

"Right."

"C'mere."

She looked back at him.

He reached out, fisted his hand in the hem of her scrubs shirt, and pulled her down onto the edge of the bed. Then, quick as lightning, he hooked that hand around the back of her neck and pulled her down, capturing her mouth with his. Those lips of hers were just as soft and kissable as he imagined they'd be. They parted with her surprise, and he took full advantage, his tongue sweeping inside for a taste. It only lasted a second, before she was pushing off him and out of his reach. But that second told him all he needed to know—there was fire there, for both of them.

"You've got some crazy ideas if you think I'm interested in the likes of you. I'm no scared little virgin who's going to go along with whatever you want."

"You're a real wildcat, you are."

"You've misjudged me badly. I will never want a biker like you."

"Never say never, angel."

"You're too much like my brother-in-law and this bunch to suit me, and I'm an expert on him."

"Can't blame a man for trying, sweetheart."

"Don't do that again."

"Now that's a promise I won't be making."

She folded her arms and sat in the chair, glaring at the wall.

"What do you do at the hospital?"

"I'm a nurse," she replied, like he was a moron.

"I know you're a nurse. What department? What's your specialty?"

"I work in the departure lounge."

His brows shot up. "The what?"

"It's what we call the geriatric floor."

His mouth pulled up. "Cute."

"Want to know what we call motorcycles?"

"What?" He could hardly wait to hear this one.

"Donorcycles. It's where we get most organ donations. Motorcycle fatalities."

"Well, that's morbid."

She looked up at his IV bag. "You need another one."

He watched as she got up and switched it out. He reached for a bottle of water and chugged it down while she worked. With her arms over his head, he had a perfect view of her chest. Naturally, she caught where his eyes were when she pulled back. In any other circumstance, he'd have wrapped one strong arm around her waist and lifted that top, helping himself to her breasts with his mouth. It was damned strange being in a fucking situation where the woman had the upper hand.

She stepped back and took the empty bottle from him. "After this bag, I can probably switch you over to oral antibiotics."

"You got any of those?"

"Actually, no."

"Hmm. Sounds like someone might have to make a run to the hospital."

She blew out an exasperated breath. "Are you hungry?"

He shook his head. "But I bet you are. Ask them for some food. If you don't, I guarantee they aren't going to think about it."

"Maybe I don't want to remind them I'm up here."

He nodded, taking her meaning, and looked toward the hall. It was a wonder they hadn't come up for her yet, but that wouldn't last for long. He needed to get her out of here. "They'll be rousing in a couple hours. When they do, tell them you need more supplies."

She looked toward the hall, but made no promises. She got up and stretched, then moved to the window again, peering out. The sun was up now, and the temperature was rising quickly. "What I really could use is some Vitamin X."

Blood frowned, studying her. "That's a new one."

She looked over absently at him. "Sorry. Xanax."

"More hospital humor. Cute."

Their eyes met, and a small smile formed on her face. He answered it with one of his own.

***

Hours passed and the temperature in the room climbed. Blood continued to try to draw Cat in with conversation.

"You're accent. It sounds more like Texas than New Orleans."

She looked over at him. "That's because I'm from Beaumont."

"Beaumont, huh? How'd you end up here?"

"My dad died when I was seven. That's when everything went to hell. We lost our house and ended up living in a rundown trailer in a crappy trailer park. My mom hooked up with one loser after another. Last one took an interest in Holly. That's when I decided to get her out of there."

"How'd you end up a nurse?"

"When I was in high school, I got a job at a small diner. The owners took me under their wing, telling me I could be anything I wanted. That I could rise above my upbringing and the bad start I had in life.

"With their help, I worked my way through a nursing program at the community college. I knew I wanted to get away from Beaumont. As far away as I could get."

She moved around the bed and leaned over to check his wounds as she talked.

"Stacey never had that kind of help. She took off at sixteen and hooked up with that low-life loser, Dax. They got married. He started dealing drugs."

She prodded at the wound after taking off the bandage. He groaned as the pain flashed through him.

"I need to change out the packing. I can give you something for the pain, inject it into the IV," she offered.

He shook his head. "I've got to keep a clear head right now. I can't be foggy from pain meds."

She looked toward the closed door.

Blood followed her eyes. The men had started to rouse about an hour ago and the man in the hall had locked them in again.

"All right, then. I'll get started." She moved to set up her supplies, laying out a sterile pad, donning gloves and a mask, and ripping open new gauze.

Blood watched her, noticing—like he hadn't when he was feverish—just how competent she was at what she did.

She moved toward him with a pair of tweezers. "I've got to pull the packing out. You may want to turn your head for this."

He gave her a flat look. Did she think the sight of a little blood and gore would have him heaving over the side of the bed?

She shrugged. "Suit yourself."

He watched as she dug out the wad of gauze bandaging she'd packed in his wound. It pulled on the healing, clotted tissue. He sucked in a breath as she pulled it free, and he hissed, "Jesus Christ! It didn't hurt that bad getting shot."

"Sorry. I'm trying to be gentle."

He caught her look as she attempted to fight a grin. *Gentle, my ass.* Maybe it was a test to see just how much of a badass he was. He clenched his jaw as she prepared to repack the wound with gauze squares she'd dipped in saline.

He gritted out, "Finish your story. Take my mind off the torture you're inflicting on me, Nurse Hotty."

She grinned, but complied. "Dax got hooked up with the local biker club—our friends downstairs—the Death Heads."

"They ain't my friends."

"Stacey died because of them. An accounting issue, they'd said. I can't prove it, but I know that's what happened. She called me the night before, begging me to help them. I pleaded with her to leave him, to come home. She wouldn't.

She died the next morning."

"Sorry," he whispered.

Her pretty blue eyes looked up from what she was doing and met his. "Are you?"

Then her eyes returned to what she was doing, and he hissed in another breath at the jolt of pain.

"Sorry," she whispered.

"*Are you?*" He gave her words back to her and watched the corner of her mouth pull up. There was the slightest little dimple there.

She finished by placing a new square of gauze over his wound and taping it in place.

"Thank God, you're finished."

Apparently, she didn't like where she'd applied the tape, because she pulled it off and reset it. He sucked in at the sharp yank. "Fuck." He glared at her. "You did that on purpose."

She rolled her eyes at him as she pulled off her gloves with a snap. "If we were in the hospital, I'd write BFB on your chart."

"What the hell is BFB?" he glared at her, still pissed about what he was sure was intentional roughness on her part. And maybe, if he were being honest, he deserved it for grabbing and kissing her earlier.

"Big Fucking Baby."

"Ha ha. Very funny. You know what I'd call you?"

"I can only imagine."

"Nurse Sweetcheeks."

She actually grinned at that—she tried to hide it from

him, but he saw.

"How 'bout a sponge bath?" he said. "Is that in your skill set? Maybe you can redeem yourself. Show me you've got a gentler touch."

Her eyes skated down his body. "Well, you *do* stink."

His brows shot up at that. "Thanks a lot."

She moved to the other side of the bed and poured the last bottle of water into the empty ice bowl. Then she dipped a towel in, sat on the edge of the bed and began to wipe down his face and arms.

He watched her as she did it. Occasionally her eyes would flick up to meet his, but mostly she was all business, focusing on what she was doing. She swiped over his neck and then down his chest, over his abs to the edge of his low-riding jeans. He watched every little emotion on her face. She swallowed, the towel slowing its stroke, and he pounced.

"See something you like?"

Her eyes flicked up to his, and she quickened her movements. "I'm a nurse. I've seen it all."

He grinned. He could tell his close scrutiny was making her nervous. She moved the towel over his armpit and the cuff rattled as he jerked.

She smirked up at him then. "Ticklish?"

"Hell no. It's cold, is all."

She lifted his other arm and repeated the motion. He grit his teeth, trying to keep from jerking under her touch.

"You *are* ticklish."

"I get these cuffs off, maybe we'll see how ticklish *you* are," he threatened as she stood to wring out the towel in the bowl.

Her eyes connected with his, and they both knew it was a long shot that those cuffs would ever be coming off. It was also a reminder that she needed to decide if she was going to take a chance and help him.

"You gotta trust somebody, angel," he murmured, reading her like a book. He lifted his eyes to the IV bag that was now empty. "Now's your shot."

Her eyes followed his and then moved to the door. He watched her stare off into space, considering her options.

"I would happily keep the world on the other side of that door for you if I could," he whispered.

She looked at him with those big blue eyes—eyes that had seen too much in her young life, that still held a touch of vulnerability that called out to him to protect.

"C'mere." He beckoned her softly.

She moved toward him as if pulled by a force she couldn't fight, perhaps didn't even understand.

He reached up and grasped her fingers, tugging her down on the edge of the bed. Then his hand moved to her cheek. His thumb brushed over her cheekbone, just a soft stroke as they stared at one another. Her eyes dropped to his mouth, and that was all the invitation he needed. He slid his hand into the hair behind her ear and pulled her to him.

He was gentle with her this time, just a brush of his lips over hers, but he came back again and again, until her mouth was opening under his, her tongue sweeping out to lightly explore. He let her take the lead. *Just this once*, he told himself.

Maybe it was the fact that he didn't push or demand, like everything inside him was screaming for him to do, or maybe it was the fact that he was chained to the bed that made her feel safe with him. He didn't know. He didn't care. He was just glad she did. He didn't want that to ever change, but in the back of his mind, he knew it would. He knew if he ever got out of here, if they ever *both* got out of here that would change. Because he wouldn't be able to hold back with her anymore. The kid gloves would come off.

She angled her head, continuing the slow soft kisses that were getting him aroused, his dick pressing hard against the zipper of his jeans. It wasn't used to being denied. Ever.

Eventually, she pulled back, and he stared up into her wide eyes. She looked as confused as he was by all this, but he saw desire there, too. She may not like bikers very much, but she was attracted to him. That much was plain on her face. Then her eyes dropped to his crotch.

"I may be injured, but I ain't dead," he explained with a grin.

She flushed.

The sound of footsteps in the hall had both their heads twisting toward the door. The footsteps moved on past. He looked up at her, brushing the hair back from her face. "It's dangerous to be doing this."

"I know."

He wrapped his hand around her ponytail and pulled her down for one more kiss, unable to resist. Then he released her, letting the silk of her hair slip through his fingers as his hand dropped to the bed.

They heard footsteps again, and this time the doorknob rattled as it was unlocked. She jumped from the bed and pretended to fiddle with the IV bag above his head as one of the Death Heads came through the door.

Blood feigned sleep.

"How is he?" the man bit out.

CHAPTER SIX

Cat glanced down at her patient, only to see his eyes closed. "He needs more antibiotics. I need another IV bag. This one's empty."

"So give him one."

"I'm out. I only grabbed two. I need to go back to the hospital to get more supplies."

"Are you fucking serious?"

She whirled then, her hand on her hip. "Look, I didn't know what I was walking into here. I had no idea he was this bad off. You want my help or not? If he doesn't get a full cycle of antibiotics, he won't make it. The infection will just flare back up worse than before, and he'll go into a coma." She didn't know if he'd buy the story, but she gave it her best shot. "Now who's taking me? You?"

"Goddamn it. Let me go see." He slammed the door and marched down the stairs.

Blood cracked an eye open at her. "Damn, girl. You can be a real hard-ass when you put your mind to it."

"You think they'll take me?"

They heard arguing coming from the first floor and then boots pounding up the stairs. "We're about to find out. Remember... make that phone call and then you *don't come back*, understand?"

She turned toward the door, but felt a tug on the leg of her scrubs.

"Hey?"

She looked back at him.

"Understand?"

She nodded. "Wait. The number?"

He rattled off the phone number, and she said it over and over in her head, trying to commit it to memory as the lock rattled again and the door flung open.

"Get your bag and come on." The biker jerked his chin.

"Okay." She looked back down at Blood one last time as he once again feigned sleep, and then she turned, gathered up her duffel, and followed the biker out.

***

Twenty minutes later, she darted up the hospital stairwell no one ever used. She was able to make it to the third floor employee break room without being seen. Quickly moving to the phone on the wall by the lockers, she punched in the number Blood had given her. "Come on. Come on. Pick up."

"Clubhouse," came a bark on the other end of the line.

She swallowed, not exactly sure how to begin. "Blood told me to call."

"Who is this?"

"A friend."

"Blood ain't got no friends."

"He gave me his club ring," she babbled, not sure why she said it, but hoping maybe that bit of information would keep the man from slamming the phone down on her.

"He what?" There was silence for a long moment. "Describe it."

"Three skulls. Says Evil Dead. Just listen to me, I don't have much time."

"Who the fuck is this—"

Obviously he wasn't used to being snapped at by a woman, but she didn't have time for long explanations. She cut him off. "He's in trouble. He's being held in a house in the Quarter by the Death Heads MC."

Cat heard the break room door opening behind her and two women's voices. She hurriedly hissed out the rest of the information. "Corner of Henriette Delille and St. Anthony. Hurry."

"Is this bullshit? Who is this?"

She hung up the phone just as the two nurses came into view. They stopped short when they saw her.

"Hey, girl. I thought you were out on vacation this week," one of them said.

Cat frowned, pretending the woman was wrong. "No. You're mixed up. That's next week. I've got to go. See you later." She hurried past them, noting their confused faces. She wasn't sure she'd fooled them, but it didn't matter. She just needed to buy a few minutes to grab some supplies and get the hell out of there.

CHAPTER SEVEN

Blood grimaced as the hand around his throat tightened, he tried to pull it free, but with one arm still cuffed and the other with an IV catheter stuck in his hand, he didn't have the strength to overpower his attacker.

The door opened, and the hand around his neck released as the Death Head standing over him, the sadistic motherfucker they called Ratchet, backed off.

Blood coughed as the biker named Stoner shoved Cat into the room ahead of him, the duffel bag clutched in her arms.

Blood's surprised eyes swept over her, taking in the guilty and perhaps traumatized look on her face that somehow said she'd fucked up. His jaw clenched. She knew better than to come back here. *Goddamn it.* If they ever got out of this, he might just be tempted to beat her ass red for this.

His tormentor turned to look at her with a sick grin. "Well lookie here. If it isn't Nurse Feel-good."

She looked from Blood to him.

Ratchet strolled toward her. "You get everything you need?"

She nodded.

He tore the bag from her arms and tossed it to the floor, his attention staying on her. He backed her to the wall, one palm pressing against the plaster by her head, the other lifting to wrap around the lanyard her badge hung from and sliding slowly up until he had it tightened around the slim column of her neck.

"Leave the fucking girl alone. It's me you came up here to torment," Blood growled from the bed, drawing the man's attention from Cat.

Ratchet looked over at him with a curled lip. "Shut the fuck up. You ain't in any position to tell me jack shit."

Cat's stricken eyes glanced to Blood, and he could see she was scared shitless.

Stoner leaned a shoulder against the doorframe, a dirty grin on his face that said he planned to have a turn with her next. There was a pecking order in every club. Apparently Ratchet outranked Stoner. Blood had a feeling everybody but the Prospect outranked Stoner. He seemed to have the brains of a sixth grader.

Ratchet on the other hand was dangerous. He was smart, and he didn't have an ounce of remorse in his body.

With his arm cuffed to the bed, Blood knew the only weapon he had was his mouth. The only thing he could do was to anger Ratchet so badly he'd turn his attention from Cat to deal with Blood.

"Don't worry, girl. Bet he can't even get it up," Blood taunted.

Ratchet's head swiveled to him. "Shut your damn mouth or I'll shut it for you. I'll yank that damn IV tube out and wrap it around your fucking throat."

"I'd like to see you try," Blood challenged.

A split second later, Ratchet had jerked a handgun from his back waistband and aimed it at Blood's head. "Try me, motherfucker."

"Go ahead. Do it," Blood growled. He caught the terrified look on Cat's face as she let loose a loud piercing scream that had to have carried outside.

Blood stared down the barrel of the semi-automatic. "Do it, asshole! Fucking do it!"

Booted feet pounded up the stairs, followed by a booming voice. "What the fuck is going on? Shut that broad the hell up!"

A moment later Snake shoved past Stoner to shoulder his way into the room, taking in the scene. "What the fuck are you doing, you fucking idiots? You trying to bring down every cop in the parish on us?"

"He needs to shut his goddamned mouth," Ratchet announced, his gun still aimed at Blood's head.

"Put your motherfucking gun away, Ratchet. I told you before, you're not shooting anyone in this house. Deal with it."

"He keeps running his fucking mouth, I will."

"Just leave him alone. We've got a goddamn meeting to get to. Now! Move!"

It was a long tense moment of standoff as Ratchet glared at Blood, and Blood glared right back. Finally, Ratchet backed off, jamming the gun in his waistband.

Snake grabbed the duffel bag off the floor and shoved it at her chest. "You open your mouth again or cause anymore trouble, you're done. Understand?"

She nodded, her terrified eyes meeting his. Satisfied, he moved out of the door, followed by the others. She stood frozen as they left. Before he closed it, Stoner grinned at her as if to tell her this wasn't over, and he'd be back. Then he locked them in.

She slumped against the wall in relief, and Blood could finally breath again. "Jesus Christ, girl. Come here."

She moved on shaky legs toward him. He pulled her to sit on the edge of the bed and the duffel slipped from her hands to fall with a thud to the floor. And then she was clinging to his chest, sobbing in relief. His arm with the IV came up to wrap around her, his hand cradling her head. "Shh, baby. It's okay."

"It's not okay. None of this is okay," she cried.

Something in her tone had him frowning. "What happened?"

She shook her head and sat up, wiping her eyes. "I'm sorry. Your wound."

"It's fine."

They stared at each other.

"What the hell did you come back for?" Blood growled in a hushed tone.

"My sister. You're right. Everything you said is true. I

think you're the best shot I've got at saving her."

"You make the call?"

She nodded, but the look in her eyes wasn't reassuring.

"What?" he bit out.

"I don't think they believed me."

Blood clenched his teeth and stared off. He'd been MIA for a couple days now. They had to be looking for him. "You give 'em the location?"

"Yes. But we got interrupted. I had to hang up."

"They'll come. If not enforce, they'll at least send someone to scope it out, see if it's a trap." He saw her doubting eyes. "They'll come, baby. I promise."

About that time, they heard motorcycles firing up in the yard, and they both paused to listen. He lifted his chin toward the window. "See how many pull out."

She moved, watching for a moment as the roar of engines shook the glass and then thundered out into the street.

"How many bikes are left out there?" Blood asked from the bed.

"I only see one."

Blood looked to the door. "They may have left us with just one guard." His eyes met hers. "This may be our shot. Might be the only one we get."

"What do you mean?"

He motioned her closer with his fingers, and she sat on the bedside.

"Not sure who they left here. Might be a Prospect. Might be that idiot, Stoner. Whoever it is, he comes in the room we got one shot. We draw him to the bed, and I'll try to get his gun."

Cat looked at him and said nothing, but he could see the wheels turning in her head. She was coming up with a plan of her own. Blood grabbed her forearm. "You listen to me; we do this my way or not at all." The stubborn little wench wouldn't agree, wouldn't even nod.

She wrenched her arm free and stood.

"Damn it, Cat—"

Before he could stop her, she bent, pulled the plug to the lamp from the wall, and dropped it to the floor. Then she moved to the door and started banging on it. What the hell was she doing?

"Goddamn it, *listen to me*," he hissed as the sound of boots trudging up the stairs carried to them. The lock rattled and the door opened.

Stoner entered. Blood let out a sigh of relief. This still wasn't ideal, but he was better than Ratchet. Thinking quickly, Blood growled, "I've got to take a piss. You want to let me out of this cuff or do you want me to just hang it over the side and piss on the floor."

Stoner's attention was all on Cat with a grin that told Blood he planned to put his time alone in the house to good use. But he swiveled his head to snap, "Like I'd fall for that. No way in hell I'm letting you loose."

"So, I guess I go with Option B and piss on the floor." Blood made a move to roll to the side.

"Gross!" Cat bit out and glared at Stoner. "You're not really going let him do that are you? I'm supposed to stay in this room with him after that? No fucking way!"

Blood almost grinned at Stoner's reaction. He just didn't know how to take her.

"At least find him a container he can use as a urinal for God's sake!" she snapped.

"Like what?"

"I don't know. A milk jug. A pail. Anything."

"We don't have anything like that."

"Then take him to the bathroom, or aren't you man enough to handle one guy sick with infection and two holes in his side?"

Goddamn it. Blood grit his teeth. Didn't she know that if she pushed the wrong buttons, it'd be her who paid the price? He had to give her credit though, she stood her ground, stood up to these guys. It was only after the confrontation was over, when she'd melted against him like a wilted flower, that she'd let the vulnerable fear show.

She was holding it together now, though, going toe-to-toe with Stoner, glaring at him as if that alone would bend him to her will.

Stoner stared her down, like he was contemplating backing her against the wall with a hand at her throat. Instead, he whirled to move out the open door, grumbling about fucking bitches. In that split second, Cat grabbed the lamp off the side table and smashed it over the back of his head.

He dropped like a bag of rocks.

She didn't stop there. She pulled the gun from the back of his jeans, stood over him and shot him in the back. *Bam!*

Bam!

Holy fuck!

Blood stared, stunned, and then watched as she turned her eyes on him. For a split second, he wasn't completely sure she wouldn't turn that gun on him. They stared at each other, both in shock.

"Holy shit, babe. You just shot him."

She looked down at the gun in her hand and then, as he watched, she took the hem of her scrub shirt, and calmly as you please, wiped her prints off the weapon and tossed it to him. "No, I didn't. You did."

He caught it to his chest, his heart in his throat, hoping the damn gun wouldn't go off on him. His brows shot up. Now his prints were on the damn gun. One that had just been used in a homicide. "Yeah, o-kay. Remind me never to fuck with you."

She looked back down at the body, and Blood could see her start to tremble as the ramifications of what she'd just done started to sink in.

"Well, since you're not going to shoot me," he paused to rattle the cuffs. "You want to let me go?"

That broke the spell, and she bent to dig through Stoner's pockets. Coming up with the key, she quickly moved to the bed and worked the cuff free.

Blood paused to shake his hand out, the muscles in his arm stiff from being in one position for so long. "Hurry, babe, give me his phone, and then get this damn IV out of me."

She moved quickly to comply, tossing him the phone.

He grabbed it and quickly punched in a number, putting it to his ear.

"Who are you calling? The police?" she asked.

"No. Since *I just shot a guy*, I'm not calling the police."

She rolled her eyes. "Ha ha. Very funny. Then who are you calling?"

"The cavalry. Now get this damn IV out quick. We've got to get out of here."

She bent to grab a pair of surgical gloves out of her duffel.

"We don't have time for that," Blood snapped, waiting for someone to answer the damn phone at the clubhouse.

"I didn't spend all this time getting you well, just to…" She paused as the roar of motorcycles coming up fast carried to them both.

"Shit!" Blood growled.

She quickly bent over his arm, yanking the tape off. "Hold still."

"Hurry, babe," he whispered.

She carefully pulled the needle out and pressed a piece of gauze over it.

Blood batted her hand away. "We've got to get out of here."

He shoved the phone in his pocket, and with a hand to his bandaged wound, he struggled up to sit on the side of the bed. Cat helped him to his feet and with the gun in his hand he moved to look out the window.

"Hurry, Blood. They're coming."

"Wait a minute, babe. Those are my guys." He hobbled

NICOLE JAMES

past her and yanked open the door to the outside staircase. Leaning against it as a wave of dizziness took hold, he motioned his brothers up.

The faces of a half dozen brothers jerked up to see him. A moment later, they were scrambling up the staircase.

Sandman was the first one through the door with a sawed off shotgun. He growled low, "How many of them are there?"

"They left one guy. The rest are gone."

"Where the fuck is he? Downstairs?"

"No. He's dead on the bedroom floor." Blood led the way.

Sandman followed and stood over the guy bleeding out on the floor.

Undertaker was the next one up the stairs and in the room. He looked down at the man, taking in the patch on the back of his cut. "Jesus Christ. Death Heads."

"Yeah," Blood acknowledged.

Undertaker's eyes lifted to Blood, and his hand grabbed the back of his neck, pulling him close. "You scared the fuck out of me, Son."

They embraced. When they pulled back, Undertaker's eyes dropped to the bandage and then noticed the IV hanging from the bedpost. "What the hell happened?"

"They shot him," Cat said.

Undertaker's eyes flashed to her. "You the one who called us?"

She nodded.

His eyes moved back to Blood, dismissing her. "You

100

okay?"

"Yeah. I'll explain the rest later. Right now we need to get the hell out of here. No tellin' when the rest will be back."

"Let 'em come," Sandman growled, his hand tightening around his gun.

"Right now we've got another problem, Brother," Blood said, his eyes connecting with Sandman—the man who'd had his back through more shit that he cared to remember.

"Yeah? What the fuck's that?" Undertaker growled.

"They're holding Cat's sister. I'm going after her."

"Like hell you are," Undertaker bit out. "Only place you're going is back to the fucking clubhouse to get Doc to patch you up."

"Already been patched up." He nodded toward Cat standing there in her green scrubs.

Undertaker's gaze swept over her again.

Blood met her eyes, and he read the look in them. Now that his club had rescued him, she doubted he'd keep his word to help her sister. She was afraid he'd renege on that promise. Not a chance in hell, sweetheart. "I told you I'd get her back for you, and I will. Least I can do after you saved my miserable life."

She nodded slightly, but her eyes strayed to Undertaker and the President's patch on his cut, and Blood knew she was wondering if the decision was in his hands.

"Where's your apartment?" Blood snapped, drawing her eyes back to him.

"Tulane and Carrollton," she murmured quietly.

He looked at his club's President. "I'm going to get her. You can come or not."

"Now just a damn minute," Undertaker snapped. A moment later he was pushing Blood out of the room, ordering Sandman, "Watch her."

Blood knew his President didn't appreciate being talked to like that, but right now he didn't give a fuck. They didn't have time to stand around here arguing.

"This chick is here treating you as a favor to the Death Heads. Doesn't that tell you something?" Undertaker snapped under his breath. "She's *with* them."

"She's not. They threatened to kill her sister if she didn't come treat me."

"You sure you can take her word for it? Enough to bet your life on it? Enough to bet the lives of your brothers on it?"

"Like I said, I'm going. You don't have to come with."

"Goddamn it, boy. You think that's how this works? Since when do you call the shots in this club? I say where the fuck we go, and I say where the fuck *you* go! Seems we've got bigger problems than some bitch's sister. If we're going after anybody, it'll be Death Heads."

"She made that phone call for me. I promised her I'd get her sister back. I owe a debt to her. I'm not turning my back on her." Blood stared him down.

"Goddamn it." Undertaker looked back toward the bedroom door. "How many Death Heads were there?"

"Not sure. I saw at least four. Might be half a dozen."

"What the fuck are they doing here in New Orleans for

Christ's sake?" Undertaker mused aloud.

"No clue. But whatever it is, its big."

"Where'd they go? Got any clue on *that*?"

"One of 'em said something about a meeting."

"Jesus Christ."

"Yeah."

"We've got a fucking dead body and a town full of the enemy. Any suggestions?"

Blood grinned. "Burn it to the ground, and get the fuck out of here."

"We're not setting the damn place on fire."

"Makes a statement."

Undertaker grinned back at him, his white teeth flashing in his dark beard. Then he studied Blood. "Prospect's got the van parked half a block down. Can you make it that far?"

"What do you think, old man?"

Undertaker studied him silently for a long moment, and Blood knew he was debating whether or not to let him go. Finally, he jerked his chin. "Take Sandman with you."

Blood made to move back into the bedroom, but Undertaker pushed him back with a final warning. "If the sister's not there, you come back to the clubhouse, and we get a plan together."

Blood nodded, grateful that Undertaker was agreeing to put the weight of the entire club behind helping him get Cat's sister back. "Thanks."

Undertaker nodded. "Where's your fucking cut?"

"Bastards took it."

Undertaker turned and jerked his chin to his VP, Mooch.

"You and the boys tear this place apart. See if you can find a clue what these cocksuckers were up to, and find Blood's goddamn cut!"

The men moved downstairs.

Blood walked back into the room, his hand over his wound, and his eyes connected with Cat's. "We're going."

Undertaker followed him in.

Her eyes shifted between the men. "Where?"

Blood clenched his jaw when she questioned him. Obviously, she still didn't trust him. "To get your sister."

Her eyes shifted between them again, and she nodded.

Blood's eyes drilled into hers. "I gotta trust you, and you gotta trust me. Only way this works. Understand?"

"Yes."

He grabbed her upper arm and pulled her close, dipping his face to hers. "There's a van parked down the street. Stay quiet, move quickly, and everything will be all right."

She nodded again.

Mooch stuck his head in the door, and Blood twisted his neck to look. The man's eyes swept over Cat, but he said nothing about her. He tossed Blood his cut. "Got a couple holes in it, but at least they didn't burn it."

Blood caught it in his free hand and released Cat to slip it on. "Thanks, man."

"I don't want anymore holes in it, you hear me?" Undertaker ordered.

Blood grinned at his President's way of telling him not to get shot again. "I'll see to it." His eyes moved over Cat's head to Sandman. "You're with us."

"Ain't I always?" Sandman grinned and hefted his shotgun up over his shoulder.

As Blood passed through the door, he bumped his VP with his shoulder. "Took you long enough to find me."

Mooch grinned at him. "Hey, we all thought, 'Blood can take care of himself; it's not like he's Sandman'."

Blood chuckled and moved on, Cat's hand secure in his as he pulled her behind him.

Sandman glared at Mooch. "Nice to know I'm loved around here."

Mooch grinned and slugged him in the shoulder. "Take care of him."

CHAPTER EIGHT

A white panel van rolled quietly into the apartment complex on Tulane and Carrollton, a single motorcycle following in its wake. They pulled to the back of the lot, and the Prospect put the van in park, eyeing the building.

"How many exits?" Blood asked Cat, eyeing the setup himself. "There a backdoor Dax can run out of?"

"Just one way in or out. The front door."

Blood nodded, then looked over his shoulder from the front passenger seat. His eyes connected with Cat's. "You're waiting here."

"Oh no, I'm not."

"Cat—"

Sandman rapped on the passenger window, and Blood swiveled his head and rolled the glass down.

Sandman leaned on his forearms in the window. "Looks quiet. Didn't see no bikes."

Blood nodded, then looked back at Cat. "Stay here."

"I'm going with!" she insisted.

"No, you're not."

"Yes, I am."

"She always like this?" Sandman asked from the window.

"Apparently. Got any suggestions?" Blood asked him.

"Women are bat-shit crazy. Sorry, that's all the advice I've got."

Cat folded her arms, that stubborn jaw lifting. "Fine. Go. I'll only follow you."

"Goddamn it." Blood whirled on the Prospect. "You got anything I can tie her up with?"

The Prospect, who looked like he wasn't sure if Blood was joking or not, offered, "Uh, there's some jumper cables in back."

"You are not tying me up!" Cat snapped and threw open the cargo door.

Sandman looked through the window at the Prospect. "Jumper cables, really? That's the best you got when a member asks you for help? I'm ashamed, Prospect."

"I can pin her down, if you want, Blood," the Prospect suggested, now nervous he'd let the club down.

"Shut up and get out of the van," Blood snapped and pushed out his own door. He slid a round in the chamber of his weapon and looked at Sandman. "You ready?"

"I was born ready, Brother." Sandman grinned back.

Blood grabbed Cat's arm and hauled her to his side. "You stay behind us. You hear me?"

She nodded.

"Which one?" he snapped.

"214. Second one from the left. See it?" She pointed.

Blood nodded. "Let's go."

"Wait."

They all turned back to her.

"I don't have my keys. How are we getting in?"

Sandman looked at Blood. "Is she for real?"

"The MC way," Blood said with a grin. "We boot the door, baby."

She clamped her mouth shut, and they all moved across the lot and up a flight of metal stairs to the second level.

Blood held his index finger to his lips, signaling them to be quiet, as he leaned to the door to listen. He shook his head. Sandman jerked his head to the side, motioning for Blood to step out of the way, then he reared back and hit the door just to the side of the doorknob with his size thirteen boot.

The cheap door splintered from the frame at the lock and flung open. The men all charged through, with Cat right behind them.

Dax was kicked back on her sofa in a wife-beater t-shirt and a pizza box on his chest, one slice poised in the air halfway to his mouth. With a startled look, he tossed the box in the air and tried to run. He didn't get far, seeing as he had nowhere to go. The only exit was blocked by the Prospect.

Cat didn't waste time on him, she dashed through the apartment looking for Holly, calling her sister's name.

A moment later, she raced back out to the living room.

Blood looked up at her, his hands fisted in Dax's undershirt with the man pinned to the wall. "You find her?"

Cat looked at him, her eyes glassing with tears, and

shook her head.

Blood could see her whole body was flooding with panic, her hands shaking. He turned back to Dax and slammed him against the wall. "Where is she?"

"I don't have her."

Cat moved in next to Blood and shouted into Dax's face. "You *had* her! You promised you wouldn't hurt her!" She made a lunge for Dax, but Sandman grabbed her from behind and held her back.

"Let Blood deal with him, girl," he ordered.

She yanked and pulled, trying to get to Dax.

Blood looked over at her. She was fighting mad, but she was scared, too. He lifted his chin to Sandman, who pulled her back farther. Then he turned his attention back on Dax. "You had her. What happened to her?"

"They took her."

"Who took her?" Blood asked, praying he didn't already know the answer.

"Death Heads. They sent a couple Prospects for her."

At that, he heard Cat burst out crying, getting more hysterical by the minute. "You piece of shit!" she screamed.

"Where'd they take her?"

"I don't know."

"The fuck you don't." Blood punched him in the face.

He tried to block his face, pleading, "Stop! Stop! Okay! They said she'd seal the deal on some meeting. Something about business in the Quarter. That's all I know, man. I swear!"

"When did they take her?"

"About an hour ago."

"You fucking little shit." Blood pulled his gun and put it to the man's head. The punk really started to sweat then.

"I swear to God, it's the truth! She was here. I was taking good care of her." He looked at Cat. "I didn't touch her, I swear, Cat."

"Shut up! You don't get to talk to her. You don't get to look at her. Got me?" Blood growled.

Dax put his hands in the air. "Okay, man. Okay."

Blood glanced back at Cat. He could see the desolation and despair this punk's words had caused her. It was written all over her face. He jerked Dax forward. "You're coming with us. You make a sound, I'll drop you on the spot. Understand?"

He nodded. "It's cool. I won't give you any trouble. I'm a friend."

"You're no fucking friend to me. And any friend of the Death Heads is an enemy to me." He shoved Dax toward the door. "Move."

Sandman took hold of Dax and passed Cat to Blood. She fell against his chest, and he gathered her close, his head dipping to hers. "I'll find her, baby. I promise you."

She shook with sobs.

"You've got to be strong for her, Cat. You've got to hold it together."

She pulled back and looked into his eyes, as he willed his strength to her. She nodded and wiped her face. "Okay."

"Good girl." He lifted his chin toward the hallway. "Go grab whatever you need. You're not staying here."

She looked up at him blankly. "Where am I staying?"

"Not here. I don't want the Death Heads coming back for you. They know where you live. Ain't got a lot of time, babe. Move."

She nodded, and as if coming out of a trance, she dashed down the hall.

He watched her go. She may not like him taking control of the situation—and of *her*—but that was exactly what he was doing, and she'd better adjust.

Five minutes later, they were heading across the parking lot to the van. The Prospect had a hold of Dax. Sandman, Blood, and Cat followed behind him. One minute Dax was walking calmly and complacently toward the van, the next he took off sprinting for the road.

"And we have a runner," Sandman joked as he and Blood watched their Prospect take off after Dax and tackle him a moment later. He punched Dax in the face, and then hauled him to his feet.

"Now if he can figure out how to restrain him with jumper cables, we're good," Sandman added with a grin.

Blood slugged him in the arm. "He can always sit on him."

They secured Dax in the back of the van with some cable ties that the Prospect scrounged up out of the glove box. Cat climbed in the back and scooted across the bench seat to sit behind the driver's seat. Blood climbed in next to her, sliding the cargo door shut.

The Prospect fired up the van, and they pulled out with Sandman riding behind them.

"Are you going to kill me?" came the muffled voice from the back.

Blood twisted to look over the back of the seat. "No body, no murder, right?"

"Oh, shit," Dax mumbled.

Blood met the smiling eyes of the Prospect in the rearview, then his eyes moved to Cat. She sat staring blankly out the side window, looking absolutely shell-shocked. Blood pulled her away from the window. "C'mere, babe."

She didn't fight it, and he tucked her back against his side, his arms wrapping across her stomach and chest, one hand on her shoulder, one on her hip. He pressed his mouth to her temple, holding her tight, trying to comfort her. He knew what she was feeling. She was grieving, like she'd lost already, like she was leaving everything in her life behind, descending into a world she wanted no part of. But there was one thing she didn't realize—she had him now. And it crossed his mind that he may be *all* she had now.

"I've got you, babe. I've got you."

CHAPTER NINE

They headed northeast out of town and across Lake Ponchartrain. Then headed down some dirt back roads. Cat soon became lost and was content to stare emotionless at the scenery passing the windows: old fish camps and houses up on stilts over the water of inlets and bayous. Spanish moss hung from the trees that stretched over the road to form a canopy. At several points the narrow road ran adjacent to the bayou, no more than ten yards from the pavement.

Cat felt the vehicle slowing, and she perked up in the seat, frowning at what appeared to be a stockade. The gates swung open, and the Prospect pulled through. Once they were clear, two men scrambled to shut and secure the heavy gates again. This place was locked up like Fort Knox.

The tires crunched across the gravel as the van rolled up to the clubhouse. Cat glanced around, taking it all in: the six foot high wooden fence and the huge metal building with the extended roof that covered a cement slab with a half dozen picnic tables. There were a couple leather-clad men sitting on the tabletops, their booted feet on the wooden bench seats. Others stood around them, smoking cigarettes. They all turned when the van rolled in, eyeing it as it stopped up front.

Blood yanked on the door handle and slid the side door open, jumping out to the ground. Turning back, he held his hand out to Cat. "Come on, angel. It's okay."

She turned at the sound of the rear double doors opening, and then Sandman dragged Dax out the back. The Prospect jumped out and helped him.

She saw a biker walk up, eye Dax's battered face, and ask, "What happened to him?"

"He decided to take a closer look at Blood's fist," Sandman answered with a chuckle.

"Cat."

Her eyes swiveled back to see Blood still standing with his hand out. Everything seemed so surreal. She couldn't believe her sister was taken. She couldn't believe she was here with another MC. Would they be any better than the last bunch?

She looked into Blood's eyes. He wouldn't let anyone hurt her. She could feel his protectiveness radiating off him, had felt it as he'd held her close in the van, insisting to her over and over that everything would be okay, that she had to be strong for Holly. That he'd find her if it took him all over the state to do it. He'd track her down, and then he'd kill the motherfuckers who had her. He'd promised.

She believed him. She had no choice but to believe him, because if she didn't, she'd shatter into a million pieces.

Blood was right, she had to be strong.

She slipped her hand in his and stepped out.

Bikes, lined up in rows, sat gleaming in the hot sun, their chrome almost blindingly bright. She squinted and looked over at the men sitting under the overhanging roof.

They stared back at her blankly, and she wondered if they knew who she was and why she was here. Was that curiosity she saw or apathy? Perhaps they didn't really give a shit why she was here. Perhaps she was as inconsequential as she'd heard women were to men like these. *Cunts don't count*, she'd once heard Dax say, teasing her big sister, Stacey, with a phrase he'd picked up hanging around the MCs in Texas.

Was it true? Did she not matter at all?

Probably not to the club, but maybe she mattered to Blood. At least, he seemed to feel he owed her for what she'd done for him. And perhaps that's all any of this was. Respect. Loyalty. She'd heard those were important to these clubs. Perhaps debts owed meant something to them, too.

Blood took her hand tightly in his, almost as if he was afraid she'd bolt. Then he led her through the doors of the clubhouse, and she clung closely in the wake of his tall body and broad shoulders. Sandman and the Prospect disappeared somewhere with Dax.

It was dim inside, especially after coming in from the bright sunshine. She blinked several times, waiting for her eyes to adjust. The place was cavernous. A bar came into focus off to the right, pool tables off to the left. A staircase in the back led to what must be a second level.

A man behind the bar called out, "Blood, Doc's up with Undertaker waiting for you."

Blood nodded, and Cat half expected him to park her ass on a barstool and go meet with his President. He surprised her by pulling her along behind him toward the stairs.

When they reached the second level, he led her down a long hallway to the last door at the end. Rapping twice, he barely waited for the "Come in!" that was hollered out, before he twisted the knob and walked in.

It was a large office with a big desk on the left side. The man she recognized from earlier sat behind it: Undertaker, their President. His VP, Mooch, leaned against a credenza off to the side, his arms folded. Another man sat in one of the chairs facing the desk. He wasn't a biker; that much was plainly obvious. Although he did look pretty young. Cat figured he had to be the doctor the man downstairs had referred to. He was leaned forward with his elbows on his knees, his hands clasped between them. He'd been laughing at something Undertaker had said.

He twisted to look when they came through the door. He wore wire-rimmed glasses and his light brown hair brushed the button-down collar of his chambray shirt. He wore khakis and running shoes. Not exactly the picture of your average Intern. She wondered if he was a real doctor.

"You get her?" Undertaker asked quietly.

Blood shook his head. "Guy was alone. Sandman's puttin' him in the room."

The room. Cat wondered what that meant.

Undertaker nodded, then his eyes flicked to her. "Sorry,

kid."

The man in the chair stood then, drawing her attention. He extended his hand toward her. "How do you do? I'm Dr. Richard Sanders."

"Dr. Sanders." She shook his hand. "Catherine Randall. Call me Cat."

He glanced at Blood, then to her. "I understand you treated Blood."

She nodded. "Yes, Doctor. I'm a nurse."

"Mind if I have a look at your patient?" he asked with a nice smile, gesturing to Blood.

"Please." Cat wasn't used to doctors being so kind or respectful to nurses.

Dr. Sanders grabbed his black leather doctor's bag from the floor and gestured toward a couch against the back wall. "If you don't mind."

Blood shot Undertaker a look that said, *Is this really necessary?*

"Humor me," his President growled.

Blood moved to the couch, pulled his cut off, tossed it over the arm, and lay back.

Dr. Sanders pulled a pair of gloves and a mask from his bag and put them on. Then sat on the wooden coffee table and leaned to remove the bandage. He bent to examine the wound, front and back. "How was the patient when you first examined him, Ms. Randall?"

Cat suddenly felt like she was back in nursing school doing her nursing practicum. "Yesterday at five pm, his fever was one hundred and six. He was dehydrated with signs of delirium. His eyes were glassy. I examined the wound and found it to be a through and through gunshot wound. It appeared to have entered from the back and deflected off the rib, causing no severe damage. I irrigated and packed it. I changed the packing once, this morning. I started him on a saline IV and a course of antibiotics."

"Which one?"

"Ampicillin sulbactam, three grams IV every six hours. I was able to give him three rounds. He finished the last one"—she glanced at her wristwatch—"three hours ago."

Dr. Sanders nodded. "I'll start him on oral." He looked at Blood. "Appears to have only got the flesh and muscle. Lucky for you it didn't enter the abdominal cavity. It looks good. She took good care of you."

Blood met her eyes and grinned. "That she did."

"The packing needs to be changed out every day until its healed. I'll leave enough supplies for Ms. Randall to continue that at home until its healed, if you'd like." He looked from Blood to Cat as if to ask if she'd be around to do these home healthcare duties.

Blood answered, not giving her a chance to speak. "That would be good."

"All right then, let me write you a prescription for antibiotics and a pain killer. I'll need to see you in my office end of the week to see how its healing."

"Thank you, Doctor," Blood said.

Undertaker approached and shook his hand. "Yes, thank you, Richard. I appreciate you coming to take a look at him."

"Anytime."

Dr. Sanders quickly wrote out the prescriptions. Then he turned and shook Cat's hand. "Ms. Randall. If you're ever looking for a job. I've got a small clinic, and I'd be glad to have you."

"Thank you, Dr. Sanders."

He cocked his head at her. "How are *you* holding up? Undertaker told me your sister was missing. I could write you a script for something to calm your nerves or to help you sleep, if you'd like."

Cat shook her head. "No, thank you, Doctor. I'll be fine."

He nodded and patted her upper arm. "Well, if you change your mind, let me know."

After he left, Undertaker turned to Blood. "I had the girls come in to fix some food."

Blood nodded and patted his taut stomach. "I'm starved, and I know Cat hasn't eaten either."

Undertaker nodded then jerked his chin to Mooch. "Take her down and introduce her to the ladies. I need to speak to Blood. We'll be down in a minute."

Mooch nodded. "Sure thing, Boss. Follow me, honey."

Cat looked to Blood, unsure about being separated from him.

He lifted his chin. "I'll only be a few minutes, then I'll come find you."

She nodded and followed Mooch out.

***

Blood watched the door close, and then his eyes swung to his President, knowing the man wanted to discuss the Death Heads situation. "Find out anything?"

Undertaker lifted his chin toward his desk. "Sit down."

They both took a seat.

"There wasn't much left at that house. The boys swept it over… didn't find shit. Nothing to tell us what the hell they're up to. You want to tell me exactly what happened? How the hell did they get ahold of you?"

"Some girls by my place were getting hassled—"

"By girls, you mean—"

"Hookers. Anyway, I interceded. When I asked where the hell their pimp was, Cherry told me John had been busy lately with other things."

Undertaker stroked over his beard, taking it all in and making his own summations. He knew all the players in this town; Blood didn't have to explain who he was referring to. "And you went lookin' for him?"

"I decided it'd be in all our best interests if I knew what was keeping him busy. What did Black Jack have that was more important for John to be doing than keep an eye on the girls?"

"It's always a good idea to know what Black Jack is up to."

"Anyway, I walked down toward his compound, came around the corner, and the last thing I remember is seeing four Death Heads standing in the alley. I woke up chained to that bed."

"And the girl?"

"They brought her in to treat me. Infection was setting in. I was bad off. Thought I'd never get out of that room."

"What I'm wondering is why they kept you alive."

"Been wonderin' that myself. Only thing I can come up with is to use me to get something from you."

Undertaker stroked his beard, thinking.

"So what do the Death Heads have to do with him?" Blood asked.

"Don't know. But we're gonna find out."

Blood stared at the scarred wood of the desktop. "I'm taken near his compound. The Death Heads are right there. They don't want to kill me, or maybe someone stops them."

"I think the clue to all this is sitting in the room downstairs."

Blood nodded. "Dax. Let's go talk to the man." He started to rise from his chair, but Undertaker waved him back down.

"We will. First there's something else I want to talk to you about."

"What's that?"

"Nurse Hotty down there."

Blood's jaw hardened. "What about her?"

"You helping her find her sister... What's that about? Death Heads took her. So now it's your job to fix this for her?"

"I've had worse jobs." Blood gave him a look.

Undertaker read his look and grinned. "Jobs I've given you, huh?"

"Maybe."

Undertaker leaned forward on his elbows. "Seriously. What's in it for you?"

"Does there have to be something in it for me?"

Undertaker chuckled. "Yeah. Usually."

"I promised her. I owe her. She saved my life. That means something to me."

"It means something to me, too. And gratitude will be shone. But is that all this is? Is it just about you owing her?"

Blood had always been straight with Undertaker, since the day he'd met him. That was the one thing they had. So Blood gave him nothing less now. He shifted in his chair. "I owe her a debt, a debt I need to repay. More than that? Hell, I don't know. I suppose if I had any sense I'd know there's no shot with her."

"Why do you say that?"

Blood shook his head slowly, trying to find the words. "She's been through some shit. She blames men like me for a lot of it."

"Men like you?"

"MCs. Bikers. How do I roll around that? She's got no reason to trust me."

"Then give her one," Undertaker replied, leaning back in his chair.

Blood huffed out a laugh. "It's just that easy, huh?"

"If it's what you want, you'll bring her around. I have no worries on that. It's you I'm worried about."

"You've got no reason, old man."

"Why do you think that? Because you made it out?"

"No, because I nearly died, and that changes

everything."

"Does it?"

"Yeah. Helps you to see what's important."

"Yeah? What's that?"

"You should know. You found it once."

Undertaker studied him with that "all knowing" look that could always cut right through everything Blood ever thought about hiding. "Love? That was a long time ago."

Blood looked away, staring at a picture of a pretty dark-haired girl with sky-blue eyes Undertaker kept on the credenza. "I've seen what Shades and your daughter have. You had that once, too, with her mother."

Undertaker followed his gaze, taking in the photo of his daughter, Skylar. "And you want that?"

Blood studied him and grudgingly admitted, "Maybe."

"I want that for you, too. Son, there's nothing I want more. But this girl…" Undertaker tipped his head toward the door. "I'm not sure she fits in, and I'm not sure she *wants* to fit in."

Blood looked away and nodded. "Maybe, but she's lookin' at me to fix this. If I can't find her sister—"

"Then she'll need a strong shoulder to lean on and help her through this, and you've got that in spades, Blood."

"No matter where it might lead?"

"Bonds are created in rough situations. Don't forget that. And there's something else you shouldn't forget. Your first duty is to this club."

Blood met his eyes with a burning look. "You think I need you to remind me of that?"

"Just makin' sure you remember." Undertaker lifted his chin toward the door. "Go get some chow with your girl. Dax can wait."

"She's not my girl."

Undertaker grinned. "Your guest, then."

Blood stood.

Undertaker stopped him before he got to the door. "Hey, if she's not yours, am I having a room made up for her?"

That stopped him short, the vision of Cat in his bed momentarily flashing through his brain. While he'd like nothing more, he also knew now was not the time to press that issue. Soon, though. Very soon. He looked back at Undertaker and nodded.

Undertaker chuckled. "Fifty bucks says that doesn't last the week."

Blood gave him a look, and then he went in search of little *Nurse Hotty*.

***

Cat stood at the stove in the clubhouse kitchen, stirring a pot of gumbo. Mooch had brought her downstairs and led her through what appeared to be a big dining room to a large kitchen where three women were busy cooking. He'd gruffly introduced her to them, motioning to the one with the red kinky hair tied up in a bandana as Roxy and the other woman, who had a braid of dark hair going down her back, as Sissy. They were both middle-aged, wearing jeans and tank tops and tons of silver jewelry. Then he spoke to the third woman, who turned from the stove.

"Mama Ray, this is Cat. She's with Blood."

Mama Ray was an older woman dressed in jeans and a faded black tank top that read *Support your local Evil Dead MC* on the front in fading white lettering. She had short, gray curly hair and dark brown eyes.

"Mama Ray was Jaybird's ol' lady. She takes care of the clubhouse now."

"Was?" Cat asked.

Mooch nodded. "He was killed a couple years back."

"I'm so sorry," Cat said, looking to the woman.

She gave Cat the once over, peering through her glasses. She noted the scrubs but didn't reference them. Instead she asked, "Cat, huh? That a nickname or short for something?"

"It's short for Catherine."

"Huh. Can you cook, Cat?"

"Some."

"Some good? Or some bad?"

"I'm okay."

"Guess we'll see." She set a head of cabbage on a cutting board with a big knife. "Here, make yourself useful. Cut this up. You can make the coleslaw."

She had picked up the knife and began chopping away, scooping up the shredded cabbage to toss in a stainless bowl. The three women began to chat and soon were including her in the conversation. They were down-to-earth women, all committed to the club. They gave her what amounted to an interview, putting her through the wringer with question after question, wanting to know who or what she was to Blood and why she was there.

Her answers didn't seem to appease them, or at least didn't seem to sound plausible to them. *Blood, in need of help? Their Blood? Not possible.*

They were sad to hear about her sister, but were equally as curious at the fact that Blood had promised to get her back for Cat.

Roxy frowned, while Mama Ray openly laughed.

"Our Blood? Right. Sure he is, honey," Sissy insisted.

"What's keeping you here?" Mama Ray asked, her hand on her hip. "I was you, I'd hightail it out of here and go find my sister."

"He told me he doesn't say shit he doesn't mean. That sound like 'your' Blood to you?" Cat gave it back with a snap in her voice.

That had Mama Ray lifting her chin, her eyes narrowing as she studied Cat. Then without another word on the subject, she snapped, "Food's ready."

Cat watched her pick up a large pan of pulled pork and storm off into the other room.

Roxy picked up the bowl of coleslaw, held it out to Cat, and then picked up a large pan of baked beans. "Her bark is worse than her bite, and she's protective of the guys. Don't worry. If Blood wants you around, she won't make trouble for you." She winked. "Come on, sweetheart."

CHAPTER TEN

Cat watched Blood as they all sat to eat. He was a man back once again in his natural habitat, back within the clubhouse he obviously felt at home in. Back again with the men of this MC he'd pledged his loyalty to, brothers he loved and trusted. It was as if she was seeing him clearly for the first time, and she studied him closely. The way he joked with them, the way he felt at home and totally relaxed in their company...It was eye opening. Yes, he was like the other MCs she'd been exposed to, and at the same time, he was nothing like them. She also observed how respected he was within his club. He held some rank or importance, it seemed.

He caught her eyes on him across the table as he reclined back in his chair, pushing his empty plate away, and he winked.

The other men were still going back for second helpings.

"I went and saw Carlos Santana Saturday night. He was amazing," one of them said between bites.

Another slapped a spoonful of coleslaw on his plate. "If I cared what you did on the weekend, Bam-Bam, I'd put a gun in my mouth."

"That so, Easy? Well, what's stopping you?"

"And if I gotta hear *you* drone on about another 90's hair band, Easy, *I'm* gonna eat a bullet," Blood retorted.

"Who is Carlos Santana?" the twenty-something Prospect asked and everyone at the table went silent.

Bam-Bam turned on him. "Oh, now you're just trying to piss me off."

Sandman scrapped his plate clean. "Can we get this meeting going? I've got to get out of here soon."

"Oh, like *you've* got plans." Blood laughed at him.

"Okay, enough, boys. Sandman's right," Mooch said.

"That'd be a first," Easy teased him.

Sandman reached over and, with a flick of his fingers, dumped the man's plate upside-down onto his lap.

Easy looked down. "You fucker."

"Meeting's in twenty minutes. Got something to take care of first," Undertaker said, standing. He glanced at Blood and jerked his head toward the door. Blood nodded and turned to Cat. "Got something to do. Stay here with the girls."

He rose from the bench, as did the rest of them.

Cat's hand closed around his forearm, stopping him. His eyes dropped to her hand, then lifted to her eyes. She knew where he was going and the reason. They stared at each other, a thousand questions in her look. None he would answer, and she understood that, too, but she had to try.

"She's my sister. Let me talk to him. Please."

"She *is* your sister. But what happens here in this clubhouse, babe, that's club business."

"Blood—"

"I won't be long." With that he pulled her hand from his arm, stepped over the bench, and strode out of the room along with the rest of the men.

***

Blood followed Undertaker into the room. There was only one piece of furniture—a chair—and Dax was cuffed to it. The other men shuffled in. Sandman stood on one side with his arms folded, Mooch stood on the other side. Bam-Bam, Mud, and Easy stood around the room.

Undertaker nodded to Blood to take the lead on this interrogation. It wasn't anything new to him. He was the club's Enforcer and, therefore, handled a lot of beatings.

He stepped forward.

Dax's eyes lifted to him, and Blood could see he was already shaking in his boots. He had a black eye from earlier.

Blood slammed his fist into the side of Dax's face, sending his head spinning to the side. He had no problem doing it—not when he knew this slime ball had been responsible for leading the Death Heads straight to Cat's door and for whatever horror her sister, Holly, was currently enduring.

Blood had seen a picture of the girl at Cat's apartment—

a small framed picture of the two of them together. He'd slid it in his pocket while Cat was stuffing some clothes in a bag. It was obvious the two were sisters. The girl was young and sweet and innocent looking. He doubted they'd killed her; not a pretty girl like her. They'd find a use for her. Sell her. Trade her out for a favor. Put her on the streets. But the thing Blood didn't understand was why they'd taken her before they even knew he and Cat had escaped.

He was about to find out. He was sure Dax knew more than he'd claimed to know at Cat's apartment.

"Please," the asshole begged. "I told you everything."

Blood hit him again. Dax's lip split open, and red splatter flew all over Sandman.

"Goddamn it, man." Sandman stared down at the stains on his vest.

Blood grinned at him. "You might want to move, dumbass."

***

Half an hour later, the club filed into the second floor room they used for Church, the club's weekly mandatory meetings. But this wasn't their usual Friday night meeting. This was an emergency meeting that had been called specifically to deal with the Death Heads situation and to discuss what they had just learned from their "guest" locked up in the downstairs back room—a guest who was currently being guarded by a Prospect.

The men settled into chairs, some standing shoulder to

shoulder along the wood-paneled walls. The room was crowded with leather-clad full-patched members incensed at the invasion of Evil Dead territory by another MC, as well as the fury they felt that one of their own had been taken and held all this time.

There were grumblings all around the room, most consisting of threats, vowing revenge and all the different ways "those motherfuckers were going to pay."

Undertaker slammed the gavel against the table and barked, "Settle down!"

The room came to an abrupt dead silence. Other than the creaking of leather vests in old worn executive chairs, they could have heard a pin drop.

"This meeting shall be called to order. We'll dispense with the usual roll call and get right to it. First up, Bug, I want you to get on the phone with our friends in Texas. Find out everything you can about the Death Heads movements. Find out the numbers still in town, how many they think may have left town on a run, and any intel they can get. I don't care if it's just word on the street or unconfirmed rumors, I want to hear it."

"Yes, sir." Bug nodded from his place toward the end of the long table.

"Wicked, Big Boy, Sly, I want you three to concentrate on our snitches in town. Get everybody on the look out for those motherfuckers. Find out any talk they're hearing. Make sure they're suitably motivated. That goes for all the hang-arounds, too. Don't divulge too much, but make sure they know to be on the look out for any Death Head activity."

There were several nods around the room.

An arm rose.

Undertaker acknowledged the man with a nod. "Tee Ray."

"That sniveling cocksucker downstairs give up anything?"

Undertaker shook his head. "He doesn't know shit. Apparently, he was trying to save his ass from a beating when he gave up the girls to the Death Heads. They had a disagreement about an accounting issue. Not the first time, according to him. Claims he doesn't know why the Death Heads were in town. He was brought along to make some introductions to other drug connections, but he believes there was something much bigger in the works. There was talk of a meeting the MC was going to, but he doesn't know the other players. He wasn't told prior that they were coming to take the second girl he'd been left guarding. Said two guys showed up, took her without a word, and left. Only thing he knows is one of them got a call; he overheard part of it. Said he heard the guy reference the Quarter, and they'd be there in fifteen minutes. He wasn't sure that was where they were headed or not."

"What about Blood being taken?"

"He didn't know shit about that except they had a guy who needed medical treatment. He cut the deal to offer up Cat, who's a nurse. The sister just happened to be there. She was a bonus, not the target."

"And now?"

"Now we find out what the fuck those assholes are doing

in our town."

Mud cracked his knuckles. "We need to get rolling ASAP and comb the city tonight."

"We wait for a few hours to gather intel before we walk blind into a trap. Then we'll move, make no mistake." Undertaker glanced around the table receiving nods in agreement.

"Other chapters?" Easy asked.

"Put the word out to Mississippi and Alabama. We may need backup on this one."

"Done."

"Let the support clubs know to keep their eyes open, too."

"You got it."

Undertaker's eyes swung to his Sergeant At Arms. "Double up security here at the clubhouse."

"You want us on lockdown?" Bam-Bam asked.

"Not yet, but let's open it up to any ol' ladies and family who would feel safer here than at home."

The man nodded. "I'll pass the word."

Undertaker looked around the room. "Any other questions?"

The room stayed quiet.

He slammed the gavel down. "Dismissed."

The majority of the men shuffled out until only the club officers remained—Undertaker, Mooch, Blood, Bam-Bam, Easy, Mud, and Wicked.

Undertaker looked over at Blood. "How're you feeling?"

"I'm fine," Blood bit back.

"Bullshit."

"I said I'm fine." The two men stared at each other. Then Blood broke the silence. "I want to go down to the Quarter tonight and search for Cat's sister."

"No."

"I can look for the Death Heads."

"And end up taken again? No."

"That won't happen again. They caught me unaware. Now I know they're here. And maybe they're long gone."

"We just discussed this in the meeting. We're waiting on intel before we move."

"I made a promise to Cat to help get her sister back."

"A promise you shouldn't have made. Your club comes first, in case you forgot."

Blood stood. "I haven't forgotten a damn thing, including the fact that I wouldn't be alive if that girl hadn't helped me. And I wouldn't be free if she hadn't stuck her neck out and made that call. She trusted me. I gave her my word. Or doesn't that mean anything in this club anymore?"

Undertaker bolted to his feet. "Don't you disrespect me or this club by suggesting that. Sit the fuck down."

Blood took a seat.

Undertaker stared at him. His officers stayed quiet, their eyes connecting with a meaning that wasn't lost on Blood.

Blood knew the conflict of the situation he was in, and he also knew the spot he was putting his President in, but he had to help Cat get her sister back and fulfill his debt to her, even though it might take time away from protecting his club.

This was a crucial time. He knew that. He saw the dichotomy, the conflicting demands on his time, but he knew he had to try. He just couldn't bring himself to turn his back on Cat, the woman who had risked everything to save him. So his eyes met his President's with clear determination and resolve. "You know I'm dedicated to this club. That's never been in question, not once since the moment that Prospect patch went on my back and through all the years I've held a full patch. My loyalty and dedication have always been rock solid. You, more than anyone, know how much this club means to me. You know how much I've done for this club. Everything you've ever asked I've done without question, without hesitation. Now I'm asking for this one thing—give me one night to search for her." He swallowed, the last word a hard one for him. "Please."

Undertaker sat back in his chair, leather creaking as he did. He ran a hand over his mouth, and then stroked the back of his fingers along his beard as he studied Blood, contemplated all he'd said, and considered his request. Finally, he spoke. "One night. But you don't go alone. Take Sandman with you, and keep in touch. I want hourly updates."

"Done. Thank you."

Undertaker jerked his chin to the door. "Get out of here."

***

After Blood closed the door behind him, Mooch turned to his President. "What the hell was that about?"

Undertaker ran a hand over his mouth. "A whole lot of questions in his head he doesn't have the answers to."

***

Blood found Sandman out in the hall, leaning against the wall, just like he knew he'd be. Blood could always count on Sandman to have his back. The man probably knew exactly what Blood was in there requesting, and he was ready and waiting.

"Don't think you're going alone," were the first words out of the man's mouth, proving Blood's thoughts were correct.

Blood nodded and laid his hand on Sandman's shoulder. "Thanks, Brother. You ready to roll?"

"Ain't I always?"

Blood shook his shoulder and continued down the hall toward the stairs. "Let me get Cat taken care of, and I'll meet you outside."

Two sets of boots tromped down the stairs.

Blood found Cat in the kitchen, cleaning up with the other women. He liked the fact that she pitched in. He stopped in the doorway and every eye turned toward him. Cat paused, her hand clutching a dishtowel, stilling the motion as she dried a plate.

He spoke to Mama Ray. "I'll be out for a few hours. Take care of her for me."

"She'll be fine," she said, her voice raspy from years of cigarette smoke and her arms elbow-deep in soapy water.

"Go on, now."

Blood's gaze shifted to Cat, and their eyes held a moment. He lifted his chin to her in acknowledgement. She returned the gesture.

The side of his mouth lifted in what some might consider a tiny smile, at least for him. And then he turned and walked out to his bike where his brother waited.

He had just swung his leg over the seat, when Cat came dashing out the door. She stopped short, her eyes searching the dark until she spotted him in a sea of chrome shining in the moonlight.

"Get back inside," he growled, not pleased she'd followed him.

Moving toward him quickly, she blurted, "Where are you going?"

"Club business."

"Are you going to look for my sister?"

"Cat, get back inside. Not gonna say it again."

Her hands landed on her hips in the classic "you're not the boss of me" pose Blood was familiar with, but not often the recipient of.

"Don't think you can order me around. You don't own me."

That had Blood swinging his leg off his bike and moving toward her with such speed it had her stepping back. He got right in her space, his large presence looming over her. "Until this is over, I do." He pointed to the ground at his feet. "Here, on Evil Dead property, I'm responsible for you. How you behave reflects on me. I expect you to show respect to me, my brothers, and everyone else here. We clear?"

She looked pissed, and her chin came up, but she had the good sense to concede. "Crystal."

"I made you a promise. I'll do what I promised. What I won't do is be questioned about it by you. I'll let this little display go. *This time*," he warned.

She stared back at him with fire in her eyes, but had the good sense to keep her mouth shut.

"Get inside. Now."

Her jaw tightened, and Blood half expected her to argue, but she turned and did what she was told.

He got back on his bike and fired it up. He looked over at Sandman, who grinned back at him.

"Bitches, huh? Can't live with 'em, can't leave 'em on the side of the road."

"Speak for yourself," Blood growled as he roared out of the compound and onto the pavement, gunning the throttle.

Sandman followed, laughing as he let out a, "Yeehaw!" Gravel spewed up as he roared out of the lot and tore after Blood's fading taillight.

CHAPTER ELEVEN

Blood and Sandman rolled slowly through the French Quarter. Night had fallen. and the revelry the Big Easy was famous for was in full swing. Music poured into the neon-lit streets from a dozen bars. The two men had already done one full swing down Canal, along the river and up Esplanade to the east bordering the Faubourg Marigny section and up through the Treme neighborhoods, skirting the section where the house Blood had been kept stood looming in the darkness. The place looked deserted and quiet. Undertaker had informed Blood that he had some informants in the area keeping an eye on the place, and no activity had been reported.

The two bikes rode slowly up and down each one-way street, traversing back and forth like a search team clearing a quadrant. There were a few bikers in the French Quarter, like there always were, but they were civilian, just out having a good time, their bikes parked, rear-wheel to the curb, the owners standing on the sidewalk within sight.

Blood and Sandman finally circled back and parked in the courtyard by Blood's place. They backtracked toward Bourbon Street, showing Holly's picture around to some of the bouncers that stood in open doorways. No one had seen her.

Blood noticed that none of Black Jack's girls seemed to be out on the streets in the neighborhood by his place. He thought that odd.

The more he thought about it, the more it ate at him.

"Sandman."

"Yeah?"

"The Treme neighborhood is where Black Jack's compound is. It's where I was headed the night I was jumped. Now the Death Heads were supposedly headed toward the Quarter with Cat's sister. I can't help but wonder if this is all tied to Black Jack somehow. Or is it just a coincidence?"

"Do you believe in coincidence?"

"Fuck no."

"You think Black Jack's involved?"

"He hates bikers. Can't stand the fact that the Evil Dead MC exists here. I just can't see him getting involved with the Death Heads. Besides, he's runs all the prostitution from the Ninth Ward to Canal St. and all the way up to Lake Ponchartrain and out toward the Vietnamese section."

"Little Saigon?"

"Yeah. What do you know about it?"

"I know they have the best Bahn Mi."

"The Vietnamese version of a po-boy?"

"Yeah. They're awesome. There's this little place off Michoud Blvd. Been there a couple of times."

"I'll take your word for it. Can we get back to the problem at hand?"

"Right. Black Jack."

"My point is, he sure doesn't need an MC cutting into his business."

"Maybe they sold her to him."

Blood nodded, eyeing the end of the street. "Guess we should go ask him."

"Fuck, I was hoping you'd say that. I've always wanted to see his place."

"Don't be so eager. His compound is well guarded. We'll be outnumbered. He has a lot of men. Some you'll see, some you won't, so don't go doing anything stupid."

"Me, stupid?" Sandman scoffed, holding a hand to his heart. "I'm wounded, Brother."

"Shut up and come on."

They walked the eight blocks toward the compound, pausing halfway down the street to observe. They watched for twenty minutes to be sure there were no Death Heads anywhere near the compound. Blood wasn't about to be caught off guard again.

This time when they approached, they skirted the alley and went in through the front entrance. Inside a small courtyard was the front door.

Blood hated the setup, with its one way in and out; they could easily be cornered here. His eyes darted around the area and up to the windows and galleries above. There was a set of French doors two floors up that opened into a gallery. Sheer curtains were softly billowing in the breeze. Quiet classical music drifted down.

"Watch our backs," he ordered.

Sandman kept an eye to their rear. "On it."

Blood used the old doorknocker; its loud banging echoed around the small courtyard and up to the French doors above.

There was a tiny square window in the heavy wooden door covered by intricate iron scrollwork in a fleur-de-lis design. A shadow moved at the glass. and after a long moment the door swung open.

A large bull of a man stood in the doorway. "Can I help you?"

"Here to see Black Jack."

"Mr Boudreaux isn't receiving visitors this late."

"Tell him Blood is here to see him."

The man's eyes ran over him, and he stepped back, gesturing them into a parlor. "Wait here."

Another man stepped forward to guard them as the big bulldog went to inform his boss. Blood smirked, sizing up the man who watched them. He was quite sure Sandman was doing the same thing, thinking just where he'd stick his knife—just under the ribs where it could do a lot of damage.

The big man returned.

"Follow me."

Blood noticed, as they headed up the stairs, that the second man brought up the rear, his eyes on them the whole time. They were led down a long hallway with beautiful décor, old world paintings, soft lighting, and polished woodwork.

The big man tapped on a door to the left and opened it. He motioned them inside. Once they were in, the two men took their positions just inside the door.

Blood glanced around the room. He'd been here before, and not much had changed. Black Jack sat at his large antique desk, surrounded by all the trappings his ill-gotten wealth had afforded him. The man was in his early sixties, his still dark hair was slicked back, and he had a moustache that came down along the sides of his mouth.

His fathomless eyes lifted to Blood and moved over him before skating over to Sandman. "Well, look what the cat dragged in. Something I can do for you, boys?"

"How's business?" Blood asked snidely. If looks could kill, the one Black Jack gave him back would do the job.

"I've got things to do. How 'bout you just tell me what you want. I've got no reason to be nice to you, so let's not screw around."

Blood reached to his vest to pull the photo of Holly out of the inside pocket. When he did, the two men behind him drew guns. He put his hands up. "Easy fellas. Just got a picture to show your boss." When they didn't move, Blood looked Black Jack in the eye. "You want to tell Frick and Frack to relax?"

Black Jack's eyes shifted to his men, and he nodded. The guns were holstered.

Blood slowly lifted his cut and reached inside. He held the picture up for Black Jack. "Have you seen this girl?"

Black Jack leaned forward and held his hand out. "May

I?"

Blood handed him the photograph.

Black Jack studied it with an appraiser's eye that made Blood's stomach turn. "She's lovely. Yes, quite lovely." His eyes moved to Blood, and he handed the photo back. "In answer to your question, no, I've not had the pleasure. And who is she to you?"

"A friend."

"A beautiful, *young* friend," Black Jack elaborated with a twisted smile. "Is she a runaway, perhaps? You do seem to have a penchant for 'taking up their cause,' now don't you?"

Blood's jaw tightened. He supposed Black Jack knew every move he made around here. Talking to Black Jack's girls apparently had not gone unnoticed. Blood didn't like the insinuation that he had no business sticking his nose in. Or perhaps it was a warning. Blood didn't take too well to those either.

"We're looking for her. And we're going to find her. And God help anyone who's harmed her."

"My, my." Black Jack made a fake tremble. "I shudder to think. I do so hope you find her. I'll be sure to keep my… *people* informed of the missing woman. If I can be of further assistance, don't hesitate to ask. Was there anything else I could do for you?"

Blood leaned forward, his hands on the desk. "Do not misjudge me."

Black Jack held his eyes. "I wouldn't dream of it."

Blood stared the man down, wanting to rip the smug smile off his face. His eyes shifted to the balcony. There was another man out there smoking. Blood could only see his shadow, but he'd bet anything it was Big John, Black Jack's right hand man, lurking like the scum he was.

Blood grit his teeth and cut his eyes back to the man seated at the desk. "I'm sure we'll see each other again."

The man smiled. "I'm sure we will. I look forward to it."

Blood straightened. "If I were you, I wouldn't. My next visit won't be so pleasant." With that, he and Sandman moved toward the door. The two men guarding it didn't move aside. They looked to their boss. Blood swiveled his head back in time to catch Black Jack's nod, and then the men moved out of their way. The door was opened, and they were escorted out the front door.

As they moved through the courtyard, Blood's eyes shot up to the gallery. It was empty now, and the French doors were shut tight. He caught the scent of cigar smoke lingering in the air, a sickly sweet cherry cheroot—an unmistakable scent.

They moved out onto the street and headed back toward Blood's place.

***

"He's going to be trouble."

Black Jack looked to his second in command. "Let me worry about him, John."

"You gonna put the girl out on the street?"

Black Jack leaned back in his chair, his elbow on the armrest, his hand running across his chin and moustache, deep in thought. "No, I have something special in mind for this one. After all, she's quite the prize, isn't she?"

"Yes, sir."

"I have a buyer in mind for her. He's been looking for someone just like her—innocent, young, beautiful, and blonde." Black Jack's eyes lifted, piercing into John's. "Contact Mr. Yamaguchi. Tell him I've found what he's requested. He'll be in town next week."

"There's also that Saudi prince," John reminded him.

"Khalid?" Black Jack considered it. "A bidding war? That could be interesting. Of course you'll have to get some pictures of her. You can't make a sale without showing the goods."

"I'll see to it."

"I have an additional job for you."

John chuckled. "Who am I killing?"

That got a small smile from Black Jack. "No one dies. We'll save that for another day. For now, I want you to have him followed." He nodded toward the door the two MC members had exited. "I want to know everything he does."

John grinned. "Yes, sir."

CHAPTER TWELVE

It was late when the two motorcycles rolled back into the Clubhouse compound. They parked their bikes and cut the engines. Sandman threw his leg over his seat and stood, pulling his helmet off.

Blood was a little slower climbing off. His side was aching. He'd taken a couple of painkillers and could think of nothing better than falling into bed. His eyes drifted across the compound, seeing two women standing in the moonlight, one smoking a cigarette. The other one turned to look at him, and he realized, even in the darkness, that it was Cat.

Sandman headed inside, and Blood strolled toward them. His eyes connected with Marla's for a moment. She took the hint, dropped her cigarette, grinding it under her high-heeled boot, and headed inside.

Cat stared up at the moon, ignoring him. He wrapped his arms around her, pulling her back against him as he dipped his mouth to her ear. "We still speaking?"

He could feel her bristle, trying to hold her silence, but

in the end she couldn't. "Am I your captive now?"

"You're my guest."

"So, I can leave whenever I like?"

"No." He felt her body stiffen. Blood wasn't a man who usually explained himself, but he felt the need this time. "It's for your own good."

Her head turned toward the bikes.

"I take it you d-didn't find her." Her voice came out shaky, like she was on the verge of breaking down.

"No, babe. Showed her picture all over the Quarter. Put the word out to all my connections. She's out there; we'll find her."

She trembled in his arms. "I'm so scared for her. What if they've killed her?"

His arms tightened. "They wouldn't do that. She's valuable to them."

"She must be terrified."

"I'll get her back, Cat. I promise you."

She stayed quiet, and he wondered if she believed him. There was no sense trying to convince her—he'd have to prove it. And that was unfortunately going to take some time—time he wasn't sure he'd have much of. He knew he couldn't put off club business. It was going to have to take precedence over the next couple of days. At least until they got a handle on what the Death Heads were up to.

His eyes moved to the low hanging full moon bathed in a red-orange hue, shining just behind the black shadows of the tall cypress trees. "That's called a Blood Moon."

"So now you have a moon named after you?" she asked

with a trace of sarcasm.

"It's called that because of the color."

She stayed quiet, staring up at it.

He didn't want to tell her that some thought it was a bad omen—a signal of foreboding. Blood didn't want to believe that shit, but he couldn't deny the bad feeling he had that the worst was yet to come. Christ, things were already bad; he hated to think they'd get worse.

Cat didn't need to hear any of that, so he racked his brain for something to lighten the mood. The midnight blue sky behind the dark shadowy outline of the cypress reminded him of a poem. For some odd reason that he couldn't quite wrap his brain around and didn't want to examine too closely, he found himself reciting it to her.

When the day turns to dusk
And the first stars emerge
When the mist is forming yonder
In a ghostly mystic blue
When the cypress trees turn black
Like phantoms rising up
Let the golden moonlight shining
Illuminate your heart
And think of me with longing
Until no more we are apart

She turned her head to look up at him like he'd unexpectedly grown two heads, and he suddenly felt like an idiot, standing here reciting fucking poetry like some geek.

"That's beautiful."

He looked down at her upturned face, his eyes moving over every inch. "Don't get too excited. It's the only one I know. My mama taught it to me. It was a poem in a book she loved."

The door to the clubhouse opened, breaking the moment. Blood looked up to see Undertaker strolling toward them, and he dropped his arms from around Cat.

Undertaker paused next to them, dipping his head to light up a joint before blowing out a stream of smoke toward the sky. His eyes fell to Cat. "Past your bedtime, little girl. Marla made up a room for you. She's inside."

Cat looked at Blood, and he lifted his chin. "Get some sleep."

She turned and headed inside.

When she was gone, Undertaker took another hit and passed it to Blood. "Give her space. I need your eyes on the Death Heads, and your head in the game."

"It always is."

"Take it you came up empty?"

Blood took a toke, his eyes on the sky. "Unfortunately."

"And the Death Heads?"

"No sign of them."

Undertaker nodded.

"Any intel yet?" Blood asked.

"Got a couple leads I want to check out tomorrow. Still waiting to hear back from Texas. They're out scoping out the Death Heads' numbers tonight."

Blood nodded. "I stopped by Black Jack's."

That got Undertaker's attention. He huffed out a breath, and Blood knew he was pissed he'd gone in with just himself and Sandman. "How'd that go?"

"Claims he doesn't know anything about her. I don't trust him."

"Imagine that."

Blood's eyes snapped to him. "I'm not satisfied with his answers. He'd sell out his own mother if it got him something."

"Don't disagree."

"You don't think it's odd that I ran into the Death Heads near his place?"

"I think he's worth keeping an eye on."

"And…?"

"I'll put the Prospects on it. How are you holding up?"

Blood took another toke. "With painkillers and pure grit."

Undertaker glared at him. "Don't need you thinking you're Superman."

Blood tried to suppress a smile. "You mean I'm not?"

Undertaker shook his head with a chuckle and changed the subject. "What do you want to do with our friend in the back room?"

"What do you think?" Blood wanted to kill him, preferable with his bare hands.

Undertaker grinned, his white teeth flashing in the moonlight, and clamped his hand on Blood's shoulder. "Get some rest. We'll figure that out tomorrow."

CHAPTER THIRTEEN

Eighty-eight miles west of New Orleans

Blood, Sandman, Bam-Bam, Easy, Wicked, and So-Cal stood in a line taking a piss in the grass at the edge of the gravel parking lot. The hot afternoon sun beat down on them.

Sandman looked over at Blood. "Ever since you made that remark about the pin in my dick, I've been having a hard time getting it up."

Blood chuckled as he zipped back up. "The voodoo bullshit? It's all in your head, bro. Or maybe you're just getting old and need a little blue pill to get your dick stiff."

"Bite your fuckin' tongue," Sandman snapped back. "This isn't funny. Don't anyone laugh." At which point, the line of men all burst out laughing.

Blood replied with a chin lift to the man on his right. "Hey, Bam-Bam here swears by 'em."

"Don't drag my name into this fairy tale you're tellin' him." Then he peered around Blood. "Sandman, the bitch put a hex on you, and your dick's gonna fall off. Hate to be the one to tell you, but there it is, the sad truth."

Sandman looked down. "Fuck."

Blood's phone went off, and he pulled it from his pocket. "Yeah."

Undertaker's voice came through. "Where are you?"

Blood scanned the area. "About ten miles from 'wouldn't be caught dead living here.' Why?"

"Quit fucking around."

Blood chuckled. "I'm standing in the parking lot of some dive bar called *Whiskey-a-go-go*. It's on Bayou Teche in Morgan City. Been all up and down the area; there's no sign of 'em."

"Got a tip on a place about twenty miles west of there. An old body shop off Highway 90 and Kemper Road."

"Yeah? What's the tip?"

"Lot of bike activity in the area. Guy thought he saw a couple patches with Texas bottom rockers. Couldn't get close enough to see the club insignia."

"We'll check it out."

"Be careful."

"Ain't I always?"

Undertaker huffed out a breath. "Not lately."

Blood disconnected. "Mount up."

"What? I thought we were having a beer? It's hot as hell out here."

"It just ain't your lucky day, Sandman. Move."

A minute later, six bikes turned right out of the gravel lot and gunned it down the pavement.

***

Fifteen minutes later, they rolled into another gravel lot in the middle of bum-fuck nowhere. There was a large metal shed to the right of a one-story brick office. A faded metal sign read Topper's Body Shop. Broken down vehicles filled the lot, but no motorcycles.

The men dismounted.

Bam-Bam looked around. "This place looks more like a junkyard than a body shop."

They walked to the glass door. Blood pulled on the handle. "It's locked." He cupped his hand and peered inside. "Looks deserted."

"Let's try the shed," Sandman suggested.

The men walked over, their eyes scanning the lot.

"You see any bikes?" Bam-Bam asked.

Blood looked down at the dusty ground. "No, but I see tire tracks." He bent and examined them. "Definitely big touring bikes."

They moved carefully to the door. Blood drew his gun, and the others followed suit. The metal door was open two feet. They moved carefully inside, peering around.

"Easy, Wicked, So-Cal, sweep the yard, the back, everything. Search for any trace," Blood whispered. The men nodded and backed off.

Blood, Sandman, and Bam-Bam entered. They looked around the cavernous space. Didn't look like a lot of bodywork was done there. In the back was a wooden board set up on saw horses. Jugs of chemicals sat on top. Blood strolled over and examined the setup.

A man darted from behind a wall, a gun firing. Blood and the other men ducked for cover and returned fire. A moment later, the man dropped to the ground. Bam-Bam knelt next to him and rolled him over. His face was shot up. "He's done."

The other three bikers yanked open the big metal double doors. "What the fuck? You guys okay?"

"Yeah. Stay out there and keep watch." Blood glanced over the table again.

Sandman moved to stand next to him. "Meth lab?"

Blood studied the jugs. "Hydrochloric acid, sulfuric acid, and hydrogen peroxide."

"Hydrogen peroxide isn't used in cooking meth," Bam-Bam offered as he joined them.

"That's because he wasn't cooking meth," Blood replied. "He was making a bomb." He gestured to the two five-gallon metal drums sitting on the floor, one filled with ball bearings and the other filled with nails.

There was a small sound from the left, behind some old equipment. Blood put his finger to his mouth and signaled Sandman, who crept up and yanked a skinny girl out. She was dressed in jeans, a tank top, a ruffled apron, and rubber gloves. A paper-breathing mask hung around her neck. She looked terrified.

"What the hell are you doing here?" Blood barked.

She stayed mute as Sandman dragged her forward. Her eyes fell to the dead man on the floor.

Blood's eyes moved over her again, taking in her pink ruffled apron. "What are you, Betty Crocker, meth cooker, or homegrown terrorist? Or maybe you're all three. A real renaissance woman, you are."

"Me and Gib, we were just making a little extra money. That's all."

"Making bombs?"

"No, making meth."

"That ain't meth."

"They made us do it."

"Who?"

"The bikers."

A loud beep and a click sounded, and the men all looked at each other puzzled. "What the hell was that?" Blood swung back to the girl. "There someone else here?"

Tears streamed down her face, and a moment later, the building exploded.

The men all hit the dirt floor as the entire shed caved in.

***

Cat stared at the clock above the bar. Blood had been gone the entire day. She'd heard not one word from him. He'd ridden out earlier with one of the three different groups who had left that morning. She knew they were looking for that other MC; they weren't looking for her sister.

She wished Blood would call and ask to speak to her. Something about the sound of his voice had a way of calming her, and she needed that.

She chewed her lip, wondering if Holly was okay, worrying that right this minute she may be enduring a rape or beating. Blood had told her she was too valuable to kill, but Cat wasn't sure she believed him.

She felt so helpless, and Mama Ray's words from that first day kept coming back to haunt her. *"If that were my sister, I'd hightail my butt out of here and go find her."*

Cat glanced around the main room. The place was deserted except for the Prospect at the bar. There was one old landline phone behind the bar, but he'd been ordered to keep her away from it.

"You want a Coke or something, sweetheart?" he asked when he caught her looking at him.

She shook her head. "I think I'll go sit outside and get some air."

"Stay away from the gate."

Cat nodded and moved outside. She sat atop one of the picnic tables and studied the compound, the wheels already turning, formulating a plan of escape she hadn't realized she was contemplating until right that moment. She couldn't wait any longer. Her sister had been missing for days and must be out of her mind with fear. Cat had to do something.

She eyed the gate. Two men stood near it. One smoked a cigarette; the other was animatedly describing something to him until they both were laughing. Cat's eyes strayed to the back. There were a couple of metal garbage dumpsters in the back corner. If she could find a way to get on top of them, she might just be able to pull herself over the tall stockade-like fence. It would be quite a drop to the other side, but she couldn't worry about that.

She looked around again. There were a couple of old plastic milk crates behind the building. She could use them as a step up onto the dumpster. She glanced back at the gate. The men seemed oblivious to her. She slowly edged down off the table and darted behind the building. They couldn't see the dumpsters from where they stood. As long as she didn't make any noise, she just might have a shot.

***

Blood lifted his head and shook it. He couldn't hear a thing besides the ringing in his ears. Dust filled the air. Something heavy was on top of him. He managed to roll to his back and shove the sheet of metal off him, the whole time thinking that if he ripped open his wound, Cat was going to kill him. If it didn't hurt so badly, he'd laugh at the irony of that.

"Sandman? You okay?"

He heard a muffled groan to his right and crawled beneath the twisted metal that formed a low cave around them. "Sandman!"

"Yeah," came the weak reply. It sounded like it was coming from underwater, but then Blood realized his hearing was just messed up.

He heard the shouts of the men he'd left outside to guard their backs.

"Blood! Sandman! Bam-Bam! You guys alive?"

"Over here!" Blood yelled back. He looked around.

There were spots of daylight coming through the pile, but he knew there was a good chance they were trapped under all the debris. He got to Sandman and pulled him out from under a twisted metal pipe. He only had strength in one arm, but somehow he managed.

Sandman rolled over and started cursing. "Motherfucker, that hurts."

"Tell me about it."

"Are we trapped?"

"Not sure."

"Who the fuck's idea was it to come in here?"

"Yours," Blood replied with a grin.

"Bullshit. I deny all involvement."

"Yeah, right."

"You still got those painkillers in your pocket?"

"Let me check." Blood finagled his hand into his hip pocket and came out with the bottle. "Yeah."

"Give me a handful."

"Fuck no. I need them. You can have two."

"I always knew you were a stingy bastard, even in my hour of need."

"Fuck off. I was shot."

"I think my leg's broke."

"Shake it off, you big baby. You're fine."

"We were setup."

"No shit."

"I'm gonna kill the motherfucker. Who gave Undertaker this tip?"

"He didn't say."

"Call him and find out."

"Now?"

"Uh, yeah."

Blood dug his phone out. "No service."

Easy yelled out, "I found Bam-Bam. He's okay. We're gonna get you guys out. Don't worry!"

"Shut up and let me die in peace!" Sandman yelled back.

"Relax," Blood told him.

"Hey, do me a favor please, and for once in your life admit how bad the situation is."

"I'm aware of the situation."

"Really? Because I think we're fucked."

"Calm down."

"You know I hate small spaces."

"That's just a state of mind. You've got to work through it."

Sandman groaned and rocked.

"You all right?"

"No, I'm not all right."

"Quit moving around so much. This pile is very unstable."

"Thanks. That's encouraging."

They were both quiet as the others continued to try to dig them out.

"How'd they know when to detonate, Blood?"

"Maybe pizza-face called someone."

Sandman looked around. "Let's dig him out so I can kill him all over again."

Blood fell to his back, breathing heavy. "Maybe Betty

Crocker detonated it. She gave me a weird look."

"That's just the way all women look at you."

"Ha ha. You're hilarious."

"I know. It's a gift."

Blood stared up at the tiny slivers of sunlight shining through the debris and tried to move some of it. The metal pieces were all twisted together in an interlocking pile like some giant Jenga game. He shifted one piece, and another board fell on Sandman.

"Fuck!"

"Well, that could have gone better," Blood said, trying to stifle his laughter.

Sandman glared over at him. "Ya think?"

Blood tried again.

"Please, for the love of God, stop before you kill me."

He finally gave up, impatience gnawing at him, and fell back, breathing hard.

Sandman shoved the board off himself. "I hate you right now."

"You'll get over it."

They were quiet for a few minutes. Blood looked over at Sandman who could never stay quiet for long. "You alive?"

"Unfortunately."

"Remember last week when you wanted to tell me the meaning of life? Now's your chance."

"You sayin' I babble?"

"Endlessly."

"Fuck off," Sandman bit back then rolled his head to look at Blood, picking a topic of his own choosing. "She's pretty."

"Who?" Blood frowned over at him.

He turned his head back to look at the bits of blue sky. "Cat. You can tell she really cares about you, too."

Blood looked up at the same spot. "Yeah, I'll probably screw it up like I do everything else. It's not in my DNA to be happy."

"What a bunch of bullshit."

"I'll run her off just like all the rest. It's what I do."

Sandman huffed out a laugh. "Yeah, so…quit doin' that. Boom. I'm your life coach."

Blood fought to give in to the humor, but soon they were both breaking down into laughter. He clutched his side. "You fucking asshole. Damn that hurts."

That only made Sandman laugh that much harder.

CHAPTER FOURTEEN

Dusk had fallen when the group finally made it back to the clubhouse. Blood, Sandman, and Bam-Bam were slow getting off their bikes. Undertaker and the rest of the club were waiting for them.

Blood straightened, his hand holding his side.

Undertaker stepped over. "You okay?"

"I'm fucking fine." He hobbled past him, wanting nothing more than to collapse into bed.

"Got some bad news."

"Jesus Christ, what now?"

"Cat's gone. I was just about to send someone to look for her."

That brought Blood up short. "What do you mean she's gone? Gone where?"

Undertaker shrugged. "We've searched the property. She's gone. I'm guessing she's on her way to the police."

"Goddamn it. How the hell did she get out? There are guards on the gate. Did the fucking Prospects fall asleep on the job? Where are they? I'll kill them."

"Calm the fuck down. She didn't go out the gate. In our search we found a couple of crates stacked up near the dumpsters. Guys found tennis shoe prints on the ground on the other side of the stockade."

Blood limped back toward his bike.

"Where the fuck you think you're going?"

"I'm going after her."

"No, you're not."

"She's my responsibility. I'm going."

Undertaker huffed out a breath, seeing it was pointless to argue. "Fine. Take one of the boys."

"So-Cal!" Blood barked. "Let's go."

The man, whose nickname stemmed from the fact that he'd transferred from one of the club's Southern California chapters, stepped up.

Undertaker put a hand in So-Cal's chest, halting him. "Mud said the tracks led to the left."

"The left? The road heads through the swamplands in that direction. Why the fuck would she go that way?"

Blood snapped back sarcastically, "Let's find her and ask her."

"Better hurry before the gators make a meal out of her," Undertaker suggested with a grin.

Blood glared at him as he threw his leg over the seat.

They both fired up their bikes and headed out.

***

Cat stumbled down the road. She hadn't seen a car pass since she'd left the clubhouse. There was nothing in the direction she'd gone. Just trees as far as she could see. A few feet to the right she could make out the reflection of the bayou. She trudged on, slapping at mosquitoes. Dusk had fallen, and the pests had come out in full force to feast on her. And that's not all she was afraid could be out looking for an evening meal. With every sound she glanced around, terrified an alligator would come out from the water.

She was really rethinking her decision to leave the compound. And where the hell did this road lead anyway? Nowhere? She'd been too afraid to go in the direction the bikes had left, thinking maybe she'd run into them returning.

A sudden noise in the trees made her jump. She looked up to see a large white egret lift from the upper branches and take flight; its snowy wings spread three feet across as it flapped away.

She kept walking. A few minutes later, she saw a large shadowy shape stretched across the highway about twenty yards ahead. It stopped her in her tracks. *Oh, crap!* If that was an alligator, could she outrun it?

She backed up a step, not taking her eyes off it. It moved, and as she watched, she realized it wasn't a gator, but a huge greenish-black snake. Probably one of those Anacondas she'd heard had become such a problem with idiots releasing them into the swamps. *Good God, the thing had to be fifteen feet.*

As she watched, it slithered slowly into the brush on the other side of the road. Still, she waited, not sure she wanted to pass the spot just yet.

As she stood there contemplating returning to the clubhouse, she heard the distant unmistakable rumble of motorcycles. She looked back the way she'd come and saw two tiny headlights in the distance. As she stood waiting, they quickly grew closer and louder. A moment later they were upon her.

Blood rolled up next to her, parked, and dismounted. She was never so happy to see anyone in her life… but he didn't look happy at all.

"You're a fucking handful. Just how far did you think you'd get? And where the fuck did you think you were going? This road leads nowhere you want to go!"

He studied her, and she could tell he wasn't sure what to make of her. A man trying to figure out the female mind— she'd seen that look before. Like they were trying to understand a foreign language, a puzzle, a map they couldn't read. They knew there was something important, but they just couldn't figure it out.

"Babe, you want something, you need something, spell it out. Tell me. No shit, just fucking tell me. I don't have time to try to figure out the female mind. I'll fuck it up every time."

She rubbed the sides of her upper arms. "I'm going to the police."

"Well, it ain't this way. The only place you're going is back to the clubhouse." He made to grab her arm, but she yanked back.

"No! I'm going to find my sister. I'm not waiting around

that damn compound any longer!"

He yanked her to him. "You're a real fighter, you are. I'm trying to help you."

"No you're not!"

"You have to trust me, Cat."

"How am I supposed to trust you? You're only concerned with getting revenge on the Death Heads. You eat, sleep, and breathe it."

"You're right. Revenge is the reason I get up each day. But don't fool yourself, darlin'. The police can't find your sister, and when the Death Heads find out you went to the police, they'll hunt you down."

"I'll take my chances."

Blood shoved her away. "Fine. You wanna run, then run. But if you do, you better keep on runnin'. Change your name, cut your pretty hair off, and go into hiding. And just maybe you'll be safe. 'Cause I'll tell you one thing, the police can't protect you from the Death Heads MC. They'll come lookin' for you. And God help you when they find you."

"I don't care," she said petulantly, turning away.

He yanked her around. "You damn well *should* care!"

She shoved him away. "You're exaggerating just to…to scare me."

"Really? So you're an authority on the Death Heads now?"

"I know you're just like them."

He grabbed her upper arm and yanked her to him, fury written all over his face. "I'm *nothing* like them, Cat, and if you haven't figured that out by now I don't know why I'm here wasting my time." He shoved her away again.

They glared at each other.

"You're not really gonna leave her out here, are you?" So-Cal asked, glancing around the darkening woods.

Blood looked back at him a second, before capturing Cat's eyes with his. "Thinkin' about it."

Her chin came up.

There was a tick in his jaw, and then he finally growled, "Come back and promise me you'll stay put."

Cat bit back, "Promise me you'll find my sister."

"I said I would, didn't I?"

"But you haven't, have you?"

"Goddamn it, woman!" He ran his hands through his hair in frustration, and stepped away before spinning back to her. "Don't you get it? I find the Death Heads, I find your sister!"

She was stunned by his words and stood, considering the truth in them. Maybe he wasn't just out for his own benefit, maybe he really was doing it for her. Her chin came up again, and she murmured, "I didn't trust you. I'm sorry."

Blood shook his head and looked away. When his eyes met hers again, he huffed out, "Just what does it take to earn your trust?" He turned and moved toward his bike like he was giving up, like he was planning to leave her, and she panicked.

"Blood." Her soft voice stopped him, and he turned back. Her eyes glazed over with tears as she whispered shakily, "I don't know what to do."

Blood stared into her eyes a long moment. "Come here."

She moved toward him, and when she was within arm's length, he reached out and pulled her to him. She was enveloped in the smell of leather and motor oil and his own special scent, calming her somehow and reassuring her in some odd way she didn't want to examine too closely.

His head dipped, and he spoke into the hair at the top of her head.

"You need to fall in line. I know you're scared, babe, but I've got enough shit on my plate without having to worry about you, too."

She clung to him, needing his strength. She didn't know how much longer she could bear the weight of fear and worry all alone. She wanted so badly to share the burden, if only for a little while, and have someone tell her it was all going to be okay. A moment later, he tilted her head up, holding her face in his hands.

"Look at me." His voice was low and certain, and as he looked deep in her eyes, she felt compelled to believe whatever he told her. "All you gotta do is trust me."

If only it were that simple, she thought. But she had to take the chance, so she nodded, giving him the answer he wanted.

He studied her a long moment before releasing her.

They climbed on his bike, and she pressed against his back, holding him tight, hoping she was right to put her faith in him.

***

When they got back to the clubhouse and climbed off the bike, Cat looked at how stiff and slow-moving Blood was.

She frowned. "Are you in pain?"

"Had a building fall on him," So-Cal put in and saw the glare that Blood gave him. Cat didn't miss it either. Her mouth dropped open.

"*A building fell on you?* Are you okay?"

"I'm fine."

"I'll be the judge of that. I need to look at your wound. It could be bleeding."

"I said I'm fine."

Her hands landed on her hips. "Don't give me the attitude. The packing needs to be changed anyway. Come on." She pivoted and headed inside.

Blood's brows shot up. "Attitude? Look who's talking about throwing attitude?"

So-Cal chuckled until Blood turned and gave him a death stare.

A few minutes later, Blood was sitting shirtless on the side of his bed, Cat peeling off his bandages.

She glanced around. "This is your room?"

"When I'm here, yeah." His eyes watched her, waiting for her to lift her baby blues from her task and meet his gaze. When she did, he looked into those expressive eyes he was quickly finding so easy to lose himself in. "The bed's real soft if you want to try it out."

He got the corner of her mouth to turn up as she fought a smile.

"You're a beautiful woman, Cat. Why aren't you

married? I'm sure at least one idiot has tried." She chose that moment to yank the bandage off, hard, and he winced, groaning, "Oh, right. That."

"Ha ha. Very funny. You're a real comedian."

"I have my moments."

"This would be easier if you were on your back."

He grinned as he complied with the request. "A woman's never had to tell me that twice."

She rolled her eyes. "Thank you."

"I aim to please."

She changed out the packing.

"Cat."

His quiet voice had her lifting her gaze.

"Why'd you leave?"

She dropped her eyes back to her task, one shoulder shrugging. "I needed you, and you weren't here. I started to worry about my sister, and the anxiety took over."

"Sorry. I know you're worried. I should have called you. I *meant* to call you, but, ah…"

"Save it. I've heard that whole trapped-under-a-building excuse before."

He started to chuckle, but the pain caused him to suck in a harsh breath. "I'd laugh, only it hurts too much."

***

After she'd finished tending to Blood, Cat stood back. "Surprisingly, you didn't do any damage. It's healing nicely."

"Great." He sat up.

"I notice you have a few new bruises, though."

"Comes with the job."

"Is that all the explanation I get?"

"Yep. Club business is club business."

"How's the pain?"

"Tolerable."

"You're not eating pain pills like candy, are you?"

He slid off the mattress to stand, slipping his arms into a new denim shirt. "Now would I do a thing like that?"

"Uh, yes."

He stared at her as he buttoned up the shirt, noticing her gaze followed his movements. He darted a look to the bed. "You sure you don't want to take me up on my offer?"

She rolled her eyes again and moved toward the door. "Honestly, is that all you men think about?"

He chuckled as he followed after her. "Mostly."

***

Late that night, while Cat slept in her room, Blood sat at the bar in the clubhouse. The light of the neon bar signs on the wall reflected through the glass in front of him, turning the whiskey a glowing amber. Undertaker walked up and took the stool beside him. Blood leaned over the bar, grabbed a second glass, and poured his President two fingers from the bottle in front of him.

"Thanks." Undertaker picked it up and took a sip.

"So where do we find the asshole who gave you that

great tip today?"

Undertaker lit up a cigarette and dropped the lighter on the bar. He blew the smoke toward the ceiling. "That'll be handled tomorrow."

"Damn right it will," Blood guaranteed vehemently.

"Mooch is handling it."

"My crew is in on it. That's our fucking payback."

"Thought you wanted to concentrate on the Death Heads."

"Apparently, it's all tied together. Girl at the shed said bikers made them switch from making the meth to building bombs. Had to be them."

"Yeah, but you're not going to find them at this guy's house."

"You never know. We might get lucky."

"Lady Luck doesn't seem to like you very much lately," Undertaker observed with a grin.

Blood stared him straight in the eyes. "Well, that's about to change."

Undertaker nodded. "Maybe so. That all that's got you stewing tonight?"

Blood turned back to his drink, downing it with one gulp. "What do you mean?"

"Nurse Hotty."

"What about her?"

"I suppose you think she proved your theory right today, with that stunt."

Blood looked over at him and cocked a brow. "My theory?"

"That women can't be trusted. That they all run out on you."

Blood looked back at the mirror behind the bar. "Don't they? Ain't found one yet to prove me wrong."

Undertaker chuckled. "Maybe. Maybe not."

"Way to take a position."

"I'm just saying the world isn't always black and white. Sometimes it's a thousand shades of gray."

"Cryptic as usual, Undertaker. I can always count on you to philosophize. But when I want pointless conversation, I'll let you know."

Undertaker smiled and poured himself another shot. "I was hoping this one was different. I think you were, too."

"I don't give a shit one way or another. She's nothing more to me than a debt I owe."

Undertaker held the bottle over Blood's glass and refilled it with a grin. "Right, Blood. Keep tellin' yourself that."

Blood downed the drink, a tick in his jaw.

"Just do me a favor."

"Yeah? What's that?"

"We got a shitload of trouble goin' on now. I need you focused. Don't let that little damsel-in-distress get in your way."

CHAPTER FIFTEEN

Cat sat outside in the late afternoon sun. The men were off on club business that no one would talk about, but that didn't mean the clubhouse was quiet. There were several more ol' ladies than had been there before, some having brought their kids with them—kids who were now either goofing around trying to play pool—if they were old enough to hold a cue—or in a game room on the second story, playing video games.

Cat couldn't help her eyes from straying from where she sat at one of the picnic tables over to the gate. The thought of running, this time in the opposite direction, crossed her mind briefly, but she'd promised Blood she's stay put. After everything yesterday, she couldn't break his trust again.

Undertaker, who'd stayed behind when the group of men pulled out earlier in the day, strolled out the door and joined her at the picnic table.

He sat across from her and lit up a cigarette. "Mind if I smoke?"

She grinned. "Seeing as you already lit up, I guess not."

He grinned back. "How're you holding up?"

She tucked a lock of hair behind her ear and looked off. "Okay, I guess. I'm worried about my sister. I feel like the chance of getting her back is dwindling with each passing day."

"Hey."

She met his look with eyes that were starting to sting.

"Never bet against Blood."

She nodded, but he looked at her strangely, like he was trying to figure her out.

"You don't like the MC life, do you, babe?"

She shook her head. "I don't want anything to do with this life."

"How about Blood? You want anything to do with him? Because, *this life* saved that man." He waved Marla over.

Cat frowned, but held back her question as Marla approached.

"You need something, boss?" She laid her arm across his shoulder, smiling down at him.

"Get us a couple of cold ones, doll."

"Sure."

He wrapped his arm around her waist, pulling her back against him as she tried to move away. "Hey."

She looked down at him. "Hmm?"

He grinned at her and warned, "You bring me the wrong beer, and I'll beat your sweet ass."

She rolled her eyes. "You say the most romantic things."

He smacked her ass as she moved away to do his

bidding. Then he looked back at Cat, took a drag off his cigarette, and spoke. "I'm gonna tell you a story. This is between you and me, understand?"

She nodded, having not one clue what he was about to tell her.

"Not because it's your business, but because maybe it'll help you understand things better."

"Okay."

Marla came out with two bottles of beer. Undertaker took them and slid one to Cat. Then he waited until the girl walked off to continue his story.

"Blood's father ruled him with a tight leash and an iron fist. I met Blood about the time he got big enough to fight back. When he was in his teens, he took to lifting weights and learning to fight. One day he eventually had enough of the abuse his old man doled out on a regular basis, and he turned on his father. Then he ran. His old man found him and dragged him back. He beat him. This cycle went on for awhile, and I think Blood came to realize he'd need some men at his back if he wanted to escape."

"That's where the MC came in?"

"Smart girl." Undertaker paused to take a long drink. "I was in a diner and saw it happen, saw the way his old man treated him. After some verbal abuse, he shoved Blood and walked out, leaving him there... told him he could walk home. After his old man left, I approached the kid." Undertaker grinned. "His eyes got as big as saucers when he saw me. I tapped my vest and told him if he ever got sick of his old man beating him to give me a call. I scribbled my number on a cocktail napkin and shoved it in his pocket. He called me the next day."

"And?"

"I took him in. He turned eighteen soon after and became a Prospect for the club. There's a deep level of personal commitment and self-discipline a man has to demonstrate and sustain in order to earn a patch. Blood was one of the best Prospects we ever had, and you know why? Because he wanted it so badly. He's one of my best guys. He's like a son to me. This club is his family now—the only one he's got, the only one he *needs*."

Cat took a sip of her beer, beginning to see Blood in a different light, but unsure why Undertaker was telling her all this.

"Maybe now you'll understand him a little better. Men come to this MC for a lot of different reasons. Blood, he *needs* this club in a way a lot of my guys don't." He studied her eyes. "His path… it hasn't always been easy. His actions result from some deep personal impressions that left a huge mark on his personality and on his view of women. That aside, he's got some good qualities if someone cares enough to look for them."

"Meaning me?"

"You tell me."

"Will he find my sister?"

"Don't worry, sweetheart. You've got a good man looking out for you—the best guy in my crew. He says something, he does it."

A couple of the younger girls came outside. One stopped

at the table. "Undertaker, do you mind if we do a little target practice?"

Undertaker grinned. "Just as long as you're careful."

"We will." They started to move off, but Undertaker stopped them with a hand. He looked at Cat.

"You know how to shoot?"

She shook her head. "Not really."

He jerked his chin, indicating she should go with the girls. "Tammy will show you the basics." He paused to wink at the girl. "She's our best shot, aren't you, gal?"

The girl, while pleased by Undertaker's compliment, looked less than enthused with her new assignment. She gave Cat a cold look, but obeyed Undertaker. "Sure. Come on, honey."

"That's okay, I really don't want—"

Undertaker cut her off with a warning look that told her she had better comply.

"Um… yeah, sure. Why not?" She got up and followed the girls over to the makeshift targets at the back of the compound.

Twenty minutes later, Cat was trying to get the hang of it, but she was less than interested. The gun was heavy and loud and scared her to death. Yes, she'd shot that Death Head, but that had been all the adrenaline, fear, and anger pumping through her body. She'd reacted without thinking. This was entirely different. She was more aware of what she was doing and realized how out of her depth she felt.

There were several paper targets nailed up on the back of the stockade wall. She'd hit all around hers, but only hit the white paper once and not even on the circle.

Tammy looked over at her as she took aim. "So what's the story with you and Blood?"

"There is no me and Blood."

"Well, your loss, sweetie."

"You mean he hasn't fucked you yet?" one of the other girls asked.

"Not that it's any of your business, but no."

"What the hell's wrong with you, girl?" Tammy asked.

"Yeah, you're missing out."

Tammy smirked. "Maybe she's just not Blood's type." Her eyes ran down Cat's body dismissively.

"Honey, you let that man in your bed, you're gonna feel like you've died and gone to heaven," said a redhead at the end.

They all started giggling.

Tammy loaded anther clip in her gun and looked over at Cat. "Hey. Best three out of five. You in?"

"I can barely hit the target."

Tammy chambered a round. "You chicken?"

That had Cat's chin coming up. "I'm not afraid of shit."

Tammy's brow shot up. "Then prove it."

Cat lifted her gun, took aim, and pulled the trigger. She barely hit the edge of the outer ring.

Tammy smirked, aimed, and fired. *Bam*! She glanced over at Cat triumphantly. "Bullseye."

The sound of motorcycles could be heard approaching from a distance. It grew louder and louder until it was a rumbling roar as a horde of bikes pulled through the gates, kicking up a cloud of dust.

Cat looked over, but the girls yelled for her to take her turn.

***

Blood and the rest of the men dismounted and headed over to the picnic table where Undertaker held court. Many of their eyes strayed to where the women were shooting.

"How'd it go?" Undertaker asked.

"Fine," Blood replied, his eyes on the girls, surprised to see Cat among them. As he watched, he realized she couldn't shoot worth shit.

"According to plan, for once," Sandman elaborated for Undertaker.

"Good. Any sign of the Death Heads?"

"Nope," Blood bit out, his attention still on Cat

"Ten bucks says she misses the next three shots," Undertaker bet, his eyes on Blood.

Blood turned to him, "Ten bucks says I get her to make a bullseye."

Undertaker chuckled. "I've been watching her shoot for the last hour. You sure that's a bet you want to make?"

"Afraid you'll lose?"

Undertaker grinned. "You're on."

Blood walked toward the women, Sandman trailing behind. They both came to stand behind the girls, their muscular arms folded.

"Who are you two? Thelma and Louise?" Sandman

asked as Tammy and Cat accelerated their shots until they were shooting right after each other. *Bam. Bam. Bam. Bam.*

Blood stated, his eyes on Cat, "That is a woman resolved never to be fucked with again."

Cat turned at his words, noticing him standing there. She paused, lowering the gun. "Hi."

"Hi," he replied, his mirrored shades sweeping down her body to the gun.

"I can explain," she said sheepishly.

He smirked. "You can?"

She shook her head. "Nope. Not at all."

He looked at the target that was mostly unscathed. "Well, you scared the hell out of it, at least."

"I suck."

"Looks like you could use a few pointers."

"No, that's okay. I'm done."

"Nope. Not till you get a bullseye."

She looked at him like he couldn't be serious. "You're joking right?"

"Nope."

"Then I guess we'll be here all night."

"Nah. I've got faith in you."

Her brows shot up. "Oh, you do, do you?"

"Yep. I've seen you in action, remember?" He stepped behind her, wrapped his arms around her, and showed her how to hold the gun. Then his hands dropped to her hips. and he re-positioned her stance. His mouth was at her ear. "Eyes on the target. Take a deep breath, let it out, and slowly squeeze the trigger."

She did as he said.

Bam.

She hit low and to the left.

Blood adjusted her arm. "Again."

She repeated the steps he'd taught her, breathing in and out slowly, and then fired.

Bam.

She hit the outer edge of the center circle.

"Again."

Her next shot hit the center circle.

"Again. Take your time."

She hit the center circle about two inches left of dead center.

"I did it!"

He grinned, taking the gun from her hands. "Thanks, babe. You just won me ten bucks."

"Hey, Thelma."

Cat turned to find Tammy staring at her. The girl winked. "Nice shot."

Cat smiled. "Thanks, Louise."

Tammy almost smiled before turning away.

Blood met Cat's eyes, having caught the exchange. He gave her a chin lift, a smile tugging at his mouth as well. She gave it back.

"You teach all your women to shoot? Fatal mistake, bro," Sandman said. "She may put a bullet in you."

Blood answered, his eyes still on Cat. "Nah, she wouldn't do that. Besides, she already had her chance to put a slug in me." He pulled the clip out, loaded a new one, stepped to the line, chambered a round, and fired off several shots at the target.

Bam. Bam. Bam. Bam.

Blood turned to see Cat watching him with a new regard. After a moment, she murmured, "I don't know if it's what you were going for, but I'm really turned on right now."

Blood took the clip back out and handed the gun back to one of the other girls. Then turned back to Cat with a cocky expression on his face. "Baby, that's *always* what I'm going for."

She smiled.

He stepped over, grabbed her hips, and pulled her flush against him. "You want to take me up on my earlier offer?" She put a hand to his chest, pushing back, but he had no intention of releasing her. "We can only circle the flame for so long, Sweetness. And waiting's not in my nature."

Sandman stepped to the line with a machine gun, breaking the moment. "You have a funny way of picking up women." He fired the gun at the target, round after round until there was nothing left.

Cat put her hands over her ears, the sound deafening.

When Sandman was done, he hefted it up, barrel toward the sky and turned back to them. "The 240 Saw; she's a badass bitch. Carried it in Iraq. Nothing like humping around 25.6 pounds of pure chaos."

Blood shook his head. "Did you have to blow our eardrums out and put a hole in the stockade?"

Sandman cupped his hand to his ear pretending not to hear. "Sorry, I can't hear you over two hundred rounds of awesome."

"Seriously, dude. Waste of ammo."

"Hey, they wouldn't put two hundred rounds in an ammo belt if you weren't supposed to use 'em."

Blood shook his head. "You'll have to excuse my compadre. He spent too much time in Iraq."

Sandman grinned. "Haters gonna hate."

"Why do you need one of those?"

"I didn't until I found out it pissed *you* off," Sandman teased him.

Blood huffed out a laugh. "And you're gonna carry that heavy ass bitch when we go out on a run?"

"Maybe."

"Blood!" Undertaker called from the picnic table. Blood's eyes lifted over Cat's head to the man who held up a ten-dollar bill. Then his eyes dropped back to her.

"Guess I need to go collect my winnings." He looped an arm around her. "Come on, let's get a beer."

***

Blood set a shot on the bar in front of Cat. "Shoot it down."

Cat picked up the glass and downed it.

He poured them both another.

"Blood, enough."

"You drunk, yet?"

"No."

"Then it's not enough."

"Can I talk to you, in private?" she bit out, and Blood could sense her anger. Just when he thought he was loosening her up. *Damn*. He huffed out a breath and followed her up the stairs, away from the crowded main floor.

When they were a few feet down the upstairs hallway, she turned to him and snapped, "I don't need to be drunk right now, Blood! And neither do you!"

"You don't get a say in what I do!" They stood a foot apart, both fuming, tempers clashing. At least she knew better than to say this shit in front of the club, but still, a man like him didn't like hearing any criticism, least of all about his drinking.

"I can handle my liquor, Cat." He wasn't drunk, not even close; she didn't have a clue how much alcohol that took.

"You'll be useless tomorrow when you've got a hangover. How're you going to go out searching for my sister when you're hung-over?"

"I don't get hangovers. Ever."

Apparently, the nurse in her found that hard to believe. Her hands landed on her hips. "Oh really? And you'd better not be mixing pain killers with alcohol."

"Haven't had a pill all day, Nurse Hotty."

Blood could see the fire in her eyes, and suddenly more than temper flared to life in him as he imagined her in a sexy nurse's costume. He drew in several deep breaths, trying to get control of his emotions; unfortunately all he drew in was the scent of her. It was sweet, floral, honey, and sunshine. Was that the shampoo she'd washed her hair with? His eyes strayed down the waist-length cascade of corn silk. It gleamed against the black scooped neck t-shirt she wore.

He ached to run his hands through the soft tresses. The ponytail she sometimes wore it in had played center stage in a hundred fantasies he'd had since he'd met her. He itched to wrap it around his fist, control her with it as he drove his dick in her mouth, her pussy, her—

"*Blood.*"

Her voice broke into his fantasy, and his eyes flicked back up to hers. He knew he should give her space, stay away from her, because keeping his hands off her was becoming impossible. But giving her space was the last fucking thing he wanted to do.

So, he did what he did best—he acted on his impulses and backed her to the wall. Her wide eyes came to his as he pinned her there. He didn't ask, he didn't pause, he just took—something he'd always been good at.

His mouth came down on hers, crushing her lips under his. Her hands came up to fist in the material over his chest, gripping, clutching the fabric. She'd been startled at first, but her mouth was opening to his, her head falling back, submitting and letting him drink his fill. Her tongue skated against his as she moaned into his mouth.

She pressed against him, and her hips brushed the hard-on that strained against his zipper. A growl rumbled up from his chest. That only seemed to drive her on, but he wasn't satisfied with the grazes and brushes she managed.

He dropped his hands to her ass and hauled her up against him, grinding that erection into her. Her arms naturally slid over his shoulders, her fingers threading into his hair.

Jesus Christ. He wanted to rip her clothes off and fuck her right here.

He needed to touch her, to do what he'd dreamed of since the first time he'd kissed her. He wanted to smell her scent, to taste her. Before he could think better of it, he had her pants open and his hand inside. She broke the kiss to gasp out her surprise, but he quickly captured her mouth again. She whimpered softly as his fingers reached their goal, finding her wet. He stroked his fingers through it, dying to yank her jeans down and bury his face between her legs.

He pulled back to stare down at her with hooded eyes. "You're fucking soaked, baby." He moved his fingers in slow circles around her clit and watched her eyes flutter shut as her breathing started to come in short pants. "You like my touch."

She tried to shake her head, but they both knew it was a lie. He kept at her.

"No, we shouldn't do this." She glanced down the hall, and he saw the panic start to form in her eyes. She was afraid someone would come. He smiled. Someone was going to come all right.

"Blood, stop, please."

He ignored her pleas, choosing instead to follow the contradictory signals her body was giving him. It called out for more, *begged* for it. She was riding his hand now, unable to resist the instinctive thrusting as she tried to chase that elusive climax. He shifted to stroke with his thumb while his fingertips teased her entrance. She almost hyperventilated, and he couldn't pretend her reaction wasn't making him hard as a rock.

"Shh, babe. Relax." He kept stroking, and her breathing changed again. The short pants stopped as she sucked in her breath and held it. She was close, so close. It was written all over her face. "There's my girl. Let go."

She did, jerking against his hand and clutching his shoulders as her body slumped against the wall. He had a thigh pressed between her legs, keeping her from sliding down to the floor in a puddle.

They heard boots on the stairs and the muffled sound of talking.

He slid his hand free and quickly did up her pants.

She looked confused and stunned and disoriented as he gave her a wink and walked away to talk to his brothers.

When he glanced back, she was still where he'd left her, staring after him, her lips parted and swollen from his kisses, her face flushed and her eyes dilated.

CHAPTER SIXTEEN

It was barely dawn when Cat snuck out of her room and headed to the kitchen in search of coffee. She'd pulled on a pair of jeans and a tee, slipping her feet into tennis shoes. A few minutes later, she had her hands wrapped around a steaming mug when she heard some conversation through the screen of the window over the sink. It was barely light out, the first traces of pink and yellow lighting the horizon.

She peered outside and saw Blood and Sandman already dressed and standing near their bikes. Sandman lit up a smoke and shoved the lighter back in his hip pocket.

She ducked back out of sight, but stayed close enough to listen.

"Blood, we're rolling out at four. Mooch is taking one team, and you're supposed to lead the second. We don't have time to be searching all over for this chick."

"I fucking know what the plan is. I'm just asking for a few hours. We'll sweep the Quarter, check in with some bouncers, follow up with our contacts, and show her picture around again."

"We did all that. They know to call if they see her."

"I can go alone, then."

"Bro, we've got bigger fish to fry than some missing chick. Get your priorities straight."

Cat heard a boom, and the wall shook. She peeked out to see Blood with his fists in Sandman's leather cut, pinning him to the side of the building.

"Don't you ever fucking question my priorities or my dedication to this club," Blood growled into his face.

Sandman held up his hands. "Okay, man. Lay off."

Blood released him with a shove.

"I'm just trying to tell you, Blood. You go too far with this, guys are gonna start to wonder."

"You been hearing talk?"

"No... I mean, other than wondering why you brought a fine piece of ass back to the clubhouse and ain't touched her. But you start to blow shit off, you're just gonna stir the pot."

"I can go alone. Go back to fucking bed."

Sandman let out a frustrated breath. "You can be a real dick, you know that?"

Blood got on his bike.

Sandman huffed. "Fine. I'll fucking come with you."

"Thanks."

"Yeah, yeah. Like I'd let you go alone. Somebody's got to watch your fucking back."

Cat stood back, thinking, her eyes darting frantically over the Formica. Then she put her mug down and dashed through the club and out the door.

Both men looked startled as she rounded the corner on them.

Blood frowned. "What are you doing up so early? Go back to bed, Cat."

"I'm going with you."

"You don't even know where we're going."

"You're going to look for my sister. I heard you." She jerked her chin to the window ten feet down the wall.

"Shit," Blood grumbled. He and Sandman exchanged a look.

"Don't look at me, bro. She's your fucking problem."

"I'm going with you," Cat reiterated.

"The hell you are," Blood snapped back.

"Yes, I am."

"Get inside."

"No."

"Anyone ever tell you that you're a stubborn thing?"

She glared, her hands landing on her hips. "Yes, and it's a good thing I am. Maybe that stubbornness was what saved your ass when the Death Heads had you."

There was a tick in his jaw. He knew she was right, but he didn't like being reminded. "Cat, not gonna say it again. Get inside."

She folded her arms and glared back at him. "Fine. You go and I tell Undertaker where you're going."

Sandman shook his head. "Well, she's a hellcat, ain't she?"

Blood ignored him. "You won't be telling anyone anything when I gag you and tie you to the bed."

"Don't you threaten me!"

"Not a threat, it's a fact."

Sandman whistled. "Girl, you better be careful."

She bit her lip and changed her approach. "Blood, please. Take me with you. I can help. Maybe I can get people to talk. People who won't talk to you."

He said nothing, but he stared at her, like maybe he was considering, so she pressed. "Please, Blood. She's my sister. I need to feel like I'm doing something."

Sandman looked to Blood for his answer, almost like, he too, was pulling for her. "She might be right."

Blood glared at him. "Stay outta this."

"I can go back to bed and let you two fight it out."

After a long moment, Blood reached back, dug in his saddlebag and jerked out a spare helmet. "Put it on and be quick about it."

She gave him a big smile as she reached for the helmet and scrambled on the back of his bike.

***

"I'm starved," Sandman whined.

"When are you not?" Blood snapped as they walked down one of the side streets in the Quarter.

"Come on, don't that smell good?" he asked as they passed another restaurant.

"Christ. Shut up about food," Blood growled.

"Come on, man. Can't you smell that Etouffée? Hey, maybe we could split a Po-boy or some Red Beans and rice. I know. We could stop at Central Grocery for a Muffuletta or Pat O's for some shrimp and grits, or Jambalaya. Come on, I'm dyin' here. Just a quick bowl of gumbo, anything."

Blood ignored him and kept walking.

"Come on, I'm starved, and every place we pass smells so fucking good."

Blood came to an abrupt stop and glared at him. "You're not gonna shut up about it, are you?"

Sandman grinned. "Nope."

"Fine." Blood pivoted on his boot and pulled Cat into an establishment with a courtyard.

They sat at a table and watched people walking past. After they placed their orders and each had a beer, Blood murmured low to Sandman, "Black Jack's involved, I feel it in my bones."

"You want to pay him another visit?"

"I'm thinking maybe we need to get inside without them knowing. Search the place."

Sandman rubbed his hand over his jaw. "That's gonna take some doing. The place is guarded well."

Blood nodded.

Their food came, and they ate.

Blood wiped his mouth with a paper napkin and tossed it on his plate.

Sandman pushed his plate away and looked over at him. "Come up with a plan, yet?"

"To get into Black Jack's? Not in the light of day. Anything I can come up with involves darkness."

"Definitely." Sandman finished off his beer.

Blood glanced over his shoulder at the people passing by on the street. A second later, he was stiffening in his chair. "Christ, there's Ivy."

Sandman and Cat watched stunned as he bolted out of the courtyard after some woman walking past.

"Fuck. Come on, girl," Sandman snapped to Cat as he dug into his hip pocket, pulled out a wad of cash and dropped it on the table. They both ran out after Blood.

They made it to the street in time to see Blood dash around a corner. They tore down the block after him and spotted him down an alleyway.

Cat could barely keep up. She was huffing when she came to a stop in what appeared to be a dead-end. A scared woman was backing away from Blood.

"You're running out of alley, Ivy," he said to her.

"What do you want?" The woman continued to back up, stark fear written on her face.

"Take it easy, girl. I just want to ask you some questions."

Her eyes darted frantically between him and Sandman, who was also closing in on her. She made to dash past them both for a small gangway that led between two brick buildings.

Blood was on her in a split second, pinning her against the wall. "Easy, babe. I'm not gonna hurt you."

"I'm not supposed to talk to you."

"And who told you that?"

Cat saw Sandman glance back down the alley, watching for anyone who might have seen them chase the girl back here. Cat followed his eyes, but no one in the crowd of people traipsing down the street seemed to care. She turned back to Blood and the girl.

He shook her. "Who told you, Ivy?"

"Big John."

Blood pushed the hair back from her face, examining it. She tried to pull away. "Easy." Then he looked in her eyes. "He the one who gave you that shiner?"

She looked away.

"You can't cover everything with makeup, darlin'. Did he do that?"

She nodded.

Blood pulled Holly's picture from his back pocket and held it in front of her face. "Have you seen this girl?"

She studied the picture, and then shook her head.

"Why are you so nervous, Ivy?"

"I told you, I'm not supposed to talk to you."

"You ever wonder why that is?"

She stayed mute.

"Because they don't want you girls thinking anyone can help you."

She looked away, and Cat saw her eyes glaze with tears.

"Please," Cat pleaded softly. "She's my little sister."

Ivy met her eyes, and her bottom lip trembled.

"Tell us what you know," Blood said.

"I don't know if it's her, but…"

Cat felt her heart jump to her throat, and she took a step toward her.

"But what?" Blood pressed.

"I heard Big John talking on his cell phone. It was something about 'the young blonde.'"

"What about her?"

"Nothing, I don't know, just that she'd be ready Friday when the buyer came."

Cat looked to Blood with a stricken expression. "That's two days from now."

"What buyer?" Blood shook Ivy again.

"I don't know," she pleaded. "He's flying in. That's all I know."

Blood let her go and turned to Sandman, running a hand down his face. "We need to get into that compound."

"She's not there."

Blood turned back to Ivy. "What?"

"She's not there. I was at the compound for a party last night. There's no girl being kept there. They must have her somewhere else. But Big John knows where she is. He knows everything."

"And where can we find Big John?" Sandman asked.

"It's Wednesday. He makes collections in Little Saigon on Wednesdays."

"Collections?"

"The Pho Yen Restaurant. Cherry says they collect protection money for Black Jack from all the Vietnamese businesses."

Blood dug in his pocket, pulled out a couple of twenties, and pressed them into Ivy's hand. "You don't say a word about seeing us, you hear?"

Ivy clutched the money to her chest and nodded.

"You see Holly, you call me."

"I promise."

Cat met her eyes, her own filled with tears, and whispered, "Thank you."

***

They jogged back to the bikes parked side-by-side on St. Peter. Cat put her hand on Blood's arm, halting him from climbing on his bike. "Maybe…" She looked toward the street. "Maybe we should go to that compound you were talking about."

"Hey, look at me." When she did, he stared her in the eyes. "I can kill Black Jack. I have no problem doing that. But it's no guarantee it would get Holly back for you." He slid his hand to her nape. "Our best bet is finding Big John."

She nodded and climbed on the bike with him. They wove through the city until they picked up Chef Hwy heading east, which rode right through the Vietnamese section.

They passed Michoud Boulevard and slowed down. A couple blocks down, Blood turned left onto Alcee Fourtier Boulevard, then turned into the lot of a strip mall and parked near the entrance to the Pho Yen Restaurant.

Cat climbed off and stared at the establishment. There was a glass store front, the bottom half of the windows covered in red curtains. A neon sign in the window read, *OPEN.*

Blood looked at Sandman. "Stay here. Keep an eye out."

Sandman nodded, his eyes like a hawk moving over the building, the lot, and the adjacent side street.

Blood grabbed Cat's hand and led her toward the door. "We're just a couple grabbing some lunch, got it?"

She nodded and kept quiet.

The inside was pretty generic with linoleum floors, small red Formica tables, and metal chairs. There was a *seat yourself* sign. Blood led her to a table in the middle. She noticed his eyes scoping out the place.

A young Vietnamese girl came and took their order. Blood ordered for both of them. It was mid-afternoon and there were only two other people in the restaurant, the lunch rush apparently having died down.

"I didn't realize there was such a large Vietnamese presence in New Orleans," Cat asked, her eyes moving around the décor.

"They're the largest immigrant population in the state." Blood grinned at her. "I'll have to bring you back in January. Most still celebrate the Tet holiday around here."

After the table behind them finished and left, Blood leaned forward and instructed, "Wait here. Any trouble starts, run out the door to Sandman."

Before she could ask what trouble he anticipated, he stood and headed toward the hallway that led to the restrooms, leaving her glancing around nervously. She could tell the hallway led toward the back, and she assumed he was doing a little recon to see if Big John was back there.

A few minutes later, he came back to the table. He didn't sit, instead he motioned her to stand. "Come on."

She stood, her eyes searching his as he gave her a slight shake of his head. Damn, she'd really hoped this lead would pan out.

Movement from the hallway caught her eye, and she turned her head to see three angry Vietnamese approaching. They looked at Blood.

"Who are you? Why you here?"

Blood turned to face them as they closed in, pushing her behind him and against the wall. The first one shoved him back a step with two hands planted in his chest.

Blood quickly responded, jamming his palm into the man's jaw and forcing his head to the side while he reached up with his other hand and grabbed him by the back of the neck. He spun him violently around, face-first into the edge of a table.

As that man went down, he grabbed an empty beer bottle off the recently vacated table and with a backhanded swing, smashed it into the forehead of the second man, dropping him to the ground. Then he turned on the third man, kicking him between the legs and watching him drop like a rock. As the second man was coming around, he kicked him in the face then jumped to avoid the multiple slashes the third man was making with a knife.

Blood grabbed one of the small pedestal tables and rammed the edge into the man's face, knocking him to the ground. Then he pounded the edge into the man's face twice. Spinning, he threw the table at another man coming at him from behind. It diverted attention long enough for him to grab up a chair and fend him off like a lion tamer as the man repeatedly slashed with a knife, trying to get to his face. Fortunately for Blood, his arms were longer, and he was able to keep out of the man's reach with ease and knocked him to the ground.

"Watch out!" Cat yelled.

Spinning, Blood saw the last man coming at him with another knife. He quickly grabbed a bottle and broke it on the edge of the table with a loud crash, turning to face his next assailant. The man made several slashes—right, left, right again. Blood dodged each one, then took his broken bottle and quickly slashed back and forth four times. The man's face was a bloodied mess. He didn't stop there; he grabbed the man's head and brought his face down to violently knee him in the gut. Once. Twice. Three times, dropping the unconscious man to the ground.

Then he grabbed Cat by the wrist. "Come on."

He pulled her out the door, and they ran across the lot toward Sandman, who drew his gun to cover them as they climbed on the bike.

"You had a gun and knife. Why didn't you use them?" Cat asked.

"I just had to hurt them, not kill them. No need adding to the trail of bodies for the Homicide Division, right?"

"Right." She understood his veiled reference to the one she'd already left behind.

The two bikes tore out of the parking lot and down the highway. They darted in another side street across the way and stopped on the other side of the old Folgers Coffee Processing Plant. The smell of roasting coffee filled the air.

They paused, the bikes idling.

"What the fuck happened?" Sandman asked.

"They didn't take too well to me snooping in the back."

"What'd you find out? Is he there?"

Blood shook his head. "No, but they were getting together a protection payment. The cash was stacked up on the table they were all huddled around."

"So, maybe Big John's on his way to pick it up," Sandman suggested, his wraparound sunglasses aimed at the road back the way they'd come.

Blood shook his head. "They'll have called and warned him by now."

"So, now what?"

Blood's eyes shifted down the highway. "I say we keep surveillance on the place and—"

Cat turned to look at him, wondering why he'd stopped talking. His eyes were like a hawk, trained on its prey. She looked back to see a ninja bike, moving fast down the highway, a young Vietnamese boy riding it with a large canvas duffel bag strapped to the back.

"Bet you ten bucks there goes this week's payment. Let's go," Blood ordered.

They pulled out after him, staying well back in traffic and trailed him to a low-rent section where they watched from a lot half a block down as he entered a second floor apartment, its exterior door facing a side lot.

"See the black Mercedes parked in the third spot?" Blood asked Sandman.

"Yup."

"Pretty sure that's Big John's."

"You think there's a back way out of those places?" Sandman eyed the building.

Blood shook his head. "No, they're backed up to that other office complex."

"Guess we're goin' in the front then," Sandman mumbled as he chambered a round, bent, and dug a roll of duct tape out of his saddlebag.

A moment later, the young boy bounded down the steps empty-handed.

"Bet he wasn't delivering lunch," Sandman said.

They waited until the boy had pulled out before moving in on foot. "Stay with the bikes," Blood ordered Cat over his shoulder.

The two men dashed across the street and toward the stairs, keeping their backs to the wall and out of sight of the upper windows. She watched them dart up the staircase and take up positions on either side of the door.

CHAPTER SEVENTEEN

Blood kept his back pressed to the wall. That sickly-sweet scent of a cherry cheroot—the same as he'd smelled in Black Jack's courtyard—hit his nose. Big John was inside, guaranteed. He nodded to Sandman, who knocked twice and shouted something in Vietnamese.

Blood gave him a questioning look and whispered, "Since when do you know Vietnamese?"

Sandman grinned and whispered back, "I pick shit up."

The door opened, and they pushed their way inside, catching a stunned Big John completely by surprise. The duffel sat on the coffee table.

"Blood," Big John said as he took a step back from the two guns pointed at his face.

Blood's eyes shifted to the bag. "Since when is Black Jack in the protection business? Or is this a little side business you're running all on your own?"

Sandman grinned. "Maybe he's supplementing his retirement fund."

"What do you want?" Big John asked, ignoring their questions.

Blood grinned, but the smile didn't reach his eyes. "Unfortunately for you, not the money."

Big John's chin came up. "Then *what*?"

Blood motioned for Sandman who stepped forward, dragged a dining chair over, and shoved Big John down into it. He pulled the duct tape out of his pocket and quickly had him secured to the chair.

Blood gave a jerk of his chin to Sandman who moved off to conduct a search of the place while Blood kept his gun trained on Big John. A couple of minutes later, Sandman returned, shaking his head.

"What's this about?" Big John asked, his eyes moving between the two.

Blood pulled out the picture of Holly. "Where is she?"

Big John's eyes slid from the picture to Blood. "You just don't give up, do you?"

Blood punched him in the face.

Big John's head snapped to the side, but he smiled, revealing teeth now stained red. "You think that's gonna make me talk?"

Blood smiled as he pulled out his phone. "I think your loyalty is misplaced. You really think Black Jack gives a shit about you? You think he'll cry over your grave?"

Big John's jaw tightened, his eyes falling to the phone in Blood's hand as his thumb moved over the screen, scrolling.

Blood looked to Sandman. "How many Prospects we got watching the house where I was held?"

"Two. Leroy and Pac Man."

Blood nodded as he chose a contact, put the phone to his ear, and waited for the call to be answered. His eyes met Big John's as he spoke. "Prospect. Got a job for you. I need you to get a hold of a van, one big enough to load a dining chair into. Once you make the pickup, I want you to take it out to the Five Mile Bridge at midnight tonight and throw the chair over the side. And heads-up, there's gonna be something heavy attached to it." He paused a moment, studying Big John as he listened to the voice on the other end. "I don't know. Let me ask." He spoke to Big John. "What do you weigh, big fella? I'm guessing 280, 290?"

The color drained from Big John's face as the fate that awaited him became clear.

Blood listened to the voice in his ear, and then spoke. "You want to know if he's going to be alive when he goes over? Hmm, good question. Let me ask." He tucked the phone under his chin and asked Big John. "You want to go into the water dead or alive?"

Big John didn't say anything.

Blood grinned and spoke into the phone. "He's not feeling too well right now. Let me get back to you on that. Just get the van. I'll text you the pickup address." He disconnected the call and leaned over Big John. "Can you imagine it? As you're sinking, the light from above fading away as you descend to the murky bottom, your lungs exploding with the need for oxygen, the screams that won't ever be heard as your mouth fills with water. What a way to go, huh?"

Big John turned a shade of green.

"Tell me what I want to know, and I'll make sure you're dead before you go over the rail."

Big John stared at him.

"Nothing on this earth makes any difference to you anymore. Are you starting to comprehend that? You might want to do one good thing on your way out. Tell me where the girl is. Did he put her out on the street?"

The man grit his teeth, his eyes shifting to the side before he finally shook his head. "No. He has something special in mind for her."

"And what's that?"

"A buyer is flying in from Japan on Friday. She's gonna bring in top dollar."

"Where is she now?"

"Black Jack has her."

"According to my sources, she's not at the compound."

Big John shook his head. "No. He had her moved after you showed up. Hasn't even told *me* where he stashed her."

"You see, John, he's already cutting you out. So no need to protect him in your last hour on this earth."

"I guess you're right."

"How did he get his hands on her?" Blood asked.

"The Death Heads MC brought her to him."

"And why would they do that? They sell her to him?"

"Nope. She was a peace offering for a little fuckup. You see, he's working with them."

"What?" Blood asked stunned.

There was a knock at the door. Sandman quickly put his

hand over Big John's mouth to make sure he didn't say anything. Blood stepped to the window and drew the curtain to the side an inch to peer out.

Cat. *Damn it, she was supposed to stay put, like she'd been told.* She was glancing all around like something was wrong. He quickly opened the door a crack. "Not now, babe. Go back to the bikes."

"I can't. Those men drove by," she hissed in a whisper.

Blood opened the door, yanked her in, and slammed it. Her eyes got big when she saw Big John taped to the chair.

"Stand there and be quiet." Blood got in her face, drawing that wide-eyed stare up to him. She nodded mutely, and he turned back to the job at hand, snapping, "The Death Heads. Explain."

"It's true," Big John stated.

Sandman huffed out a laugh. "Black Jack, the man who *hates* the Evil Dead MC with every fiber in his being, is working with the Death Heads? Bullshit. No way."

Big John glared at him. "I never said it was smart."

"What was the fuck up?" Blood pressed.

"You."

"Me?"

"They found out the man they'd shot was none other than Black Jack Boudreaux's son."

"What?" Cat whispered.

Blood turned to see her stunned eyes on him. He pointed to her. "Stay the fuck out of this, Cat." He watched her mouth slam shut, the expression on her face filled with a new wariness. He turned back to Big John. "Explain."

"I'm guessing that's why they patched you up. They realized their mistake. Then the girl, well, she was...compensation for fucking things up."

"The girl?" Cat took a step forward, her eyes moving between Big John and Blood. "He has my sister?"

Blood whirled on her. "Not one more word, do you understand?" He pointed to the couch. "Sit down!"

She sat.

Big John huffed out a laugh. "I'm guessing the little lady didn't know you're the son of the biggest crime boss in the city. Surprise, surprise."

Blood whirled on him and punched him in the mouth again. "What was the deal?"

Big John spit a mouthful of blood out and laughed. "Why not? Might as well tell you all of it. He made a deal with them. They're going to stock him in women."

"And in return?"

"They want a foothold in Louisiana—New Orleans, specifically. But then, you knew that, right? They've wanted an 'in' for a long time. Black Jack's giving them one. Six thousand oil rigs in the Gulf... That's a lot of lonely men away from shore for weeks at a time. Then there's the drug traffic in and out of the port. It could be a lucrative business for both parties. And I think he figures if it destroys your club in the process, you'll come crawling back to him. You'd have no other choice."

"No way in hell that's ever happening." Blood stared at the man. "Why now? After all these years."

"Your father has always been pissed you turned your

back on the *family* business. But with you having the Evil Dead at your back, there was little Black Jack could do, and that drove him crazy.

"When you started messing with his business, trying to *save* his girls, it pushed him over the edge. That's when he made that deal. You see, the Death Heads and your ol' man had the same goal—to push the Evil Dead MC out of New Orleans and out of Louisiana."

Blood stared at him. "That son of a bitch. None of that will ever happen. I'll see to it, personally."

"As long as I'm making my last statement, there's more. It's time you knew."

Blood noticed Cat's reaction to the part about this being John's last statement.

"Blood?" she whispered.

He pointed a finger at her, not even turning his head, his eyes staying on the man. But he got the intended effect. She shut up.

"Speak," he ordered Big John.

"Your mother didn't run off."

That was the last thing Blood expected to come out of his mouth. Before he could even formulate a question, Big John continued.

"Black Jack killed her."

Blood tried to jive this up with the story he'd always been told as a child—that his mother had abandoned him. Blood knew what kind of a man his father was, knew all too well just what the man was capable of, but he'd never once considered this possibility. His eyes drilled into the man.

"Why?"

"She was going to leave him."

"Then why not just let her go?"

"Because she was going to take you with her. He wasn't about to lose his son." The corner of Big John's split lip lifted in a smirk. "Guess he lost you anyway, huh? He wanted me to dump her body in the swamp."

Oh my God. Blood thought he was going to be sick at the vivid image that flashed through his brain of his mother's body disposed of in such a horrible way. His eyes burned into Big John's. "You son of a bitch. You let him kill her."

"I couldn't stop him, but I made sure she had a decent burial. I couldn't dump her like that. She was an innocent. She didn't deserve any of the shit he did to her. She's got a nice grave in Metairie Cemetery. Paid for it myself. I lay flowers on it every year on her birthday."

"You think that makes it okay? You think that washes your sins away? You think any of that is going to save you?"

Big John shook his head. "No. I know I've got sins to pay for. I know I've got retribution due me. I feel like I've been running from it all these years. And I'm tired, Son. So, you do what you gotta do."

"Black Jack know any of that?"

Big John shook his head. "No. He thinks I followed orders."

"And why didn't you?"

"She was a sweet girl. I... cared about her."

"And yet after he killed her, you continue to work for him."

Big John nodded. "I did. I shouldn't have, but I did. If he had suspected I had feelings for her; I'd have been the next to die."

"Anything else you want to confess?"

His eyes slid to Cat for a moment before shifting back to Blood. "I don't know where the girl is, but there's something you might be able to use to get Black Jack to bargain with you. Something your mother had."

"What's that?"

"A ring."

"A ring?"

"Yeah, a stupid ring. That's how it all came to a head—over a stupid ring. It was his father's ring. He was sentimental about it. Only thing he ever gave a damn about. It infuriated him when she took it. I think she was going to use it as a bargaining chip to win her freedom and yours. Things just didn't work out that way."

"Where is it?"

"I don't know. She wouldn't tell him, right to the end. I thought maybe you had it."

Blood shook his head. "I don't know shit about a ring. Maybe she didn't have it."

"He believed she did." They studied each other. "You remember that last day? The last time you saw her?"

"Yeah. I remember." It was burned in his brain, an image he'd never forget.

"Remember that strange thing she said to you? Maybe it was a clue. Maybe she was trying to tell you."

"What thing?"

"About the poem. I thought it was an odd thing for her to bring up, considering… well, considering the circumstances."

"She knew, didn't she? She knew she was about to die."

Big John nodded. "I thought maybe it was in that book of poetry she always carried around. Black Jack thought so, too. We went back to the old house, tore it apart, but we never did find it. You find that ring, you might be able to make a deal."

Blood thought about the book of poetry. This was the second time in days he'd thought about it. Prior to that, it had been years. Black Jack and Big John hadn't found it because they didn't know the spot his mother always hid it in. But Blood knew.

He glanced back at Cat. If he could find that book, if it was still hidden behind the loose board where his mother kept anything she didn't want his father to destroy in one of his rages, then maybe he had a shot at getting Cat's sister back for her.

Big John interrupted his thoughts. "Think what you will, but I loved her."

Blood's eyes bore into the man. "You used her."

"One wolf recognizes another," Big John taunted, his eyes shifting to Cat as he did.

Blood's eyes flared in rage, then strayed to the laptop sitting on the table, it's power cord connected and charging. He jerked his chin at Sandman and ordered, "Take her outside."

Sandman nodded, understanding exactly what was about

to go down and the reason Blood didn't want Cat to witness it.

"Come on, girl. Let's go." Sandman grabbed her by the upper arm and hustled her out the door.

When they were gone, Blood strolled over to the laptop and yanked the cord from the wall.

Big John began talking. "Your mother did love you, whatever you thought about her, Son. Emeline was—"

"Shut up. I ain't your son, and you don't get to say her name," Blood growled. Then he calmly moved behind Big John, wrapped the length of the cord around each fist, and strangled the life out of him.

CHAPTER EIGHTEEN

Cat stood with Sandman next to the parked motorcycles, waiting for Blood. They didn't have long to wait. He jogged across the highway to them a few minutes later, the duffel bag thrown over his shoulder.

Sandman looked at him. "You need anything?"

Blood shook his head, tossing the bag to him and pulling his phone from his pocket. "Just need to text the address to Leroy."

Sandman strapped it to his bike. "Fucker's heavy."

Blood's eyes flicked up. "Shoved his laptop and cell phone inside. Figured it might have some intel we could use."

"Smart thinking," Sandman replied.

"I have my moments. Let's roll."

Cat climbed on the back of Blood's bike, her mind whirling with everything she'd seen and learned. Those men had her sister, and one of them was Blood's father. She thought back to everything Undertaker had told her about the man, how cruel and abusive he was to Blood. But Undertaker had neglected to mention the fact that the man was Black Jack Boudreaux.

As they pulled out, roaring onto the street, her eyes moved to the second floor apartment they'd just left, and she wondered if Blood had killed Big John. He was involved in kidnapping her sister, so she could hardly blame Blood after what he'd done. She'd kill the man herself if it would get Holly back.

The apartment building faded into the distance, and she tightened her hold on the man who was doing everything he could to keep his promise to her.

***

A half hour later, they rolled up to the clubhouse gates. Blood watched as a line of bikes was pulling out. Mooch waved the others on before pulling over next to them as they coasted to the curb to let the bunch pass.

When the thundering bikes had roared down the street, Mooch said, "You're late. First crew already left with Undertaker. I'm taking the second. You and Sandman are taking the third; they're still waiting for you." He jerked his head back toward the compound.

Blood nodded. "Go on. We're right behind you."

Mooch nodded and gunned his throttle, peeling off down the road.

Blood and Sandman pulled their bikes into the compound. There were still six bikes parked, waiting. Blood dismounted and grabbed the duffel Sandman tossed to him. Then he approached Easy who stood near the building waiting to head out. Pulling the laptop and cell phone out of the bag, Blood shoved them into the man's chest. "I need you to stay behind and go through these. They're from Black Jack's second in command and bound to have all kinds of intel."

Easy looked down at the electronics. "Yeah, sure thing."

Blood tossed him the duffel. "And lock this is the safe."

Blood walked back to where Sandman stood by his bike. "Gotta ask you to do something."

"You're just full of requests today, aren't you?"

"I need you to cover for me."

"And what are you gonna be doing?"

Blood gave Sandman a penetrating look. "I'm heading to the swamp. I have to at least try."

Sandman looked disbelieving. "No fucking way. You're going to look for that fucking ring? Now?"

"It could be the only chance I've got to get this girl. You heard the man. In two days she'll be on a private jet to Japan. I've got no clue where she is. This may be the only shot I've got."

"To do what? You don't have the fucking ring to trade."

"But I do know where that poetry book is… at least where it used to be. If I can get my hands on it, then it may lead me to the ring."

"And where the fuck is that?"

"The fish camp."

"That old shack in the swamp you told me about? Are

you fucking kidding me?"

Blood stared him down.

"Brother, we have our orders."

"Just this one night."

Sandman shook his head. "Look, man. I know that asshole dumped a lot of shit on you tonight. Finding out your father killed your mother—"

Blood grabbed him with a fist in his leather vest. "Shut up about that. Understand?"

Sandman shoved him off. "I've been your brother for a lot of fucking years, Blood. So, I'll let that slide, but don't fucking push it."

Blood ran a hand through his hair in frustration. "Sorry, man. I just need to get through this week. I just need you to cover for me on this, Sandman."

Sandman looked at the horizon and shook his head. "Goddamn you." He looked back at Blood. "Fine, but you better be back and done with this shit tomorrow morning."

Blood grabbed his shoulder, patted it, and headed to his bike.

Cat watched him swing his leg over. "Wait. I'm going with you."

"Aw, not this shit again," Sandman grumbled.

"No, you're not," Blood bit out, firing his bike up with a twist of his wrist.

She approached him, putting a hand on his arm. "Please, Blood. I can help you." She didn't know to what extent the information that Big John had told him would affect him, but she knew he might need her when it all started to sink in.

Plus, she'd just watched him put finding her sister before his club duties again, and that meant something to her. "Please."

He huffed out a long frustrated growl. "Damn it, Cat. You don't even know where the hell I'm going."

"To a fish camp?"

"Yeah, and it's in the middle of the fucking swamp. With bugs and snakes and gators. And all that that implies."

"I'm not afraid."

Sandman chuckled. "Only thing you've got to be afraid of darlin' is Blood."

Blood glared at him.

Surprisingly, Sandman threw his weight behind her and backed her plan, telling Blood, "You want me to cover for you, then you take her ass with you."

Blood stared him down. "What the fuck for?"

"'Cause I'm worried about you, Brother. You've got a lot of shit in your head right now you're gonna have to deal with. And as soon as you take a moment to breathe, all that shit's gonna come crashing down on you. I think it's a good idea if she's with you when that happens."

"No. No fucking way." He shook his head.

"You want my help or not?" Sandman gave him the ultimatum.

Blood grit his teeth, his jaw tightening, but gave in. Pinning her with a look, he ordered, "Get the fuck on. But I don't want to hear any bitching. The first complaint out of your mouth, I'm dropping you flat, I don't care where we are. We understand each other?" She nodded her acceptance of his terms, but Blood could see she was wondering if he was serious about leaving her. He didn't bother to ease her mind. "Get the hell on, then."

Before she did, she ran to Sandman and kissed him on the cheek. "Thank you."

Sandman grinned. "Go on now, girl. Before he leaves your ass behind."

CHAPTER NINETEEN

Dusk was falling as the bike rolled up to a tiny run-down shack on the edge of the bayou. There was a rusted sign that read *J&P Bait Shop*. The building was made of corrugated metal with a faded red roof.

"Why are we stopping here?" Cat asked as they dismounted.

Blood strode toward the door. "We need a boat, come on."

Cat frowned at him as he held the door for her. She walked into the tiny building. There were a few shelves with merchandise, motor oil, fishing line, bait cans, Styrofoam coolers, all of it coated in dust. She followed Blood as he moved to the counter and pounded on a bell.

"Jean Michel? Pierre? Get your coon-asses out here!" There was a small curtained doorway that led to a back room where some banging stopped.

"Who dat?" A heavily Cajun accented voice carried to the front.

"Come find out, boy." Blood walked over to an upright cooler and pulled two Cokes from the top shelf. He passed one to Cat and twisted the cap off his, tilting it up and guzzling down a third of the bottle.

A moment later the dingy green curtain was shoved aside and a man stuck his head out. He was about Blood's age, from what Cat could surmise, about a foot shorter, and dark haired. His brown eyes crinkled as he smiled, then turned to shout back into the room behind him. "Coo-wee, Pierre, gar ici. Cousin Etienne."

"Dit mon la verite'!" came a voice from the back room.

"I'm tellin' you da truth, Couillon!"

Blood grinned as the two men argued, then he moved forward to embrace the first man, slapping him on the back. "Been a long time, Jean Michel."

"True, dat."

A second man came out and stopped in his tracks. "Well, hot damn. Etienne!"

Cat could see that the two men had to be identical twins.

Blood moved to embrace him as well. "Pierre. How's your mama an' them?"

"Bon. Bon. Still makes the best crawfish gumbo in Terrebonne Parrish. You should come round."

Blood nodded. "Oui."

The man's eyes moved to Cat. "Qui C'est q'ca, Boo?"

"That's Catherine Randall. And you call me that nickname again, I'll beat your ass."

"What? Boo? I always call you Boo, since I was dis high." The man held his hand knee high.

"Beck moi tchew!" Blood snapped with a grin.

The man grinned over at Cat and informed her, "He just told me to bite his ass."

Cat laughed, her eyes moving to Blood. She was amazed at how quickly he slipped into the Cajun language he must have grown up around.

"Cher, pay him no mind."

Cat smiled at the man and held her hand out. "Pleased to meet you, Jean Michel. How do you do?"

The man looked at her hand, and then grinned over at Blood. "Owee. She's a formal one, eh?" Then he took her hand and pulled her in for a hug instead of a handshake. "You with Boo, then you family. We family, we don't shake hands, we hug."

"I see, Mister…?"

"Jean Michel Robichau."

The second man came forward and extended his hand. "Some of us have manners. Pierre Robichau, Cher."

Cat shook his hand.

Jean Michel looked to Blood and jerked his head toward her. "Gaienne?"

Blood let out a huff of laughter. "Non, Jean Michel. She's not my girlfriend."

"You been out to see Tante Marie?" Pierre asked.

Blood shook his head. "Non. Headed to the old place. If it's still standing."

"Oui, it's still standing."

"Co faire? You ain't been back in years."

"None of your business why, Jean Michel." Blood

looked to Pierre. "I need a boat."

The man nodded. "Mais yeah, we got those. You wanna take da pirogue?"

Blood shook his head, grinning. "I was thinking something with a motor."

"I make you a deal. I loan you da boat, you promise to go see Tante Marie."

"Mais yeah, if I've got time."

"You make time, Boo."

Blood rolled his eyes. "Oui."

***

Fifteen minutes later, Cat sat in a small motorboat with Blood behind her, his hand on the outboard, steering them through the bayou. They rounded a bend, coming into a wider body of water, and Blood opened up the motor, moving them quickly across it. There was the heavy scent of salt in the air, and Cat turned to the west to see a dark wall of gray clouds on the horizon as a storm rolled in, and with it, Cat felt a sense of foreboding.

Finally, Blood slowed the boat and turned down a narrow inlet. He seemed to know the terrain like the back of his hand, and she supposed that made sense considering he grew up here.

Still, she didn't know how he did it. It seemed like just a mass of twisting turning jumble, one bayou leading to the next. They moved deeper and deeper into the swamp. The Cypress trees stood black against the darkening sky as the storm blew in off the Gulf like the scent of smoke warned of a forest fire.

The scent of the salty ocean breeze mingled with the smell of the bayou, a mix of decaying wood and flowering blooms. They coasted past large swaths of Water Hyacinth that covered the water with green waxy leaves and pale lavender blooms. Cat spotted purple Iris near the shore. They moved through the water, following a narrow path of clear glassy water that seemed to be cut through the trees and lily pads by years of boats traveling through. The trail twisted and snaked through the swamp like one of the anaconda that were taking over.

The thought of the snake—and what else may be lurking under the surface of the murky water—had Cat tensing a bit.

"Afraid of something, Cher?"

"Like what?"

"Oh, I don't know, the swamp is the prowling ground of North America's largest reptile."

"Are there…many?" Her gaze darted around.

"About two million in the state."

She shivered, and he chuckled. "Largest one ever recorded was more than nineteen feet long."

"Stop. Please."

He chuckled again, but kept quiet.

They moved through a tunnel of overhanging branches and low hanging trails of silvery Spanish moss. Cat reached out and touched a feathery branch, surprised to discover how soft it was.

Journeying out to the swamp was like going back in

time, back to an uncivilized primitive time. And she supposed for Blood, he *was* going back in time— returning to the home of his childhood, one she was pretty sure he hadn't returned to before now.

The dark waters they moved slowly through gave an eerie feel to their trip. They turned one way and then another, winding this way and that, as Blood led them so far into the dark swamp Cat wondered if he'd ever find his way back.

It made Cat think of his twisting journey to get to the truth of what had happened to his mother. To think that his father had killed her was so horrible; she couldn't imagine how he focused on anything right now, let alone help get Holly back. How could that be more important to him?

Maybe it wasn't. Maybe this trip was a way to keep his mind off dealing with everything Big John had revealed to him. But she couldn't help but wonder what was going to happen when he came face-to-face with his childhood home. That would have to bring up all sorts of memories.

As a chill blew across her exposed arms, she ran her hands back and forth over her skin and thought of her sister. Big John said a buyer was coming on Friday. That was just two days from now, and the clock was ticking.

And it all boiled down to this trip out into the swamp.

Blood steered the boat around another bend and slowed the engine. Cat looked around, almost missing the shack all together. A house up on stilts sat just back up the shore from a dilapidated pier. It was so overgrown with vines that it was barely visible.

She swallowed as Blood coasted the boat to the pier,

jumping off to tie it to one of the posts that stood listing to the side.

Cat's eyes moved over the property. There were several old appliances rusting in the yard to the side—a stove, a refrigerator, and several motors. Old gas cans and a plethora of junk littered the ground. Cat couldn't imagine Blood's life as a child growing up in a place like this.

"Come on, Cher."

She turned to see Blood holding his hand out to her. Slipping her hand in his warm, firm grip, she let him help her out of the boat and up onto the pier.

"Watch your step."

She followed him up the shaky pier, onto the soft, spongy ground, and then up the stairs. He opened a screen door from the small porch that led into another covered porch. The door was unlocked, and she followed him inside. It was a bare bones structure with a small kitchen area off to the right, the main room with a living and dining area, and two small bedrooms whose walls only went up about eight feet. The walls were bare wood with no insulation. There were no ceilings, just open wood rafters to the roof. An old wood-burning stove sat against the wall between the two bedrooms and must have served as heat for the entire place.

Cat noticed only kerosene lamps sitting on tables, and she could only guess the place didn't have electricity, and she wondered if it ever had.

Blood moved to open some windows, exposing the screens and letting the cool breeze blow through. Cat was grateful for the storm blowing in with its cooling effect, but she worried about getting back out before they were caught in it.

The light of day was fading quickly. If they were going to search the place, they needed to move fast, but Blood seemed to know exactly where he was looking. He moved to a board in the floor. Taking his knife from his belt, he flipped the blade open and jimmied it loose. It popped up after a moment, and he yanked the board up, tossing it aside. He put his hand in and pulled out what was hidden in the space. Moving to the table, he set the items down—a leather-bound book of poetry and a bible with a rosary wrapped around it.

He moved back to the hidden space and turned on the flashlight app on his cell phone, shining it into the darkness.

"Is it there? The ring?" Cat asked hopefully.

He leaned forward, running his hand over the inside, and then sat back on his haunches. "Nope."

Cat glanced around the room. "Maybe she put it somewhere else." The place was a mess.

"Looks like my father already tore the place apart looking for it." Blood moved back to the books on the table. He flipped through the book of poetry. Her favorite poem was marked with a prayer card—the Virgin Mary. He flipped it over and back. Just a card from the church she'd used as a bookmark. He searched the margins for any scribbled message, but found none. He thumbed through the entire book, front to back, but there was nothing but her name written on the inside cover.

He slammed the book down. "Damn it."

Cat lifted her chin. "Maybe the bible?"

Blood picked it up and unwrapped the rosary, his thumb moving over it. "She always wore this." He shoved it in his pocket and searched the bible, but found nothing. He glanced around the house. "It's got to be here."

"I'll help you look."

They both tore the place apart, searching every nook and cranny. Cat tried to think where she, as a woman, would hide something. She looked through every food container and canister, every feminine product in the bathroom, the jar of bath salts, the dust-covered box of tampons, everywhere she could think of that a man would never look.

After an hour, darkness had fallen, and Blood lit some of the kerosene lamps. A light rain began to fall outside and quickly turned into a downpour.

"I have to go cover the boat," Blood said as he moved toward the door.

Cat nodded and watched him go. She moved to the screen and watched as he pulled some kind of an old tarp from under the house and hauled it down to the pier. He looked big and broad-shouldered as he stood in the ghostly gray mist that rose up from the water as the cold rain fell on it. His muscles worked as he yanked and adjusted the heavy canvas tarp into place. Watching him, she knew she was safe with him, knew he was fully capable of taking care of her out here.

She sat at the table, waiting for him to return, and thought about her sister, wondering what would happen if they couldn't reason with Black Jack.

Blood came back inside, shook the rain off, and then

pulled out the chair across the table and sat. He picked up the poetry book and flipped through it again. As he did, a picture fell out.

Cat's eyes dropped to the photograph. It was an old Polaroid of a woman standing in front of a car, a big smile on her face, holding the keys up. "Is that your mother?"

Blood nodded.

"She was very pretty."

"Yes, she was."

"You think the car means anything? Could it be a clue?"

Blood smirked. "If it is, we're screwed. That was twenty years ago. That car's long gone."

Cat deflated. "Oh."

He opened the book of poetry and took out the prayer card with the picture of the Virgin Mary; he sat turning it over and over in his hands, staring off into space.

Cat wasn't sure what to do, so she waited, allowing him time to think.

After a few minutes, he moved to the doorway and slammed his palm into the frame. "Goddamn it. I was sure it'd be here."

Cat got up and moved behind him.

"I ain't gonna lie, Cat. It looks pretty bleak. I can't find the ring, and I've got no clue where Black Jack is. He's disappeared. Without the ring, I've got nothing to trade for your sister, nothing to draw Black Jack out with."

"He's not at the compound?"

Blood shook his head. "If he was I'd go torture him to death and make him tell me where he's got your sister. But

Big John said he left. I've had people watching the place. He hasn't come back."

"Oh."

He moved out onto the porch to stand by the screen door, watching the rain pour down. He eyed the sky. "We'll have to wait for the storm to pass."

"All right."

"You sure about that? Might mean we have to stay the night in this stinking shit hole." He watched the sky light up with a bolt of lightning. "I hate this fucking place."

"The swamp?"

He shook his head, the outline of his body dark in the shadows silhouetted by the steel gray sky. "This place... It's somewhere I never wanted to see again."

She was almost afraid to ask, but maybe Blood needed to talk about it, even if he didn't realize it himself. And Sandman had practically sent her to help him deal with all this stuff.

She watched Blood. He was definitely on edge. All this time, he'd been the one to calm her down. Maybe now it was time for her to return the favor. "Bad memories?"

He nodded.

"Tell me."

He stood stock still, and she wondered if he was debating it.

"Please."

"It's not a pretty story."

"Maybe I can help you, maybe if you talk about it—"

"Yeah, well, we all have shit we've got to live with."

"Some more than others."

"Yeah, some a whole lot more."

"Does it hurt to talk about it?"

He shook his head. "No. It's just...it's my mess, you know? Mine. I deal with it. It's like this box I carry around, packed to the brim with so much shit, when it gets opened it explodes all over everyone in the room. It's better if it stays shut."

"Does it scare you?"

"No. I just know it's there. The pain, the anger, the loss... It belongs to me, no one else."

"Share it with me."

"Why?"

"Because I want to help you."

"You can't fix it."

"Maybe not."

"There's no *maybe* about it."

"It can get better."

"Can it?" He turned to look at her then. "My mother took me and left my father. When my father found us, he brought me out here...this old fish camp out in the swamp."

"I don't understand... Did you live here or New Orleans?"

"My mother was from here. Her people were from here. But Black Jack wasn't. After they were married, when she would miss her people, he would get mad, like the nice place in New Orleans wasn't enough for her. So he bought this old place, and he would leave us out here. I think it was supposed to be some kind of punishment for her—this piece of shit shack out in the swamp. I don't think she saw it that way."

"The night you ran away, and he caught you, what happened?"

"He beat me with his belt for going with her. Then he left me out here for two weeks. Alone. I was eight years old.

"I lived off anything I could find in the cupboards— peanut butter and crackers, cans of beans, dry cereal. He finally came back for me. I wasn't sure if I was happy to see him or not. I wanted to kill him. Even then. But I was too young.

"He took me back to where he'd taken my mother—a second floor room in some shotgun house in the Quarter. A lot like the one the Death Heads had me in. I remember the narrow louvered shutters and how hot the room was. When I walked in, I barely recognized her. She was on an old iron bed. In the two weeks I'd been left out in the swamp, he'd been busy.

"He'd strung her out on heroine. There were needle tracks up and down her arms. She was shaking and sweating, begging him for her next fix. It was pathetic and heartbreaking, and not something an eight-year-old boy should have to see.

"Of course, I didn't really understand all that back then, I just thought she was sick. It was when I got older that I realized what I'd witnessed."

"I'm so sorry."

"That wasn't the worst of it."

"Oh, God. It gets worse?"

"She called my name and held her hand out to me. But

he dragged me back. He wouldn't let me near her. That's when she asked me, 'Remember the poem I used to read to you, Etienne? Remember the poetry book? Don't forget it.' I didn't know why she was talking about a stupid poem at a time like that. Then my father really twisted the knife. He nodded to a pen and paper that was lying on the bedside table and told her to sign it."

"What was it?"

Blood pinned her with a look. "My mother sold me to my father for a thousand dollars and a speedball. At least that's what he told me later. I never saw her again. He told me she'd run off and abandoned me. Years later, he told me he'd heard she'd OD'd in some motel somewhere.

"He was a monster, but he was all I had. So I did what I was told." Blood turned back to watch the rain. "You heard Big John. It's true. My father is the biggest crime boss in New Orleans.

"I remember one day he guided me in front of a mirror, his hand fisted in my hair, and he held me there. He shook my head and said, 'Look, boy! What do you see? That's Jacque Boudreaux's son.' He took my jaw in his hand and squeezed, forcing me to look. He said, 'I own you. You do what I damn tell you. And you don't ever try to run again. You do, I'll bring you back. And next time I won't stop at a black eye and busted lip, understand? You're mine. And what's mine is mine until I say otherwise. You're under my control. You'll always be under my control. Until the day you die.'"

"I looked at him with murder in my eyes and said, 'Or

the day you die, old man.' He laughed and said, 'There's the family spirit. Hate me if you want, boy, but my blood runs in your veins. You're like me, boy. Just like me. And there's no runnin' from that.' I believed him then, maybe I still do." Blood paused and shook his head, then turned to look at her. "That's always been my biggest fear—that I'd turn out just like him."

"You're not like him, Blood. You're nothing like him."

"Aren't I?"

"And your mother didn't leave you, she didn't abandon you. He killed her."

Blood nodded. "Yeah. And I didn't save her, did I? Worse than that, I thought the worst of her all these years, believing she deserted me like that. And I let that way of thinking color every relationship I ever had with women. I pushed them all away, believed they had nothing I wanted or needed beyond sex, that they couldn't be trusted, that they were all out for themselves. Everything I based that on was wrong. My mother did the best she could. *I* was the one who let *her* down, not the other way around." He stared her in the eyes. "I'm not anybody's fucking hero. See how fucked up I am?"

"Blood—"

"I had it all wrong, and maybe subconsciously, I even knew it. How am I ever gonna get around that fact?" He paused and looked away. "I can't shake it, Cat."

"You were eight years old, Blood. None of that was your fault."

"I think deep down I knew it had never added up—all

the lies my father fed me, and maybe I even thought if I helped you, if I saved your sister, somehow it'd make up for not saving my mother all those years ago."

"I'm grateful for everything you've done to try to help me, Blood, but you have nothing to make up for." She moved to him and took his face in her hands, making him look at her. She stroked over his cheeks and beard, moving her thumbs over his lips. She stared into his eyes. He looked broken and vulnerable in a way she'd never seen him before. He needed her, and that was a powerful pull for her. He'd always had that whole bad boy thing going that sucked her in. Yes, he was a badass, but he'd also been very protective of her in his own way.

She brought her mouth to his, brushing his lips softly, tenderly. She took his hand and led him to one of the bedrooms. She turned to face him, then without another word, she pulled him toward the bed. When the back of her thighs hit the mattress, he pulled back to look down at her.

"You think I want your gratitude, your pity. Is that what this is?"

She shook her head. "That's not what this is. That's not what this is at all."

"You've seen me now. The man I am, what I come from, who my father is. I won't ever be able to shake that."

"I see the good in you. You're a good man, Blood. If I didn't believe that, I wouldn't be here with you, no matter what promises you made to me."

He studied her eyes carefully, searching for the truth, and then his eyes moved to the bed. "You lead, I'm gonna follow. You give, I'm gonna take. That's just my nature, the kind of man I am."

"I know exactly the kind of man you are."

"And that's good enough for you?"

She gave him the answer, slipping her hand to the back of his neck, her fingers threading into the hair at his nape as she pulled his mouth back down to hers.

He bent, cupping her thighs as he lifted and tossed her on the bed, following her down. She tore at his vest. He lifted off her long enough to pull it off and yank the t-shirt over his head.

Her eyes moved over his body, stopping on the bandage. "Your wound. We shouldn't."

"No stopping this now, Cat."

He moved over her, yanking her shirt over her head in one quick movement. A moment later, her bra was gone as well. He paused, his eyes taking her in, and everything slowed down. His gaze came to hers, and they stared into one another's eyes, seeing… *really* seeing each other. "I need you, Cat."

She nodded, and her eyes slid closed as he dipped his head, his nose brushing along hers. Then he moved lower, his mouth trailing along her jaw, her throat, and down to latch on to her nipple. Her back arched, and her fingers dove into his hair, threading through the strands to grip his scalp.

He moved back over her, his mouth on her neck, and her hands slipped around him, the tips of her fingers tensing, digging in to the skin of his back as her mouth parted with a sigh.

He pulled back to look at her, his palm smoothing the hair back from her face, and she opened her eyes. "You're beautiful. Did I ever tell you that? The first time I saw you, I thought you were an angel, come to take me to heaven."

She smiled. "You were delirious."

"You saved me. You're still saving me, Cat."

She saw the honesty in his eyes, and it moved something in her, made her catch her breath, made her heart skip a beat. When he continued to just search her face, his eyes going all over it as he brushed her hair back, she asked, "What?"

"I'm just trying to take this moment in, how good it feels. I don't want to forget it."

"Blood." She didn't know what to say to those words. He said the sweetest things when she least expected. And then his eyes darkened, filling with desire as one hand moved down to her waistband, popping the button free. A moment later she felt the heat of his palm as it slid down the front of her pants. Her breath caught in her throat as his fingertips glided over her seam with barely there strokes.

"Open for me," he growled, his voice thick and heavy with arousal.

She did as he commanded, her thighs spreading ever so slightly, giving him the added room he needed. Still, he teased.

Her tongue came out to wet her lips as the anticipation clawed through her. She wanted his touch, *craved* it... balanced on the sharp edge of a precipice, waiting for it.

His eyes dropped to watch her tongue, and he lowered his head, catching her mouth, sliding his tongue inside as his fingers spread her open and began to stroke her clit in lazy circles.

She moaned deep in her throat, her hands clutching him as she let him play with her. Her hips lifted, attempting to rub against his hand, wanting more.

"You like that, baby? You like my touch?"

Her answer came out in barely a whisper. "Yes."

"You gonna let me play? Do what I want?"

She nodded, unable to form words at the molten look in his eyes. At that moment she'd deny him nothing.

He followed along her slit again, sliding two fingers inside her. She was wet, very wet. His thumb kept up the torment on her clit while those fingers sought out that little trigger deep inside. When they found it, she couldn't keep her head from going back.

"Bingo," he muttered, and then she felt his mouth close over her exposed neck, latching on. She couldn't help but thrust against his hand, which caused her breasts to bounce.

He soon gave up his hold on her throat and moved down to catch a nipple in his wet mouth, sucking hard.

That had her grasping his hair and holding him to her, moaning.

He lifted his head and looked at her, then pulled his hand out and brought two fingers up, coating her lips with her arousal, then swooping down to capture those lips with his mouth, lapping at them and growling deep in his throat.

She could feel the change in him. His whole body shifted over her, and she could feel his rock hard erection straining against the front of his jeans as he caged her in with his arms.

He devoured her mouth, until apparently that wasn't enough. He broke off the kiss to growl in her ear, "The taste of you just makes me want more."

His weight lifted off her. She opened her eyes, rolling her head to look at him, unsure why he was stopping. But he wasn't. He moved to the edge of the bed, grabbed each pant leg and jerked her bottoms down and off, tossing them mindlessly to the floor. He undid his own and dropped them to the floor, the whole while, his eyes zeroed in on her pink satin and lace panties—panties, she was sure were soaked through.

Her eyes trailed down his body from his blazing eyes to his muscular arms and chest to his erection standing hard and tall.

She expected him to put it to immediate use, but apparently he had other ideas. He dragged her legs to the edge of the bed and, dropping to his knees, brought his face to that pink satin, inhaling deeply.

Their eyes connected as he curled his fingers in the fabric at her hips and drew them down her legs ever so slowly.

Cat's hands fisted in the worn coverlet beneath her.

His palms glided back up the inside of her thighs just as slowly. Their eyes connected as he spread them wide, causing her to suck in a gasp.

"So pretty," he murmured and then his mouth found her and her head rolled back again. He sucked and teased and slid the flat of his tongue over her in long strokes as he groaned his appreciation and approval when she writhed and arched beneath him. He tried to pin her thighs to the bed, anchoring her with his big hands, but she was having none of it, she needed to rub against his mouth and that beard of his that was driving her crazy.

Two fingers slid deep inside her, and he started up on that trigger again while his mouth tormented her clit over and over and over until she was thrashing on the bed. It was too much.

She tried to shift free of his hold, but he held her fast and tight. "No, baby girl. Want you right where you are."

"Oh," her mouth fell open, her breath catching and holding as he continued stroking, applying deeper pressure inside her and long strokes with his tongue to her clit until she couldn't hold back, and she exploded into climax.

She barely had time to sink back into the mattress like a puddle of melted ice cream before his big muscled body and hot skin were over her, pinning her to the bed. One big palm closed around her inner thigh and hiked her leg up. Then that hand grasped his erection, and he teased her already swollen clit with the head in big wet circles, spreading her arousal all over him. He moved down to circle her entrance as his face hovered over hers.

"You ready for me, pretty baby?"

She nodded, beyond words. But that wasn't good enough for him.

"I've been going gentle with you, holding back, but I want to hear you say it."

"Please."

That was apparently good enough. A second later he

thrust inside her, his muscled arms tensing as he flexed his whole body, settling between her thighs.

His hand slid up the skin of her thigh, pulling her leg up farther.

"Damn, baby," he groaned in ecstasy, his eyes falling closed. Then his jaw clenched as he began to move in a slow rhythm.

It felt like heaven, and her legs naturally wrapped around him, pulling him close and trying to urge him into a faster tempo. He was having none of it. He was determined to set the pace he wanted, although Cat could read in his face what it cost him. Was he holding back for her? Did he think she couldn't handle anything rougher?

"Faster," she pleaded.

He shook his head. "Gonna go slow. Gonna make this last. Gonna build you up again and watch you come all over my dick, Cat. That okay with you?"

She could only nod and squeak out, "Okay."

He smiled. "Glad we got that cleared up. Now shut up and kiss me."

His mouth descended on hers, his tongue sweeping inside, demanding, coaxing, tempting... He kept her guessing, alternatingly between barely-there feather-light kisses and deep and demanding ones that took all she had to give and came back for more.

The whole while he rode her with long unrelenting thrusts that built in pace slowly over time until she was literally begging him.

"Please, Blood."

His hand moved between them, fingers brushing her clit as he lifted and changed the angle of his strokes until he was nailing her G-Spot with swipe after swipe. She was balanced on the very top of that roller coaster, about to go barreling over at rocket speed.

She clutched him, crying out his name as the powerful orgasm rolled over her.

Blood wasn't far behind. His eyes burned into hers, like a caress, until he got closer to climax. She liked the look of strain on his face and knowing he was as desperate as she was to climax. His thrust began pounding into her and then stilled as every muscle in his body tensed rock solid, his neck tightened, and he gritted his teeth as he shook with a tremor, his release shooting into her.

"Fuck," he growled, dropping down on top of her.

Cat's body was limp, but she managed to wrap her arms around him, holding him to her as his face dipped to the curve of her neck, his breathing heavy, and she inhaled the scent of the sweat on his skin. Her hands stroked up and down his powerful back.

He lifted up on his elbows and brushed a soft kiss to her forehead, her eyes, her nose, and mouth. Then he pressed his forehead to hers. "You okay?"

She smiled. "I'm better than okay."

"Good." He pulled out and dropped to the mattress beside her. She rolled and tucked up against him, immediately missing his body heat. His one arm wrapped around her while his other hand reached down to grab her knee and drag her leg across his thighs, holding it there.

They lay in the bed listening to the rain falling on the tin roof. Cat cuddled in Blood's arm, his hot skin pressed to hers. She reveled in the reassuring weight of his arm around her and his hand cupping the back of her knee. She couldn't help the smile from forming on her lips as she stared at the ceiling.

Blood traced his fingers over the skin of her back absently. "Got a question."

She turned to look at him. "What?"

"The day we escaped—you putting two holes in that Death Head—what was that about?"

She got quiet, not sure she should tell him.

"Babe?"

"I was pissed."

"No shit."

"I shouldn't have done that."

"I didn't say that, Cat. But if there's shit you're not telling me, you need to do it now."

"Maybe I shouldn't."

"Yeah, you should. We both gotta lay all our cards on the table. Only way this works. As you've figured out, I've got trust issues."

She looked up to catch a small grin on his face. "Will you be angry?"

He met her eyes. "I don't know, will I?"

"Probably." She tucked back under his arm, and his hand began stroking her hair.

"Tell me anyway."

"When we went to the hospital, the second time…"

"Yeah. What happened?"

"When we were leaving, when I'd come back to the parking garage with the supplies…"

His hand that had been stroking her head, stilled, waiting on her words.

"He…"

"He what, Cat?"

"Tried to rape me."

She felt every muscle in his body tense beneath her.

"Tried or did?"

"I fought him. He was so strong. He had me pinned against the concrete wall. I didn't think I'd be able to stop him, but then a group of people came in a van and parked. He put his hand over my mouth and told me to keep quiet. I think he was going to wait for them to leave, hoping they wouldn't see us, but then more people came, and he gave up. He dragged me back over to the bike and told me to get on."

"He hurt you?"

She shook her head. "Just scared me."

"You telling me everything?"

She lifted up to look at him. "Yes."

He studied her, and his brows rose. "That look he gave you, after you came back… He was gonna try again; he was just biding his time."

She nodded.

"I'm glad you killed the motherfucker. If you hadn't, I would have."

She put her head back down. "Can we not talk about it?"

"All right. But eventually, sweetheart, you're gonna

need to talk it through. I don't want you carrying that around, letting it fester and eat at your soul. Understand?"

She nodded against his chest, and he pressed a kiss to her forehead. They were quiet for a moment, his hand stroking her hair again.

"Blood?"

"Hmm?"

"What did Big John mean when he said you were trying to save Black Jack's girls? What did you do?"

"I tried to talk them into leaving, going back home. Sometimes I gave them some money. Not much, just enough to eat or get a bus ticket home."

"Did some leave?"

"I saved a couple." He stroked her hair. "Most don't want to listen."

"But you tried."

"Don't go makin' me out to be a hero. I'm not one."

She tightened her arms around him, thinking he was hers.

Blood kissed the top of her head. "Tell me about you and your sister."

Her fingers traced one of the tattoos on his chest. "Every girl I grew up with in that east Texas trailer park ended up married or pregnant right out of high school. My mother was an alcoholic, and my father died when I was little. If not for the old couple who owned the diner I worked at, I'd be just another knocked-up teenager going nowhere. Luckily, I had a little encouragement from the right people that there was more in life, that I deserved better, and that all I had to do was believe it. They told me a better life was there for the taking if I wanted it badly enough, and I wanted it more than anything. So, I decided I was going to get us out of that shithole trailer park. I remember telling Holly we'd move somewhere with flowers, somewhere with color, because there was no color where we lived. Everything was a dingy, depressing mud color. So, I picked New Orleans. I'd seen a picture of all the colorful buildings in the French Quarter. I thought it was beautiful, and I thought it was far enough away; I thought we'd be safe here, safe from everything we'd run from."

"Hey." Blood caught her chin and tilted it up so he could meet her eyes. "I'm sorry it didn't work out that way. But you're safe now, you hear me? And we're gonna figure a way to get your sister back, too. I'm not gonna let that son of a bitch think he's beaten me again."

She nodded.

"Don't give up. Don't ever give up, Cat. If we've got to stake out the private airfield for flights coming in from Japan Friday, we'll do it. Understand?"

She smiled, her lips quivering as her eyes filled with tears. "Thank you for not letting me do this alone."

He nodded, put his hand to the back of her head, and pulled it down to his chest. "Get some sleep, babe."

"Okay, Boo."

His chest rumbled under her head. "You want to poke the bear, keep callin' me that, sugar."

She grinned, but kept quiet. She listened to the sound of his heart beating in her ear, closed her eyes, and let go of the worry for a few hours.

***

She woke hours later. Blood was turned on his side, sleeping. She cuddled against his back, her head in her hand, stroking his arm with her other palm and staring off into space. Then her eyes moved to him, and the realization crystalized in her brain that she was falling in love with this man, flaws and all.

CHAPTER TWENTY

Cat awoke to the sun streaming in the window. She rolled her head to the side. Blood lay on his back, his body bare to her gaze. *Dear Lord, he was beautiful*. Her eyes stopped on his cock. Even in it's flaccid state, it still reached halfway to his belly button.

A grin formed on her face as an idea took hold.

She slid down the bed, taking care not to wake him. Tucking her hair over one shoulder, she lowered her mouth to him, stroking from root to tip along his shaft, and then again, repeating the long lick. Her eyes lifted to find his heated gaze.

With their eyes locked, she did it again, and felt his dick lengthen and harden under her mouth. She continued teasing and tormenting him until he slid a hand to her hair, guiding her to take him. Grabbing his erection with her hand and stroking, she brought it to her mouth, wrapping her lips around it as a groan escaped his throat. She took him deep in her throat and felt his whole body stiffen.

Up and down she caressed him—long deep strokes she could tell were really getting to him, and she loved that. She loved the hooded, dark, fathomless eyes glittering back at her when she dared to peek up at him. She loved the way his fist tightened in her hair. She loved the way the muscle worked in his jaw.

Evidently, she'd awoken the bear, and he'd had enough of the torment. He grabbed her by the arms and dragged her up his body to straddle his hips. His hands went to her waist, and he jerked her down, impaling her on his dick in one thrilling thrust that had her gasping.

"Good morning, pretty girl."

She grinned back at him and winked. "It is now."

He huffed out at laugh as his hips thrust up. "You want a ride?"

She put her hands on his chest and began to rock against him. "I thought you'd never ask."

Half an hour later, they were dressed and ready to go. As they were leaving, Cat gathered up the poetry book and bible to take with them.

"Go wait by the boat," Blood said. "I've got something to do before we leave."

She frowned, wondering what he could possibly need to do, but she did as he instructed. She walked down the pier and carefully stepped into the boat, taking up her seat again, the books tucked tight in her lap.

From her vantage point, she watched as Blood walked inside. The sound of breaking glass carried to her, and she realized he must have been smashing something. The only things she remembered being made of glass in the house had been all those kerosene lamps. He came down the stairs and moved around behind the house, returning with a large rusted gas can. He began splashing gas all along the exterior of the house, finishing with the porch and making a trail of gasoline out into the grass. Tossing the empty can into the littered yard, he stood back and lit the trail.

Igniting, it flared to life and raced toward the building. Seconds later, the structure was burning, the flames licking up the sides. A trail shot up the stairs and soon the inside was glowing with fire as Cat realized Blood must have soaked the inside with all the kerosene.

The pier shook under his booted feet as he calmly walked toward her. Untying the boat, he shoved them off and jumped aboard. As they floated backward and he fired up the outboard, Cat watched the blaze grow higher. She could now feel the heat radiating toward them. She understood his need to do this, to destroy the place that held nothing but bad memories for him. She supposed it must be very cathartic.

Blood idled the motor a moment, watching as the structure was fully engulfed, then he turned them around and headed off, the outboard shooting a plume of spray in the air as they sped away.

***

Fifteen minutes later, Blood took them out of the dense swamp and across the open water. They pulled up to another house—this one built high up on the bank with green lawns and big oak trees around it. A crushed shell drive led up to a road behind it. The dock was well kept, and a retaining wall met the water. The house was lovely—bright white with green shutters and a gallery porch across the entire front, facing the water.

He tied them up and helped her from the boat.

"This is my Tante Marie's."

"Tante?"

"Aunt. Promised I'd stop by. Pierre probably already told her I was coming, so I can't let her down."

"When was the last time you visited?"

"It's been years. Better cover your ears. She's probably gonna cuss me up one side and down the other. Though it's probably gonna be in French, so you might not understand anyway. She's a sweet lady, my favorite aunt. She was my mother's sister."

"I see."

They walked across the yard and up the stairs onto the porch. Cat glanced over to see white wicker furniture to the side. Blood knocked on the door. A moment later, an older woman with a short gray perm came to the door. She yanked the door open and screamed, her hands going to her cheeks. "Holy Sac-au-lait! Who dat standin' on my porch? Etienne!"

Cat noticed she couldn't have been more than five feet tall and came no higher than Blood's chest. She was dressed in a pair of leggings painted to look like jeans that hung on her bony legs and knobby knees. A white t-shirt that said *Hot to Trot* on the front in neon pink and red high-top Nikes completed the outfit.

Blood stooped down and grabbed her up in his arms, her feet dangling off the floor.

"Set me down, Son." When he did, she slugged him in the arm. "Poo-ey! Whass that smell? You stink like gas-leen and wood smoke. What bad bizness you been up to?"

"Good to see you, too, Tante Marie." Blood grinned.

Her hands landed on her hips. "Where you bin all dis time? Why you haven't visited yer favorite Tante Marie?"

"Don't lie, Cher. You knew I was coming."

"Course I did. Pierre told his wife, who told Tee-John who told everybody in the damn parish, prob'ly. I heard it from Sylvie at bingo last night. You oughta know, ain't no keepin' a secret in the bayou, boy." Her eyes moved past Blood to Cat. "Heard you had a pretty thing wit you, too. Ow-ee! Look at dat blonde hair. Talk about!"

"Tante Marie, this is Catherine Randall."

Cat held her hand out. "Please, call me Cat."

"Cat? Why I call you dat, chile?" She turned to glare at Blood. "Well, doan keep her out here in dis heat, Etienne! Bring her on in. It's been hot, hot, hot, even dis time of da mornin'."

Blood led Cat inside. There was a main entryway with a parlor off to the left, a kitchen to the right, and a staircase leading to a second level. Tante Marie hustled into the kitchen. She took down a faded rosebud print apron, put it over her head, and tied it on. "Get her a café au lait, Etienne. I just heated some milk before you got here. I make you sumpin' to eat."

She began bustling around the kitchen, banging a cast iron skillet on the burner and slapping gobs of butter into it. "I make you pain perdu." She peeked over her shoulder and winked at Cat. "Is Etienne's favorite."

"Pain perdu?"

"Louisiana French Toast," Blood clarified as he moved to the cupboard and took down two mugs. He picked up the saucepan on the stove with one hand and the coffee carafe with the other and filled each mug with equal measures of both the hot milk and the dark, rich chicory blend of coffee, pouring them simultaneously, the hot liquids blending together. Setting the pan and carafe down, he carried the mugs to the small table covered with a floral tablecloth, and they both sat.

"Can I help you?" Cat asked Tante Marie.

She looked over, banging the wooden spoon on the side of the skillet. "Non, petit Cher, you sit an' drink. Get the fruit I cut up out da icebox, Etienne. You like café au lait, Cher?"

Blood got up and moved to the refrigerator to do her bidding. When he did, Tante Marie moved to sniff him. "Go wash up! Bon Dieu!"

Blood looked to Cat. "Ladies first, Tante Marie." He lifted his chin toward the entryway. "You can get cleaned up if you want, Cher. There's a bathroom top of da stair."

She grinned over the rim of her mug as he slipped into the Cajun dialect.

He moved toward her with a bowl of fruit as she set her mug down. He popped one of the strawberry slices into her mouth, and they exchanged a smile. Then she slipped from her chair and went to find the bathroom.

***

Tante Marie stood at the cutting board slicing French bread at a diagonal, dunking them in batter, and then dropping them in the sizzling butter. She looked sideways at Blood.

"Heard you went out to dat old place."

Blood nodded over his mug.

"And?" she prodded.

"Lookin' for something."

"Lookin' for sumpin'? Out der? Only bad juju out der, Cher."

"You ever remember my mama having a ring that belonged to my father?"

That had her pausing and turning. "We doan talk about dat bastard Black Jack in dis house." She wacked the skillet again, then murmured, "You talkin' bout dat ugly thing, dat gaudy emerald da size of a bayou barge?"

Blood shrugged. "Don't know. Some ring that belonged to his father."

"He lose it?" She grinned.

"You know about it?"

"I remember it." Then she turned and waved a bony finger at him. "You engaged in some his bizness? You gettin' dumb or sumpin'?"

"Non, Tante Marie. Just tryin' to make a deal to get something back from him."

"Whass dat? He got nothin' you need, Etienne." She moved to slicing more bread.

"He's got Cat's little sister, Holly."

She paused mid-slice, her mouth falling open. Then she set the knife down, wiped her hands on her apron, and came to sit at the table.

"Tell me everythin'."

Blood shook his head. "You know I can't do that, Tante."

Tante Marie folded her arms and glared.

"She helped me." He jerked his chin to the second floor. "I owe her. Promised I'd help her. I need to help her."

"'Course you do." She eyed him. "She helped you? Been a long time since a woman's done something good in your eyes, huh?"

Blood stayed quiet, but shifted uncomfortably in his chair.

"She provin' all those ideas in your head wrong, huh, Cher?"

"What ideas?"

"You know what I'm talkin' bout."

And he did. Everything he'd always thought about women, Cat was proving that all wrong by doing the opposite of what he expected at every turn. She hadn't abandoned him to the Death Heads, she didn't run off again to the cops—not after she'd promised, not like he half-expected her to. She put other people before herself, time and time again.

"Mebbe she change the way you think. It's not all about a debt, eh? I see the way you smile at her." She tapped her temple. "I see what you doan see."

Blood shook his head, not willing to admit any feelings in regard to Cat yet. "There's more."

"Not good, I'm guessing."

"Non. I found out the truth about what happened to my mama."

Tante Marie folded her hands on the table and studied them. "Do I wanna know?"

"Found out she's buried in Metairie Cemetery. He killed her, Tante."

Her eyes got watery. "Knew she dint run off. She dint leave you, Son. Always knew dat."

Blood's hold on his mug tightened.

After a long moment, she whispered, "Yer mama, you gonna take care of dat, Cher?"

"You bet."

"What you gonna do 'bout dat?"

"I'm gonna kill the sumbitch and feed him to the gators."

She nodded and patted his arm. "Bon. Jist doan get caught, Etienne."

He grinned. "Nope."

She got up, moving to stand next to him, and stroked his cheek. "You look like her, Cher. You have her same eyes, same thick dark hair."

"I didn't save her, Tante Marie."

Her hand moved to tug his hair, pulling his head up. "I doan wanna hear that, understand? Dat was Black Jack. Dat wasn't you. Dat's not on you, Etienne."

"Isn't it?"

"You listen to me, now. Thass done, you know da truth. Now mebbe you can finally move past it. You got a gift, sumpin right before your eyes." She pointed upstairs. "God dropped a gift in your lap, Son. I been prayin' to St. Jude for you, and he finally come through."

"The patron saint of lost causes? Is that what I am?"

"Not anymore, mon Cher. Not anymore." She hugged his head to her chest. "When dis over, we gonna visit your mama's grave, oui? We gonna put flowers. You take me?"

"Oui, Tante Marie. I'll take you."

Cat came down the stairs, and Tante Marie moved to the stove again, wiping her eyes with her apron and hiding her upset by busying herself with cooking.

"Your turn," Cat said, smiling at Blood.

He took another gulp of coffee, tousled her hair, and went upstairs.

***

Cat took a sip of her café au lait, finding it delicious and addictive.

Tante Marie looked over at her. "You so little the crows gonna carry you off, Cher. I'm gonna feed you good."

"It smells wonderful."

"You like my Etienne?"

"I...I..."

She studied Cat. "My Etienne, he carry a burden. Carry it 'round like a stone. See, his mama, she loved da wrong man, and it killed her."

Cat didn't know what to say to that. She nodded. "My sister, Stacey, loved the wrong man, and it got her killed, too."

"I see. And you doan plan ta let dat happen ta you, huh?"

"I don't plan to love the wrong man." She lifted her chin.

"He's not da wrong man. He's the right man. Mebbe you jist haven't figured dat out yet." She went back to slicing bread. "You will."

***

When they'd finished eating and the dishes were in the sink soaking, Tante Marie suggested they take their coffee out to the gallery so her Etienne could smoke. They sat on the dingy white wicker furniture on the side porch. The laundry out on the lines flapped in the breeze.

Blood grinned. "You always did like to air dry the laundry. I remember as a child coming over here and running through it."

Tante Marie smiled at the memory. "Your mama would chase you through da rows and catch you up and tickle you. You would giggle and squirm to get away."

The laundry flapped up with a big wind, and Blood saw an old rusted car peek through. It was parked in the tall grass at the edge of the property. He ground out his cigarette in the ashtray, his eyes like a hawk. "Is that her old car?"

Tante Marie looked at him as he stood, then followed his gaze. "Oui, the rusted old Chevelle? She left it here before she disappeared. I think she was planning to take you and run

again. Didn't want your father to take it from her. I was
going to give it to you one day, den about da time you were
old enough, you took off with dem motorcycle boys." She
nodded to his black leather cut.

Blood connected eyes with Cat, his meaning clear. *The
photo of the car in his mother's book.*

Cat whispered the thought in both their heads, "Do you
think…?"

Blood moved off the porch and headed across the yard to
the car, a weird sensation moving through him as he walked
between the lines of laundry. It was almost like his mother
was leading him to it.

There were pine needles piled on the hood, and the
windshield was cloudy with dirt. The rusted door creaked as
he yanked it open. The black vinyl seats were splitting, and
dust coated everything.

He looked through the car, seeing nothing. He leaned
over and yanked the glove box open. Rummaging through it,
he found the car's registration and some old, yellowed
service receipts. As he dug through them, a prayer card fell
out. He bent and picked it up. It was the same as the one that
had marked her place in the poetry book. Then his eyes slid
from the picture of the Virgin Mary to the small statue of the
Madonna that was glued to the dashboard. He'd forgotten
about it, how it had always been in his mother's car.

There was a roaring in his ears as suddenly everything
clicked. He tore the statue from where it was mounted to the
dash. As it ripped free, the bottom tore off, and an item fell
into his hand.

Emerald green and gold sparkled up at him as a beam of sunlight shone into the car. "Holy shit." That weird cold feeling moved over him again as his fist tightened around the ring. "Thank you, Mama."

Blood studied the emerald ring. All these years this old car had sat rusting in Tante Marie's yard, and all these years this was hidden inside. Hopefully it would be enough to bring Black Jack to the negotiating table.

He took the Madonna statue and shoved it in his pocket as he climbed out of the car. His eyes connected with Cat's over the roof of the Chevelle, and he nodded. Through the flapping laundry he saw her put her hands to her mouth and burst into tears. A moment later she was running across the yard to him. He met her halfway, picking her up as she jumped in his arms.

"I found it, Cat. I've got it."

"Oh my God. I can't believe it."

He set her down and pulled his phone out, moving his thumb over the screen. He snapped a picture of the ring, and then typed out the text to Black Jack.

I've got something you want, you've got something I want. We should talk.

He shoved it in his pocket and looked down in Cat's eyes. "It's still no guarantee, babe."

She nodded. "I know."

***

As they approached the dock at Jean Michel and Pierre's

shop, Blood cut the motor and coasted the boat in. He needed to set her straight on something.

"Hey."

Cat looked back at him in the silence left when the outboard cut off. She had renewed hope in her eyes and that was a good thing. She was happy, and he hated to dampen her spirit in any way, but she needed to know.

"This doesn't mean it's a done deal."

She nodded, her smile fading a bit, her excitement tempering. "I understand, Blood."

CHAPTER TWENTY-ONE

Blood rolled into the courtyard behind his townhouse.

Cat climbed from the bike and pulled her helmet off, looking around. "Where are we?"

"My place," he answered, still sitting on his bike. He pointed to the balcony on the second floor.

She looked up to where he indicated and frowned. "You live here?"

He nodded, swinging his leg from the bike. "What, you didn't think I lived at the clubhouse, did you?"

She shrugged. "I don't know."

He headed up the stairs, and she followed, glancing around at the place. The courtyard was lovely, hidden back from the dingy street like a little gem. Blood unlocked the door, and she followed him in. The first thing she noticed were the high ceilings covered in tin tiles and the exposed brick fireplace.

Blood tossed his helmet on a chair and moved through

the living area to a small kitchen. It was tiny, but updated with tall black cabinets and a pretty glass tile backsplash. He opened the refrigerator. "You want a beer?"

"No thank you."

He pulled out a bottle of water instead, unscrewed it, and tilted it up, swallowing it down. Cat couldn't help watching his throat work as he gulped.

When he lowered the bottle, he noticed the look in her eyes. She turned away, foolishly attempting to hide something he'd already seen.

"I like your place." She looked toward the wrought iron balcony with the tall shutters.

When he didn't respond, she turned to find him stalking toward her slowly, a predatory look in his eyes.

Her mouth parted, as her breath left her. "What?"

"Sit down. We need to talk."

She sat on the couch, and he sat in the chair next to it, his elbows on his knees, his hands clasped loosely in front of him. He met her gaze with a penetrating stare.

"I need you to understand something, and I need you to be okay with it."

She searched his eyes. "Okay."

His voice was hard as he growled, "Last night, the sex, the way things were between us… I'm not usually so gentle. I don't do slow and sweet. That's not the way I fuck. That's not the way I usually like it. So, if that's what you want, you're not getting it."

"I'm not?" She didn't know sex was on the table. *Was he talking about right now?*

He shook his head. "Nope."

"How *do* you like it?" Why did she find his answer to that question suddenly more important than breathing?

He studied her eyes. "I like it rough. I like to be in control. Always."

She stared at him. His eyes were dark, filled with lust and something more, something...*demanding*. Her gaze held his for a long silent moment.

"Are you good with that?"

She felt in a daze, but found herself unable to refuse him anything he wanted. She couldn't tell him no. And she realized she didn't want to tell him no. She only hoped she could be what he needed, give him what he wanted, and satisfy his desires.

"Cat?"

"Show me," she said.

He stood and her eyes lifted. *Oh, God. She'd awakened the bear.*

The deep rumble of his voice sent shivers down her spine as he commanded, "Stand up."

***

Blood wasn't sure if she really understood what he'd been trying to convey, but fuck it, she was about to find out. He took her hand and led her to the bedroom.

"Take off your clothes," he ordered, no room for negotiation in his voice.

She turned to look at him, her expressive blue eyes

widening.

He lifted a brow, and her hands moved to her waistband. She shimmied out of her pants and kicked them aside. Next she pulled the shirt over her head and dropped it to the floor. The pink satin and lace bra and panties remained.

She hesitated, seeming a little unsure what to do. He gave her a hint.

"The rest, sweetheart. Now."

She undid the bra and dropped it. Her breasts stood out, the dusky nipples already hard, and he hadn't even touched her. He lifted his chin toward the panties, his eyes dropping to them.

She slid her fingers in the fabric at the hem and glided them down.

His gaze skated over every inch. He had to give her credit; she stood there, waiting for his next instruction, with no movement to cover herself, which he wouldn't have allowed.

"So pretty," he told her, but he knew the lust was plain in his eyes, and he knew she saw it.

He moved behind her, and his arms wrapped around her as he slid both hands down to gather her breasts in his large palms. He lifted them, kneaded them, and her head fell back on his shoulder. He tugged and pinched her nipples, his mouth coming down on hers, his tongue delving deep. He kept at her until her cute little ass was grinding back into his crotch, rubbing his thick hard-on until he growled deep in his throat. Her hair was in that long ponytail he loved so much. He grabbed it, wrapping it around his fist, and pulled her head back.

"Love your hair, Cat. I especially love the ponytail. Been fantasizing about controlling you with it."

She wet her lips and let out a soft, "Oh."

"Do you like my hands on your hair?" He gave a little tug, and she went up on her toes, but her nipples darkened and her face flushed. "Do you?"

"Y-yes. I like it."

"Good." He released it, but stroked his fingers through it. He dropped his hands to her hips and nuzzled her ear as he walked her forward until her pelvis was pressed to the rounded top of the sleigh bed's footboard. There was a quilt folded over the top of it, put there as extra padding.

His hands at her waist tightened and lifted her up, setting her on her stomach on the mattress with her legs dangling over the other side of the rail and her hips balanced over it, the quilt keeping it from digging into her hips.

She turned her head; her ass was up in the air, just where he wanted it. He ran his hand down her back and over her ass.

"Arms over your head, angel."

She complied, stretching her arms across the sheet.

"You okay?"

She nodded. "Yes."

"Spread your legs for me."

She did.

"Wider."

He opened a drawer and pulled out two black bandanas. Turning back, he bent and wrapped one around her ankle, pulling it tight and tying it to the foot of the bed. Then he did the same with the other until she was spread wide, leaving her completely open and vulnerable.

"Blood?" she began nervously.

"Easy, girl. Relax." He stroked her ass and up over her back until her breathing evened back out. "Take a deep breath."

She did as he told her.

"I'm not gonna tie your hands, just your legs. All right?"

"All right."

"You okay now?"

She nodded.

"I'm not gonna hurt you, Cat. This is about pleasure, about you giving yourself over to me, giving me the control. You want to stop, we stop."

He continued stroking her skin and massaging the tense muscles of her back, then down to her hips and buttocks and upper thighs until she was groaning, her body totally relaxed.

"Good girl," he murmured. With one palm he continued to stoke down her spine; the line of her back was graceful and enticing, as her torso lay stretched out across the mattress. He wanted to trace every inch of her luscious, silken skin with his hands, his tongue, to mark her with his teeth. He visualized the many ways he could take her, and his dick jumped. He took a breath and reminded himself they had time.

His other hand slid up the inside of her thigh, slowly, fingers finally reaching their goal.

She bucked.

"Easy, girl."

He slid his fingers inside her pussy, finding her wet. "Such a good girl. Feel how wet you are for me. Your body wants my touch, craves it, yeah?"

"Yes."

He took her wetness and spread it around her clit and folds with slow, gentle strokes.

She moaned, arching her back, thrusting her ass into the air, seeking more of his touch and pulling against the restraints. "You like the way I touch you?"

"Yes. Oh, God. Please."

"More?"

"Yes."

He bent and gave her the wet velvet stroke of his tongue on her clit.

"Oh, God." She writhed.

He loved that reaction, loved when he was able to break down the walls of a woman's inhibitions. "Look at you, baby. Making yourself so open and vulnerable for me. Do you know what that does to me?"

She shook her head.

Dominance was in his nature; it ran in his blood. He got off on it. The thought of her doing this with anyone else flashed through his brain and with it a white-hot surge of possessiveness. That was something that was *not* in his nature, at least not until Cat. She was changing everything.

He took in another deep breath. He'd never had this type of intense reaction to a woman. She was quickly getting under his skin in a way he knew he'd never get her out.

He played with her, stroking swirling patterns over her clit and slipping his broad thumb up inside her pussy. He zeroed in on that little spot that drove her crazy and pressed. With her hips pushed up against the top rail of the footboard, she had nowhere to go to escape it, and he knew that pressure just increased any sensation he was able to give her.

He applied pressure with his thumb inside her, while his fingers kept up long steady strokes to her clit. She went wild, her thighs trembling, her ass lifting as she tried to rub against his fingers, coaxing him on.

"You like that?"

"Oh, God. Don't stop. Please."

He kept at her, until she was climbing that precipice.

"Pinch your nipples," he ordered, and she complied.

She was panting hard and then gasped in and held it; he knew she was almost there. He smacked her ass with his free hand, and she screamed as she climaxed, coating his hand with a rush of wetness.

He eased his hand from her and licked his fingers, then bent and lapped at her swollen lips.

She moaned, her hips tilting, her ass tipping, her pussy straining toward his mouth. He tickled the soft skin of her inner thighs with his beard and chuckled. "My baby's greedy."

He stood and stripped off his clothes, ordering her, "Don't move."

She lay there, waiting so patiently for his next command. He loved that about her. She wanted to please him. He was about to take her up on that.

He climbed on the bed in front of her, positioning himself on his knees at her head. "Up on your elbows."

She did what he said, tilting her head back to look up at him. Her breasts stood out, jiggling softly with her breathing. Beautiful.

He cupped her chin, his thumb pressing on her lips as he positioned the head of his cock there. "Open for me, baby."

She complied, straining to reach him. She took him in, her sweet tongue caressing the bottom of his cock, sliding like silk over it. He had to grit his teeth and fight the urge to close his eyes.

She lapped and sucked and drank at him with wanton abandon until he couldn't resist taking control.

He gripped his fists in her hair and began thrusting in and out of her mouth. She moaned, and his eyes watched her breasts bounce with his motions.

"Oh, Cat," he panted as he controlled her head, increasing his speed. "Fuck baby, what you do to me." He growled deep in his throat, trying to hold back, make it last, but the sight of her stretched out before him was making it impossible.

"You want my cum?"

She opened her eyes, and he let up on his grip, giving her room to nod her head a tiny bit.

He grabbed her hand and put it to the root of his cock, allowing her some control, if she wanted to pull back. Then he thrust, went still and came. She sucked him dry, taking every drop.

"Goddamn, girl." He dropped back, pulling free.

She laid her head on the mattress, and he stroked her hair while he regained the strength in his legs. Then he slid off the bed.

She turned to look at him, her eyes following his every move. If she expected him to untie her, she was wrong. Instead he held her eyes as he dipped his head and nipped her ass cheek with his teeth. She jumped.

He grinned and smacked her ass, then began to play with her again. While he did, he stroked and worked his dick.

Soon she was writhing, rocking back against his hand, he dipped his head and ate at her pussy, giving her the attention she craved until she was bucking against his face, crying out her need, begging him to take her. That ramped up his arousal until he was rock hard again and wanting nothing as badly as he wanted to sink his dick in her and fuck her hard.

He took her ponytail in his hand, wrapping it around his fist and pulling her head back. "Up on your palms." She did as he asked without hesitation, her back curving in a beautiful arch.

He brought the head of his dick to her opening and circled it, driving her crazy.

"It's not fair. I can't touch you."

"This ain't about being fair, Cat. This is about me being in control. I want to do what I want. I want to play with you, put my hands on you, my fingers in your pussy, my mouth on your clit and lick until you can't hold back any longer and you come on my face."

And he did all those things, and she could do nothing but lie there, wriggling her ass. He wanted her desperate for it, so hungry for his dick she'd do anything for it.

"Do you like this? Me being in charge?"

"Yes."

"I don't want to hurt you," he managed to say, fighting the need to take her hard and fast. "God, I want to fuck you."

"Please."

"You ready for more?" He knew she was.

"Yes. Yes."

He slid deep, filling her completely, his strong hands wrapping around her hipbones and pulling her back against him as he thrust into her. With every stroke, he glided over that sweet spot until she was calling out his name.

He kept a firm hold on her hair and watched her breasts bounce as he continued to drive into her. He shifted, pushing and pulling her hips to meet his pounding thrusts, their skin slapping against each other.

He dropped one hand and played with her clit again, and she fired off like a piston, humping his hand and begging him not to stop.

When she climaxed, she screamed and that snapped his control. He lasted only two more deep thrusts, and then he stilled, planted deep inside her as his entire body shook, and animal growls rumbled in his chest as he closed his eyes and came.

His knees went weak. He bent over her, still firmly seated in her pussy, and bit the back of her neck, unable to resist the urge to mark her smooth skin. She was his.

She whimpered, and he kissed the spot, and then pulled from her.

"You okay, pretty girl?"

She nodded as he stroked her skin, then bent and released the ties binding her. She curled in a ball in the bed, and that gave Blood pause. Had he gone too far with her? He hadn't meant to. This was just supposed to be a taste.

He moved to the bed, hovering over her with one hand planted in the mattress near her head. He smoothed his other hand over her trembling skin. "Baby—"

"It's okay."

"You're shaking."

"I've never felt like that before."

"You were beautiful. So willing to please me."

She turned and looked up at him. He hoped the feelings he had for her were reflected in his eyes. They were so strong; he didn't know how they couldn't be.

She reached up her small hand, cupped the back of his neck and pulled his mouth down to hers. He complied, kissing her softly, tenderly, trying to show her everything he couldn't say.

***

Blood stood in the shower as Cat dozed in his bed, his mind going over every minute he'd spent with her and everything that had passed between them since she'd walked into his life. What the hell was he doing? He should put a stop to it. But he didn't want to, wasn't even sure he *could*. It was that strong, that powerful, a primal need that defied anything that wanted to stand in its way. So, he did the only thing he could. He accepted it. Flat out accepted it. And in that moment he made the decision. This was it for him. He was all in. And he was damned if he'd let her be anything less than the same.

He heard the bathroom door open. A moment later, she stepped in with him, her eyes taking in the expression on his face as he turned to look at her. He'd been struggling with it all and perhaps that was clear to her, but he tried not to let on. Instead, he smiled, and she pressed close to him, her smile bright as the sun, mirroring that same absolute, all-in position right back at him. And he felt everything inside him settle, all the puzzle pieces fall into place.

They were both in this, together, exactly on the same page. No doubts. None.

He felt bathed in a golden light, completely sure for the first time in his life. Settled. Everything inside him evened out; all the darkness, all the agitation, and all the tension fell away like a heavy weight dropping to the floor.

He held her close, his eyes unfocused on the distance. There were still things to be settled, still problems that had to be handled. Things he needed to fix.

But then she pulled back and looked at him, giving him a squeeze, and as he brought his mouth down on hers, he thought he'd let those problems wait another hour.

This time when they pulled back, breaking the kiss to stare into each other's eyes, she lifted her chin at him like he had to her a dozen times. She smiled. He lifted his chin back at her, returning the smile. Yes, they were one now.

An alpha and his mate perfectly matched.

"Baby?"

"Yes?"

"Promise me something." He cupped her face in his hands, dipping his forehead to hers. "When times get rough, and they will, I want you to go back to this moment. The moment when we realized we were meant to be together and when times get rough, you hang on to this moment."

She gave him a tremulous smile, her eyes filling with tears, and she nodded. "Promise."

CHAPTER TWENTY-TWO

Blood and Cat strode into the clubhouse. He paused to tell her to wait for him while he dealt with his club, then he went up to Undertaker's office and tapped on the door.

"Come in," barked his President.

Blood entered to find Undertaker behind his desk, his VP, Mooch, as well as Sandman, were kicked back in the chairs in front of it.

"Where the hell you been?" Undertaker bit out. "Don't you ever pull a stunt like that again."

Blood's eyes cut to Sandman, wondering how much he'd told him. Didn't matter, Blood wasn't going to lie to his President. "I found something I can use to negotiate with Black Jack. He's got Holly. Sandman tell you he's working with the Death Heads?"

"Yeah, he told me. And we'll get to that in a minute. What I want to know now is why you think you can just take off without talking to me."

"Sorry. Clock's ticking."

Undertaker ran his hand down his beard and adjusted in his chair. "Yeah, Friday. I heard."

"The cell phone and laptop... They find anything on 'em we can use?"

"Ton of shit about Black Jack's businesses. Not much about the Death Heads. There were some texts about a meet Friday, a time and location. I've got some of the boys doing recon on it now. If it's a meet with the Death Heads, we'll be ready with a little ambush of our own."

"Sounds good."

"So you contact Black Jack yet?"

"Texted him. Waiting for a response."

"You get one, we all plan the next step."

"I get Holly and kill Black Jack. Done deal. There's nothing to discuss. Club can't let him live. Not if he's dealing with the enemy."

"Son..."

Blood looked at the man who was more of a father to him than his own ever was. Undertaker had been the dominant man in Blood's life since he was a teenager.

And now that the relationship between Black Jack and the Death Heads had come to light, Blood realized—and he knew Undertaker did, too—that they had to eliminate Black Jack. There was no other way. Undertaker just didn't realize that Blood wanted the man dead for an even greater reason. Nor did he realize that killing his father would not be a burden; it would be a pleasure.

"I've asked you to do a lot of shit over the years, and

you've done every task I've ever asked of you. But, Son, I can't ask this of you."

"Yes, you can."

"No, Blood. The man... Whatever else he is, he's still your ol' man."

"He ain't shit to me."

"Blood—"

"Sandman tell you that piece of shit killed my mother?"

"Yeah, he did, but—"

"It has to be me that takes him out. You get that, right?"

Undertaker nodded. "I get that. What I'm wondering is what that's gonna do to you. You gonna be able to live with this?"

"Absolutely." He looked off into the distance. "Should've done it years ago. And maybe that's what I *can't* live with." His eyes met Undertaker's.

"Guess I knew eventually it'd come to this. Wasn't sure you were ready before. Guess you are now."

Blood nodded. "Guess I am."

"The world seems simple to you, but when you're President of an MC," his thumb pointed back to himself, "very few choices are simple. I'm still not sold on you going in there."

"I'm not afraid to face him."

"You're not afraid of anyone. Maybe this time you should be. He's a powerful man in this town, and that place of his is a fortress."

"If I die, I die."

"The club needs you. I need you."

"The Dead got along fine before I came. Dead will be fine when I'm gone."

"Your brothers need you. You were born for MC life."

"It's not so simple anymore."

"Ah, Cat." Undertaker nodded. "Women have a way of complicating things."

"Yeah, they do, I'm finding out.

Undertaker smiled. "And the sister?"

"Gotta get her out of there."

"You've got a bunch of brothers at your back for that."

"No. I need to be the one who goes in there."

"Not alone, you're not."

"I'm going alone."

"The hell you are. You've got brothers for a reason."

"He's mine!"

"Yeah, he is. But you don't go alone."

"We done?" Blood bit out.

Undertaker nodded once. "Yeah."

***

After Blood slammed out of the room, Undertaker looked at Mooch and Sandman. "Come up with a plan to get into that compound—one that takes in the possibility of Blood going off half-cocked on his own and needing backup."

Mooch nodded. "Anything else?"

"Yeah, make sure whatever you come up with"—he lifted his chin to the door Blood had just exited—"doesn't end up getting him or the girl killed."

Mooch grinned. "You don't ask for much, do you?"

CHAPTER TWENTY-THREE

A shot of whiskey sat on the bar. Bubbles rose up the sides of the glass of beer Blood had ordered as a chaser. He tipped up the shot, swallowing it down.

Cat watched all this as she walked up and sat on the stool next to him, having come back in from where she'd been chatting with Marla and waiting for Blood to finish with Undertaker.

Blood turned toward her, and their eyes met. He swiveled on his stool, his body angling toward hers, and his hand moved to the back of her barstool. Then he motioned with two fingers for the Prospect behind the bar to bring her a beer.

Once the beer was set before her, and he thanked the man, he got quiet, looking away, and she wondered what was wrong. But before she could ask, he slid a hand around the back of her neck, pulled her close, and kissed her. It wasn't a soft sweet kiss. It was demanding, in the way she was finding out Blood was so good at. He took what he wanted, and now that they'd crossed that line, all bets were off. He was no longer keeping his distance or his hands to himself—or his dirty words to himself, either.

Then, almost as soon as she thought it, he threw her for a loop by acting the opposite. He dipped his head and nuzzled her neck in a tender, gentle way, almost as if to make up for the harsh kiss, pulling back and reining himself in as if it might be too much for her, as if *he* might be too much for her.

She felt her pulse quicken and her breath catch.

Just when she thought she had him figured out, he'd do what she least expected. She couldn't keep up; one minute he was aggressive and controlling, the next tender and gentle. It was enough to make her head spin.

When he eased up on his hold of her, giving her a few inches of space, he turned his head, glancing around like he was trying to avoid smiling. She grinned and could see he wanted to grin in return, but he fought it, wanting to remain tough in front of the club. But the corner of his mouth pulled up, giving him away. It was just a fraction, but she caught it.

She pressed her forehead against his, nudging him with her nose, pulling back to smile into his face when she saw the corner of his mouth pull up even further. He couldn't hold it back, no matter how hard he was trying. He was happy. And she saw it. She pressed her knuckles to the side of his mouth, and he leaned in, his eyes closing. And that was enough. That was all she needed.

In that moment they both knew—there was something

there, something neither one of them could fight or wanted to fight anymore.

He leaned forward and kissed her again—a long slow kiss, soft this time.

The loud sound of a throat clearing broke the spell. Blood released her, and they both turned their heads to see who dared to interrupt them.

"Get a room!" one of the two men standing there said. He was grinning, his arms folded over his Evil Dead cut.

"Jesus Christ! Look what the cat dragged in." Blood stood, a broad grin plastered on his face. He moved to hug each man, slapping backs and shouting, "Shades! Ghost! Good to see you boys."

"Heard you needed some backup," the second man said.

"Surprised you could break away from the little family, Shades."

"He didn't," Ghost explained with a nod of his head. "We all piled in the van. Skylar's outside showing Undertaker his grandchild."

"That little baby big enough to travel?" Blood asked.

"She's four weeks old. Fortunately she's still in the mewling kitten phase where all she does is eat and sleep, so that makes it the perfect time to travel with her." Shades' eyes slid to Cat. "This the lady we heard so much about?"

"Depends. What the fuck did you hear?" Blood growled.

Ghost's grin got bigger. "Just that some beautiful blonde nurse patched you up and needs our help."

"Our? Thought you came down to help with the Death Heads situation?"

"We did, but as long as we're here, might as well help out with getting her sister back, right?" He grinned at Blood. "Unless you've already handled that for her."

"I'm working on it."

"You gonna introduce us or what?"

"Cat, this smug asshole is Ghost. Pay him no mind."

Cat grinned as the man took offense to Blood's words. "Blood's a grouch, if you haven't figured that out already. Pleased to meet you, Cat." He extended his hand, and she shook it.

"This other one with the baby puke on his shoulder is Shades."

Shades glanced down at his cut. "Well, damn. She got me again."

Cat reached across the bar and grabbed a napkin. "Here, let me." She moved to wipe it off his leather vest, smiling up at him as she did. "I used to work in the pediatrics unit. I'm all too familiar with the sticky stuff."

Shades grinned down at her as she cleaned him up. "Thanks, doll. You married?"

She shook her head, and he glanced at Blood. "Better snap her up quick, Blood. She ain't afraid of cleaning up puke, and she's managed to be around you longer than twenty-four hours without trying to kill you."

"Says the man who had to threaten to throw his ol' ladies suitcases in the lake to keep her from leaving his ass."

"Ooo, good one, Bro," Ghost joined in.

Blood turned on Ghost, not about to leave him out of the ribbing. "Cuff your ol' lady to any beds lately?"

Ghost grinned. "Every Saturday night. Thanks for asking."

***

Blood walked out of the clubhouse with Ghost and Shades. They moved around the side to where the bikes were parked. The club had just met to discuss the Death Head situation and catch the Alabama chapter up on what they knew. They'd spent about an hour in the chapel. It was dusk now, the last light fading from the sky.

Blood dipped his head to light up a cigarette, and as he blew the smoke out and shoved the lighter back in his pocket, his eyes sought out Cat where she sat with some of the girls at one of the picnic tables.

Shades looked over at him, followed his gaze, and grinned. "Wait a minute. Has somebody finally got to you?"

Ghost's brows shot up. "No shit? The nurse? For real? You're not just playin'?"

Blood took a hit off his cigarette. "Blow me."

"Yep, somebody finally got to you. What does it feel like?" Shades pressed, not about to cut him any slack.

"Truth? It feels good." Blood could admit it. Hell, he supposed it was obvious to anyone who gave a fuck enough to be observant. The signs were all there... The chin lift he gave and that she returned with one of her own, a small smile playing across her face, knowing they'd been intimate, like it was a precious secret they each shared and treasured, knowing they'd do it again.

Even now, as he watched her across the lot, he couldn't take his eyes off her. His gaze followed her every move and everything around him fell away. That's how drawn he was to her.

And he knew that later tonight, the moment they were alone, they'd look over at each other, and a second later they'd be across the space and in each other's arms. Clutching, grabbing... They wouldn't be able to get close enough. And even though it had only been hours, it would feel like forever since they'd been together.

They couldn't deny the pull they felt, the closeness, the rightness that just being together brought them.

It was something neither of them may have felt before, and the newness of it, the surprise at feeling it for the first time in all these years wasn't lost on him.

Blood's phone went off, drawing him from his thoughts. He glanced at the incoming number.

Black Jack.

Finally.

"I need to take this." He stepped away, moving out of earshot and put the phone to his ear. "Yeah."

"Hello, Son."

"See you got my text."

"You got my attention, and you're right. We should talk."

"Name the time and place."

"My compound, nine o'clock tomorrow night."

"I'll be there."

"Not so fast. I have an offer I want you to think over in

the meantime. There's something I want more than that old ring."

"There is always a catch with you. You've always got some ulterior motive or some agenda. What is it this time?"

"I just want you to come home, Son."

"Oh, you have got to be kidding me."

"I'm very serious."

"You have wildly misjudged our relationship."

"I don't think so. Come back and work for me. You do, and I'll let your pretty blonde girlfriend have her sister back."

Goddamn it. He knew about Cat. Obviously he had intel. Hell, he'd probably had him followed or watched. "How'd you find that out?" Blood asked tersely. "Your crack detective squad?"

Black Jack chuckled. "You know my men are dedicated to their work."

"Yeah? I also know you're short a man."

"Now that you mention it, one of my men has gone missing. Do you have him?"

"He's fish food right about now."

"Pity. He was a good man. It's hard to find such loyalty."

"Maybe not as loyal as you think."

"Perhaps."

"Funny thing about men who are about to die. They do a lot of talking."

"Hmm, so I've heard."

"Let's cut the bullshit. What do you want?"

"It's important to you to get the girl back, so I'll make

you a deal. And we'll both get what we want."

"Yeah? What kind of deal?"

"Simple. All you have to do is come home."

Blood's first reaction was to tell him to go fuck himself, but he took a breath. He couldn't afford to blow this. "And?"

"Leave that club and come back to working for me."

"I never worked for you."

"You were in line for all of this. It's your birthright."

"I don't want it."

"Sure you do. Come home, Son. I'll forgive everything you did. You can run my empire."

"I will never run a fucking thing for you."

"Well, I guess that depends on how badly you want this girl. She's important to someone you care about. So the question is, just what are you willing to sacrifice?"

"You son of a bitch!" Blood hissed out.

"Bring one man with you to take the girl home. Because, Etienne, you won't be leaving. Nine o'clock. Don't be late. You know how I hate to be kept waiting. Oh, and Etienne, you try anything, I'll have my men kill her."

The line went dead, and Blood dropped his arm, a sick feeling settling in his stomach. The last thing he wanted to do was go back to his father—a man he'd hated since he was a boy. But he knew how much Cat needed her sister back, and he'd promised her. He'd promised he'd get her back. He owed her that much. Hell, he owed her his very life. It was more than just a debt now. It was way past that. He'd begun to have feelings for her, and he didn't want to see her hurt. It would absolutely destroy her to lose her sister. Could he bear to see her go through that? She would be completely broken.

Blood looked back at the clubhouse he'd called home for all these years, and he considered Black Jack's terms. *Just how much was he willing to sacrifice to get Cat her sister back?*

CHAPTER TWENTY-FOUR

Blood shoved the phone in his pocket and turned back to the clubhouse. The parking lot and picnic tables were now empty, everyone having headed back inside as the mosquitos came out in force with the night air. He, too, headed inside and glanced around, not seeing Cat. He grabbed Marla's arm as she passed him. "Where's Cat?"

"She said she was going upstairs. I think she was tired."

He nodded. "Thanks, babe."

His brothers were gathered at the bar now, and they flagged him down with a shot. He only intended to have one, but it was hours before he finally called it a night.

When he went up to his room, expecting to find Cat, the room was empty. He strode down the hall to the room she'd been using previously. He tapped on the wood with his knuckle, his shoulder to the frame. A moment later, Cat answered. "Who is it?"

"It's me."

The door opened.

She stood there dressed in nothing but one of his flannel shirts she'd confiscated and her panties. His eyes swept over her, and then he straightened and pushed inside. She backed up a step. His brows rose, and there was a bite to his voice when he asked, "What are you doing in here?"

She glanced at the bed. "I was going to sleep. I figured you'd be with those guys from out of town, partying all night."

In a bed other than his? Oh hell no.

He grabbed her arm and pulled her out of the room and down the hall, disregarding her objections or the way she pulled back.

"Blood, what are you doing? Are you crazy?" she hissed.

He dragged her into his room and slammed the door.

She took a step back, not at all sure what to expect from him. "What the hell do you think you're doing, dragging me around like that?"

"This separate bedroom bullshit is done with. If you're in my clubhouse, then you're in my bed." He arched his brows. "And that's where I want you. Now."

She arched her brows right back at him. "Oh, really? You think you can just order me around."

"Yup. And what's more, you like it. You like me taking control. You're nipples are hard. I can see 'em right through the shirt." He lifted his chin.

She folded her arms over her chest and denied it. "They are not."

"We both know that's a lie."

Her chin came up. She knew it was.

"Done talkin'. Now drop the shirt."

Her hands landed on her hips. "After you just hauled me down the hallway barely dressed? Nuh-uh. We're not having sex now."

"That's exactly what we're gonna do. I need this. I need you." He moved to the door and threw the lock, his eyes never leaving hers. "This is how it's gonna be."

"No."

He prowled slowly toward her, his gaze sweeping over her bare legs and his eyes darkening. "No is not an option. You are a necessity."

"You can't always have your way."

"There are things we can negotiate. This isn't one of them."

She licked her lips, and he cocked a brow at her, reading her mind. She liked this—him taking control. That's exactly what she wanted him to do.

"You like this. Are you going to deny it?" He kept advancing and lifted his chin toward the shirt. He didn't have to say it again.

Her fingers moved to the buttons, and she shimmied it off her shoulders, the soft fabric pooling on the floor at her feet. His eyes swept over her, taking in every inch of that exposed skin.

Her arms lifted, her hands going to her panties, but he stopped her. His voice was low and gravelly as he leaned to her ear, nipping it. "I didn't say you could move."

Her breath caught, and he watched her pretty white teeth

bite into her plump bottom lip. His eyes swept down her body to the panties.

"Those are mine." He bent and slowly slid them down her legs, watching her reaction as he hung them on the bedpost. "They stay right there."

He took her by the arm and spun her around to face the bed. Bending her over it, he kicked her ankles wide with his boot to spread her open as he fumbled with his jeans, releasing the huge erection she'd given him. He slipped his fingers between her legs. *Fuck, yes. She was wet and ready.* He played with her for a moment, spreading her lubrication over both of them. Then he drove into her and fucked her. There were no pretty words for it. He fucked her in long, hard, deep strokes, the kind that had the bed moving every time he slammed home.

He adjusted his angle until he found the one that had her crying out and begging for more. He found the spot that had her losing all control—that spot inside her that caused those delicious moans to rise up from her throat. He answered her with a grunting rumble of his own that rose up from deep within his chest.

She was so hot, so good. He knew he'd never get enough of her. Never.

She was face down on the bed under him, her hands fisted in the sheet, her elbows tucked tight under her.

His body pressed down on her, looming over her. His left hand slid around her throat, lifting her head to him as he kissed her cheekbone.

"You there yet, baby? I can't hold back any longer." He

let go to slide his fingers between her legs. He found that trigger and a moment later she exploded in orgasm. He straightened, grabbed her hips again, and held her tight as he hammered like a piston in and out of her, then planted himself solid as his own climax detonated inside her.

He collapsed beside her, his lungs working like bellows in his sweat-covered chest. He turned his head to look at her. "You okay, babe?"

She nodded and scooted closer, her arm going across his chest.

He repositioned them in the bed, tucking her against his side, their heads on the pillow.

"Blood? Is everything okay?"

He rolled on top of her, going up on his elbows to look down at her face, his hand brushing the hair back from her forehead. "It is now."

She tried to smile, and he saw the sadness in her eyes and noticed the dried tear tracks down her cheeks. His thumbs brushed over them and he frowned. "Cat, did I hurt you?"

She shook her head.

"You were crying before, pretty girl. Why?"

"What if Holly ends up back with the Death Heads?" she whispered. "I want my sister, Blood."

"I'll get her, Cat. Don't worry," he tenderly reassured her, pressing a kiss to her forehead.

"I trust you, Blood. I believe you."

He pulled back to look in her eyes. "I told you before, I'm not like the other bikers you've known. You starting to see that?"

She nodded. "Yes."

"Good."

He needed to let it all go. Right now he didn't want to think about what tomorrow may bring. He didn't want to think about the fact that this may be their last night together. He didn't want to think about the fact that if he went back to his father, he may very well lose Cat in the process.

He knew what his father would expect from him. He'd have to run Black Jack's dirty business—a business he wanted nothing to do with. And he'd have to do it with men who weren't his brothers, men he couldn't trust, men whose only loyalty was to the almighty buck. The whole idea made him sick.

But maybe the only way to bring Black Jack down was from the inside. At least that way he could turn the tide on this alliance his father seemed hell-bent on with the Death Heads. At least he could put a stop to that. His father would no longer feel the need to drive the Evil Dead MC out. They would no longer be a threat to him, because really, the only reason he couldn't abide them was because Blood had chosen them over him.

But setting aside his club, taking off his cut, for good? Could he bring himself to do it?

He brushed the hair back from Cat's face and stared down into her trusting blue eyes. *How could he not?*

He slid down her stomach, kissing every inch of her skin, determined to make it up to her for his earlier roughness. He suckled at her nipples and then glided down farther to her belly button, and then farther, spreading her legs. He noticed some small bruises the size of his fingertips and kissed each one. Then he settled between her thighs. She groaned.

"You sore, baby doll?"

She nodded.

"Blood's gonna make it all better. I promise, baby." Then he set his mouth to her and went about keeping that promise.

***

It was long past midnight, and Blood still hadn't found sleep.

Cat tipped her head up from his chest to see his eyes were open. "Blood?"

"Hmm?" He stroked her back as he stared at the ceiling above the bed.

"I don't want you to get hurt."

He gently pushed her back down to his chest. "I won't, pretty girl."

She drew circles on the club tattoo over his heart with the tip of her finger. "Would you leave this all behind? Would you leave the MC?"

His hand paused in its motion on her back. Her question came just as he was thinking of doing exactly that, just not in the way she was meaning. "Why do you ask?"

She shrugged. "I just wondered."

"Does it bother you that I'm in an MC?

She didn't answer him. "What are you going to do about your father?"

"You ask a lot of questions."

"And you don't give me any answers."

"Answers are something I can't always give."

"You're not going to kill him are you?"

"Why? You don't think he deserves it?"

"It's not that, it's just…"

"What?"

"I don't want that for you. I don't want you to have to carry the weight of that around with you. Another stone for you to carry."

"What are you talking about?"

"That's what your aunt said—that you carried the bad things around with you like a heavy stone."

"My aunt needs to stay out of it."

"She loves you. I could tell."

"Cat, whatever I do about Black Jack won't keep me up at night. Believe me."

"He's your father, Blood."

"He's a piece of shit. Babe, I'll kill him, and I promise you, I'll have no lingering regret at all."

"You could go to prison or get killed."

"Cat, I wasn't asking permission."

CHAPTER TWENTY-FIVE

Smack!

The loud crack of a palm on skin resonated through the room, and Cat immediately felt the sting on her butt cheek.

"Ow! What the hell?" She turned her head in the pillow to find a grinning Blood stretched out next to her.

"Rise and shine, sunshine."

"I could think of better ways to be woken up," she grumbled as she rubbed her sore butt.

"Yeah, so could I, but since I didn't get woken up with a blow job this morning, I guess you're fallin' down on the job."

"Hey, I could have surprised you if you'd given me more time."

"Too late. Get up. Let's go."

She squinted into the morning light. "Go? Go where?"

"Today's the day you're getting your sister back. I'm taking you out for doughnuts to celebrate. Might be the only

time we can spend together today before the shit starts rollin'
around here and I'm pulled in a dozen different directions."

"Doughnuts? Really? Now?" Her face was still half
buried in the pillow, a tangle of blonde hair falling over her
shoulders.

"Yes, Miss Grouchy-in-the-morning! Doughnuts. Really.
Now."

"Ugh."

"Guess I found out you're not a morning person."

"And you are?"

"I don't sleep much, so makes no difference to me. And
you are the only woman I've ever met who can't be cajoled
with chocolate glazed goodness."

She huffed out a breath. "Fine."

"Hey, if you want, I can go find some other girl to go
with me."

She sat up and stuck her tongue out at him. "I'm going,
I'm going."

He grinned and yanked her to him. "I can think of some
other uses for that tongue."

***

An hour and two orgasms later, they sat at an outside
table in front of Mister Sprinkles Doughnut Shop.

Cat licked some chocolate glaze off her thumb. "You're
not going alone, are you?"

"I'm taking one guy with me."

She paused in motion. "One. Why only one?"

"Because that was one of the stipulations."

"But—"

"Look, Cat, there'll be plenty of time to explain everything later, but for now I just have to follow instructions."

"Black Jack's instructions?"

"Yes."

"I don't trust him."

"Yeah, no shit, but I really don't have a choice. He holds the cards. It's my only chance at saving your sister. It all depends on my father keeping his word. So right now I've *gotta* trust him." Blood looked off into the distance.

"Blood?"

"Yeah?"

"Can we go by my place?"

"Why?" Blood looked hesitant.

She frowned at his expression. "You think they're still watching it?"

"Probably not, but you're safer at the clubhouse."

"I just want to have some clothes." She shrugged and explained quietly, "You know, for Holly."

He gave her a small smile. "Sure. We can do that."

***

Blood paced in Cat's living room. They'd already spent almost two hours at her apartment. Cat had wanted to take a shower with her own bath products, and now it was taking her forever to sort through Holly's closet.

Blood's patience was at an end. "Yo. Come on, babe. Let's go."

"In a minute," came the response from down the hall.

His cell phone went off, and he glanced at the screen. *Sandman.* He put the phone to his ear. "Yeah."

"Hey, man. Where are you?"

"Picking up some shit at Cat's apartment. Why?"

"Can you swing by Boozer's and make a pickup?"

"Ain't that what we got Prospects for?"

"They're doin' other shit."

"Let me guess, Undertaker gave this shit job to you and now you're pawning it off on me."

"Well, if you want to put it that way, yeah."

"Asshole."

"You're five minutes from there, douchebag."

"Fine."

"Later, Gator."

"Fuck off." Blood grinned as he disconnected. "Cat, let's roll."

She came into the living room with a bag over her shoulder and a small teddy bear clutched to her chest. Blood eyed the stuffed animal and gave her a questioning look.

She hugged it to her almost shyly. "It's Holly's. I just thought, well…"

He nodded, no further words needed. They both knew that, chances were, Holly would be traumatized, at the very least, when Cat finally got her back. He held the door. "I just need to make a quick stop on the way back."

***

They rolled onto the lot of Boozer's Lounge, a seedy place on the outskirts of the quarter. Regardless of it being only noon, the lot was half full.

Blood led Cat inside the dark bar. It was loud and two guys were adding to the noise, arguing with each other, several tables over. He ignored them, with little more than a cursory glance, and headed toward the bar.

A female bartender approached. "What can I get you?"

"Two shots of Crown."

The woman moved off, and Cat looked at Blood. "We're drinking? I thought you were picking something up."

"I am. Just thought you looked like you could use a drink back at your place."

"I'm fine."

"You sure? It's gonna be a long day. I know waiting isn't easy for you."

The bartender returned and set two short tumblers down, each with half an inch of amber liquor. Blood slid a bill across the bar. "Angelo in the back?"

The woman picked up the bill. Her eyes took in Blood's cut, and she nodded. "I'll get him."

"No need. I know where his office is." He motioned for Cat to wait for him. "Get the lady whatever she wants, okay?"

The bartender nodded. "Sure thing, hon. I'll keep her company while you're gone."

"Thanks."

***

He'd been in the back for fifteen minutes listening to Angelo shoot the shit, this time going on and on about the New Orleans Saints' chances of going to the Super Bowl this year, when suddenly the *whoop-whoop* sound of a squad car siren penetrated the small paneled office and melded over the loud air conditioner. Both Blood and Angelo frowned at each other. Blood pushed his shoulder off the wall, shoved the envelope Angelo had given him into his pocket, and left the rear office.

The crackle of police radios reached his ears as he headed down the back hall toward the bar. He was met with the sight of three officers in the club's doorway, holsters undone and hands on their weapons. The two men who'd been arguing were face down on the ground. There were several tables and chairs overturned and broken glass littered the floor.

"Everyone against the bar," one of the officers ordered the rest of the patrons.

Blood's cut drew their attention. "You! Hands up and move with the others."

Blood did as he was instructed and moved toward where Cat stood. On his way, he noticed a gun lying on the floor, kicked away from one of the culprits.

When he reached Cat, he asked, "You okay?"

"Yes. You missed all the fun."

"Apparently." Blood glanced around, and then

murmured low in a voice only for Cat's ear, "Got a problem."

"What's that?" she whispered back.

"I've got a gun on me. Not supposed to have one in any place that serves alcohol. They catch me with it, they'll haul me in along with these two yahoos. I can't afford to go to jail tonight, Cat. It'll screw up the meet with Black Jack, and we may not have another shot."

She barely hesitated before whispering, "My purse is on the barstool behind you. Slip it in."

Cat had a big slouchy handbag. His gun would easily fit, but if they caught her with it, she'd be the one taking the fall.

"Babe, you know what could happen to you if they find it?"

"Just do it. You can't go to jail tonight, Blood." She moved in front of him to cover his movements, and while the officers were distracted with the other patrons, he slipped it from where it was shoved in the waistband at the small of his back and stashed it into her bag.

An hour later, after the police had taken down everyone's names and gotten everyone's version of events, they were allowed to leave. Cat grabbed her purse, and in her nervousness, she fumbled her grasp on the straps and one hooked on the back of the barstool. When she pulled, it yanked free of her hold and fell to the floor, the gun skidding across the linoleum.

Blood's eyes slid closed. *Shit.*

An officer standing nearby saw it.

Ten minutes later, Cat was in handcuffs and being taken

away. Another officer held Blood back with a hand, threatening to haul him in as well if he didn't step back. He grit his teeth and did as he was told, knowing he couldn't let anything fuck up the meet tonight.

As the police led Cat to the back of the squad car, she turned and called out to him, "Get my sister back for me, Blood! Please."

"I promise, babe. Everything's gonna be fine."

It was hard watching her being taken away, knowing she was taking the fall for him and knowing there was nothing he could do for her now except keep his promise to her.

***

Blood walked into the clubhouse with the duffel bag Cat had packed, the teddy bear sticking out. He saw Easy watching a game of pool. He passed him the envelope he'd picked up at Boozer's along with the bag. "Do me a favor and take the envelope up to Undertaker for me. Put the bag in my room."

Easy straightened and took the items. "Yeah, sure. You okay?"

"Yeah. Thanks." After Easy moved off, Blood saw Sandman sitting at the bar and approached, taking a seat next to him. A moment later, Marla brought him a beer.

Sandman turned and looked behind Blood. "You lose somebody?"

Blood lifted the bottle to his mouth. "She got hauled in, along with my gun."

Sandman huffed out a laugh. "Say what?"

Blood shook his head. "Long story."

"And you're not gonna bail her out?"

"Got something to do first."

"Yeah, what's that?"

"Meet with Black Jack and get her sister back."

That had Sandman straightening on his stool. "You heard from him."

Blood turned to find Sandman's eyes move past his shoulder to the staircase that led to the second floor, and he felt the need to set him straight. "I don't need the club in on this."

"Blood—"

"I can only bring one man with me."

Sandman lifted his chin in understanding. "I'm guessing that's one of his stipulations?"

Blood nodded. "Yeah. You on board?"

"You know I'm on board." Sandman studied his eyes. "You got a plan you ain't tellin' me about?"

"The plan is I go in and make the trade."

"The ring?"

Blood hesitated a moment. "He'll get what he wants, and Cat's sister goes free."

"And he just lets us walk out of there?"

"Something like that."

"Thought you planned to take him out. That still on the menu for the evening?"

The corner of Blood's mouth pulled up. "Depends how it all goes down. I may have to wait for another day to serve up his just desserts. The important thing right now is getting Cat's sister out of there."

"You sure she's even there?"

"Don't know. It's a gamble, I admit. But it's a chance I have to take." Blood looked at Sandman. "You want to skip this trip, I'll understand."

"Fuck off. Try and stop me."

Blood downed his beer and stood. "Let's roll."

"Yeah, I gotta take a piss. I'll meet you out at the bikes in a minute."

Blood nodded. "I need to make a call to our bail bondsman anyway. See you outside."

***

Sandman watched him go, then took out his phone and sent a text to Undertaker, who he knew was up in his office, letting him know what was about to go down.

CHAPTER TWENTY-SIX

Shades and Ghost moved to the back of Black Jack's compound, scoping out the alley.

"We need to get up on the roof," Shades said, looking up.

Ghost leaned back to look at the three-story historic building. "You're out of your mind; that's like, what..? Thirty feet up."

"Yeah, probably."

"And that's terra cotta tiles. You know how hard that is to stand on? And how unstable that shit is?"

"Quit being a whiney ass," Shades said.

"I'd like my whiney ass to stay on the ground, thank you."

"I thought you were afraid of small spaces. You got a problem with heights now, too?"

"No, what I've got a problem with is falling to my death." Ghost looked up. "Besides, how the fuck are we supposed to get up there?"

"The drain pipe."

Ghost looked over at the hundred year old ceramic pipe. "Oh, you have got to be kidding me."

"Nope. Let's go. You want to go first?"

"No. It's your stupid idea, you go first."

Shades grabbed onto it.

Ghost put his arm out, stopping him. "Hold on. Before we do this, I just want you to know one thing."

"What?"

"Whatever happens, I really, really, from the bottom of my heart... hate you so much right now."

Shades huffed out a laugh. "Love you, too, bro."

He started up the pipe, grabbing onto the metal connections and shimmying up. Ghost started up after him. "You realize you fall, you're gonna take us both down."

"Yep."

"And that pipe's gonna probably break loose and fall on top of us."

"Yep."

"Okay. Just checkin'." Ghost started shimmying up after him. "I guess there's worse people I could die under a pile of rock with, huh?"

They made it to the top and lay on their stomachs, surveying the inner courtyard and the surrounding galleries that overlooked it.

A moment later, several more club members slunk up and lay along side them.

"How many men are there?" Bam-Bam asked.

Ghost turned to him frowning. "How the hell did you guys get up here?"

"Used the fire escape on the other side of the building."

Ghost turned to glare at Shades, who just shrugged. "They said to take the back. We took the back."

"So what's the plan?" Bam-Bam asked.

"We need to take out the guy standing on that third floor gallery across the way." Shades observed.

"I can make the shot, but they're gonna hear it," Ghost said.

"Allow me, boys." Easy knelt with a crossbow to his shoulder. He fired, the steel point shooting silently through the air with deadly precision, hitting the man in the throat. He grabbed for his neck, staggered, and pitched forward over the railing to land with a splat two floors below on the stone-tiled courtyard.

The men peered over the edge down at the body.

"Gross," Bam-Bam muttered.

"Clean up, aisle three," Mud said.

Ghost turned to Easy. "Nice shot, man."

Easy shouldered the weapon and grinned. "Did I just blow your mind, or what?"

"You shoot gators with that thing?" Ghost asked.

"You two want to focus on the mission," Shades rebuked them.

***

Blood and Sandman stood in Black Jack's office.

"Let's get on with it. Where is she?" Blood asked.

Black Jack smiled up at him from behind his desk. "All in good time, Etienne. First you have to come through with your end of this deal."

Blood tossed the ring on the desk. Black Jack's eyes flared at the sight of the sparkling emerald. He picked it up and studied it. "Been a long time since I've seen this."

Sandman exchanged a glance with Blood, and both their eyes shifted to the man standing at the door behind them and another at a second side door.

"Show me the girl," Blood bit out.

"You know the ring was only part of the deal. You know what I really want." He stared down Blood, then his eyes dropped to the leather cut Blood wore, and he jerked his chin toward it. "Take it off."

Sandman gave Blood a questioning look.

Blood clenched his jaw. "Let me see the girl, first."

At that qualifying word, Sandman turned on him. "First? What the hell do you mean, first? What the fuck is he talking about?"

Black Jack chuckled. "He didn't tell you?"

At that, Sandman's eyes swung to him. "Tell me what?"

"My son has decided to leave the MC and rejoin the family business. Isn't that right, Etienne?"

"The hell he is. Tell him he's full of shit, Blood."

Blood ignored Sandman and took a step toward Black Jack. "I'm fucking here. Like you asked. Now show me the girl, damn it!"

Black Jack stared him down for a long moment before

nodding to the man behind them.

"Look around. All this—everything I've built—is all your birthright. You'll be King of the Quarter one day now that you've come back home, back where you belong, where you've always belonged."

Sandman glared at Blood. "What the fuck's he talkin' about?" When Blood didn't reply, his brows shot up. "You throwin' down your colors? For *this* asshole? You better tell me that's a fucking joke."

Black Jack, noting the increasing tension in the room, yelled out, "Tanner! Get in here!"

A moment later the door opened, and in strolled Undertaker and several of his men, guns drawn.

"Tanner doesn't work here anymore," Undertaker informed Black Jack with a smile.

Black Jack's one remaining man drew his weapon, but he was outnumbered.

Blood glanced toward Undertaker with a look that said *what the fuck are you doing here?*

Undertaker wasn't about to explain a thing in front of Black Jack and Blood hadn't expected him to, so he ground his teeth and looked back at Black Jack, hoping this hadn't fucked the whole deal up. He knew his father was capable of anything.

Maybe Undertaker thought the man was out of options, but Blood knew better than to underestimate his father. True to his suspicions, Black Jack pushed a button under his desk and several plumes of smoke shot out from the desk and walls, filling the room with a cloudy screen.

The men broke down in coughing fits as Blood dove blindly across the desk for Black Jack, but the man was gone.

Sandman threw open the French doors leading to the balcony to get some air into the room. In the few seconds it took for the smoke to clear, it became apparent that Black Jack was long gone.

"Where the fuck did he go?" Undertaker bit out, coughing. He pointed to the second door. "Search that hallway!"

Blood shook his head and felt along the walls. "He didn't go out that way. The bastard's got a secret passage. I'd bet my life on it. We just need to find it. Goddamn it."

"I've got men all around this place. He won't get far."

Blood tapped the wall and located a section that gave off a hollow sound. He grabbed a gun from one of the men and blasted a dozen rounds into the wallpaper. Then he punched his fist through the wall and began jerking pieces of drywall out. Sandman pitched in and helped him. They found a hollow section with a metal ladder that led down toward the ground level and beyond in the dark shaft. Sandman pulled a small flashlight from his pocket and peered down.

"That goes below ground."

The men were startled as gunfire resonated through the building. Black Jack's men were putting up a fight. Blood looked at Undertaker. "Find Holly for me, please. I'm going after the son of a bitch."

Undertaker nodded. "Be careful. This whole place might be booby-trapped."

Blood nodded.

Mooch tossed another gun to Sandman as he followed Blood into the shaft.

The two men climbed down the ladder, following it down thirty feet before their boots landed on wet ground. They squatted in the tunnel that was only about four feet high, and Sandman flashed his light down the only way it led.

"Shh, listen," Blood bit out. They both strained their ears. "You hear footsteps?"

Sandman looked back up at the shaft. "Can't tell if they're coming from above or not."

"Come on."

The two men moved forward, guns in hand.

***

Above them, Undertaker, Mooch, and Easy all headed down the hall to where Bam-Bam was in a gunfight with a man crouched around a corner. They all fought their way to the end, bullets ricocheting off the walls.

"You smell that?" Mooch asked.

Undertaker turned back toward the main staircase where smoke was drifting up. "They set the place on fire. Shit."

A haze of smoke rose and curled along the ceiling.

"This old place is gonna go up like a tinderbox."

They moved along the hall, their backs pressed to the wall, knowing they only had minutes to find the girl. When they reached the end, the hall opened to the left and to the right. Halfway down the hall to the left were several nervous men guarding a door.

Undertaker pressed his back against the wall around the corner. The men hadn't seen them yet. He could overhear their arguing voices.

"The place is on fire, you moron. I'm not waiting around to burn to death."

The second man put a walkie-talkie to his ear. "Jocko, come in. You there? What's going on?"

"Fuck this shit," the first man said, abandoning his post and the other two men to run down the hall toward where the MC waited. As he came around the corner, Mooch took him out with two shots. He was dead before he hit the oriental carpet runner.

Easy darted into the hall and took out the men still at the door. They slumped to the floor.

Bam-Bam peered around the corner. "They're down."

Just as he said it, more gunfire erupted from the end of the hall to the right.

"Cover me!" Undertaker yelled as he moved to the door the men had been guarding. It was locked, so he kicked it in with a boot. The door gave way and bounced off the interior wall.

His men kept firing as he moved inside.

There was a young terrified girl bound to the bed, a gag tied around her mouth. Her scream behind the dirty rag was muffled, and her eyes were wide with fear.

Undertaker holstered his weapon and put his hands in the air. "I'm here to take you home, sweetheart. I'm not going to hurt you."

Her fearful eyes dropped to his patch-covered leather vest, and Undertaker knew that to her, he was just another one of these monsters.

The smell of smoke drifted into the room with the wisps crawling across the ceiling, reminding Undertaker he didn't have much time. He moved toward her as slowly as he dared and eased onto the bed next to her. "I'm going to take my knife out and cut you loose, honey, okay?"

Her fearful eyes dropped to his hand as he pulled his knife free. She didn't believe he wasn't going to hurt her, and she began to fight against her bounds.

"Easy, girl. Easy. Your sister, Cat, sent me. Your name's Holly, right?"

She nodded.

"I'm going to take you to your sister, Holly. No one's going to hurt you again. I promise." He sliced through the rope. As soon as she was free, she scrambled back on the bed to the corner, pulling the gag from her head.

Undertaker immediately put the knife away and backed off. "It's okay, Holly. I'm here to get you out and bring you home."

She sat in the corner shaking, her eyes darting to the door as Mooch stuck his head in.

"Boss, fire's spreading quick. The lower level is about to go."

"Get the men out. We'll be right behind you," Undertaker said.

"I'm not leaving you here," Mooch protested.

"Get out!" Undertaker snapped. "That's an order."

Mooch's eyes took in the girl, and he moved back out the door.

"The building's on fire, darlin'. We need to get out. The bad men are all dead. You don't have to worry. No one's going to hurt you. I promise."

She shook her head.

Undertaker pulled the small teddy bear he'd tucked in his vest and held it out to her. "Your sister sent this for you. It's yours, right?"

She frowned, reached out, and took it from his hands, clutching it to her. "Cat? She's h-here?"

Undertaker studied her eyes. "She's waiting for you somewhere safe. I'm going to take you to her, I promise. She sent that so you'd know not to be scared."

A moment later, she was across the bed and throwing herself into his arms. He caught her to his chest, holding her tight, and murmured into her ear, "Shh, shh. It's okay. Everything's gonna be okay. I'm gonna get you out of here."

He stroked her head. Her silky hair was the color of corn silk and just as soft under his hand as he whispered, "Are you hurt?"

She shook her head.

He moved toward the door and peered out, but the fire was already coming up the stairs and down the hall. He closed the door and stepped to the window. There was a balcony, thank God. He hefted the window up and climbed out, extending his hand to her. "Come on, sweetheart. We have to hurry."

She slipped her hand in his and climbed out after him.

Undertaker glanced around. There were stairs at the far right of the gallery, but that part of the building was already consumed, the light from the flames casting an orange glow to everything surrounding it. The heat was becoming unbearable. They'd have to go over the rail and down the support post. Undertaker leaned over and studied it. Thankfully it was iron scrollwork, and so he should be able to get a foothold.

A shot pinged off the wrought iron above his head, and Undertaker spun around, drawing his gun. One of Black Jack's men fired from the second floor window of the adjacent wing.

Undertaker shoved Holly behind him, putting himself between her and the threat. He returned fire, and the man pitched forward out the window, plunging to his death.

Holly started to fall apart. Undertaker spun back to her and, with a hand to her cheek, turned her face from the broken body on the ground. "Don't look down. Keep your eyes on mine, darlin'."

She did as he asked, her wide eyes finding and holding his.

"Come on, angel. Take my hand." He climbed over the rail and extended his arm toward her. She peered over the edge and backed away, shaking her head. "Holly, you have to trust me. I won't let you fall."

She glanced toward the flames; the only other way out was no longer an option. Turning back to him with tear-filled eyes, she took a tentative step toward him.

"Thatta girl. Come on."

She took another step and grabbed his hand. His strong arm wrapped around her waist, and he hoisted her over the rail. "Grab onto my back. Wrap your arms around me."

She did as she was told.

"Good girl. Don't let go."

Her hold tightened, and Undertaker struggled down the wrought iron with her clinging to his back.

When they got to the ground, he grabbed her hand and pulled her away from the building as the other side caved in.

She clutched the teddy bear close to her with one hand.

CHAPTER TWENTY-SEVEN

Blood sat on his bike in the parking lot outside the police station where Cat had been held overnight. The club's bail bondsman was inside, bailing her out. The man knew not to speak to her about anything that had gone on, so when Cat walked outside, she didn't know if they had been able to save Holly or not.

One look at her as she walked toward him, and Blood could tell she was making all kinds of assumptions when she saw he was alone. Cat tried to hold it together as she walked, but when she got closer, her face crumpled, and she dashed the last few yards toward him.

Blood's arms opened wide, wanting, for the first time in his life, to comfort a woman and make everything better. Cat flung herself into his waiting arms. He held her tight, his head dipping to hers as she broke down. "Shh, shh… babe. She's okay. We got her."

She pushed out of his arms to stare up at him. "You got

her?"

Blood cupped her cheeks, his thumb brushing her tears away. "She's at the clubhouse. It's over, Cat. It's over."

"Is she okay? I want to see her."

Blood nodded. "I know you do. I'll take you to her. Undertaker's been with her the whole time. He's the one who found her and got her out. He hasn't left her side. She won't let him out of her sight. It's the weirdest shit I ever saw."

"Is she hurt?"

"Physically, she seems okay. Mentally, she's pretty fragile. Undertaker's been very protective of her, and she's latched onto him. But she's been waiting for you. We told her we were going to get you and bring you to her."

"I want to see her."

Blood nodded and brushed the hair back from her face. "How's my little jailbird? Are you okay?"

"I'm fine, but that place was awful. I don't ever want to go back."

"Don't plan on lettin' that happen, babe."

She stared up in his face. "What happened with your father? Did you—"

He shook his head. "He got away. We trailed him through some underground tunnels. They led to another building, but we lost him."

"I'm sorry."

He passed her a helmet and climbed on his bike. She scrambled on the back, and they roared off.

***

Undertaker sat on the bed in the room Cat had been staying in at the Clubhouse. Across from him, sat her sister, Holly, and between them a deck of cards as they played a game of War on the worn chenille bedspread.

His opponent didn't seem to have her head in the game, though, and he could understand that, considering what she'd been through. He'd brought out the deck of cards mainly to get her mind off everything that had happened. That and he was running out of ways to entertain her that didn't involve touching—something he very much wanted to do and was finding it hard to keep a tight rein on.

He'd gained her trust while rescuing her, and ever since then she'd latched onto him, not wanting him to leave her sight. He supposed it was some kind of hero worship, the kind women usually reserved for good-looking firemen, not middle-aged bikers like him—especially one old enough to be her father.

He flipped a ten of diamonds down, and she flipped a queen of hearts. When she didn't scoop up the cards right away, he glanced up at her and gently prodded, "You won, darlin'."

Those pretty blue eyes met his with a vacant stare, and he had to take a breath. She really was so young and innocent, and damned if that didn't pull at him.

He smiled. "Not the first time the queen of hearts has done me in."

That got the corner of her lips tugging up. Pretty pink lips, no lipstick, no gloss, just soft billowy lips that called out to be kissed.

Hell, pull your shit together, old man. She's half your age.

He scooped up the cards and put them in her pile. "You go first this time, sweetheart."

There was a knock at the door, and he turned his head. "Yeah?"

The door opened, and Blood led Cat in. The minute Holly saw her sister, she was off the bed like a shot, the cards scattering, along with the small teddy bear she hadn't let go of since last night.

The two sisters flew into each other's arms.

Undertaker stood from the bed, his eyes connecting with Blood's, and he lifted his chin toward the door, signaling they leave the two girls alone. "We'll let you two catch up."

The moment he did, Holly pushed out of Cat's arms to stare at him, her expression once again filled with anxiety. "You're not leaving, are you?"

Undertaker's grin communicated his patience with the girl. "No, babe. I'll be just down the hall in my office if you need me. You and your sister need some time alone." *Why did the look in her eyes make him feel like he was abandoning her?*

Cat's curious eyes moved between them.

"You'll be fine, Holly. You're safe here. I'm not going far," he assured her.

"Promise?"

"I promise."

She reluctantly nodded, and he and Blood moved out

into the hall.

Blood gave him a look.

Undertaker put his finger to his lips, signaling for Blood to stay quiet. He didn't want Holly to hear him make any comment about the state she was in. He led Blood to his office.

Instead of moving behind the desk, he went straight to a side credenza where he kept his booze. Unscrewing the bottle of Jack, he poured himself a double shot and tried to disregard the tremor in his hand. Tossing it down, he turned to find Blood standing, his arms crossed and a smug look on his face. "You want one?"

"I'm good," Blood replied with a grin.

"Wipe that smile off your face. This shit's not funny."

"Parts of it are."

"The part where a sweet girl like her would turn to the President of the fucking New Orleans chapter of the Evil Dead MC to feel safe?"

"No, the part where it makes you so uncomfortable your hands shake, ol' man."

"Fuck you. My hands aren't shaking." They both knew that was a lie.

"You say so."

"You tell anybody about this, you're a dead man."

Blood let out a rumble of laughter at that. "Right."

"What the fuck am I supposed to do with her? She won't let me out of her sight. I can barely get out of the room long enough to take a piss."

"Gee, a gorgeous young girl can't bear to be from your

side. Cry me a river."

"Bite me. This is serious."

"Cat's here now, so I'm sure she'll transfer all that clinginess—that seems to give you the hives—to her."

"You better be right. It's pretty hard to run an MC when I'm playing babysitter." Undertaker moved behind his desk.

"They come up with any intel off that laptop?"

"Yeah. There's a meet planned between Black Jack and the Death Heads in two days. We plan to crash the party."

"Where at?"

"End of Highway 23."

"Down past Port Sulphur?"

Undertaker nodded. "Wholesale seafood place down there all the way at the end."

"Strange place for a meet."

"Yup. Especially when it's scheduled for two a.m."

"Sounds like something besides seafood coming in on those fishing boats."

"Be my guess."

"How we pullin' this off?"

"We're gonna make it look like Black Jack double crossed his new friends."

Blood nodded. "So the other chapters of the Death Heads can't pin it on us."

"Exactly."

"I like the way you think. How're we getting in and out?"

"Easy's got a cousin with a boat he bought out of Navy salvage. The kind his daddy used to run up and down the

Mekong Delta back when he was a Navy Seal."

Blood chuckled. "You turning this crew into a bunch of Special Op warriors?"

"Sandman's gonna rig the SAW machine gun to it. We're goin' in hot."

"Go big or go home."

"You know it."

Blood moved to leave, but Undertaker stopped him. "Oh, and the kid you brought in, the one who gave these girls up to the Death Heads?"

Blood turned back. "Dax the dick? I'll take care of him." He moved to head for the door again, trying to decide how he'd kill the little punk. He'd promised Cat he'd handle the "Dax problem" for her, and he'd meant it.

"I already did."

Blood turned back, frowning. "What?"

"He's the one responsible for Holly being down the hall right now in the state she's in. So I took care of him. He wasn't gonna draw breath one more minute. She's just a kid. She didn't deserve this."

"You're right, she didn't."

"You good with it?"

"Yeah, I'm good with it." Blood grinned. "Thought that little girl wasn't giving you time alone to piss. How'd you find time for that?"

"I took five minutes."

Blood chuckled as he walked out. "You are so screwed."

CHAPTER TWENTY-EIGHT

Blood stood in the clubhouse parking lot talking with Sandman. The club had just broken up from a meeting about the impending Death Heads demise.

"You gonna have your head in the game?" Sandman asked him.

"Don't I always?"

"That *was* true until a certain blonde nurse showed up."

Blood gave him a look.

Sandman held up his hands. "I'm just callin' 'em like I see 'em."

"I've got some payback to dole out to these sons of bitches. You think I'm gonna fuck that up?"

"Nope. But I don't want you takin' any crazy chances either."

"Me crazy? I think you have me confused with you."

"Ha ha ha. You're a riot."

Blood took a hit off his smoke.

Sandman said, "Hey, remember that beach house we stayed at when we escorted Undertaker's daughter home that first time we met her?"

"Yeah. What about it?"

"How much you think those things go for?"

"Why?"

"I was thinkin' might be fun to have one."

"Unless you've got a million bucks stashed somewhere I don't know about, I think you're out of luck."

"Damn. That much?"

Blood blew out a stream of smoke. "Yup."

"Maybe we could rent one. Kick back with our toes in the sand and a Margarita in our hand." Sandman closed his eyes and smiled, already there.

"Maybe," Blood replied absently, his eyes moving across the lot to see Cat walk out with Marla and sit on one of the picnic tables. It had been two days since her sister was rescued, and she'd spent every minute with her, the two sharing her room.

When Blood saw what the trauma had done to Holly, he knew he didn't want that for Cat. He didn't want to put her in any danger, didn't want her to ever be used in some revenge plot. Hell, he'd almost talked himself into letting her go completely. He kept putting it off, though, making a deal with himself to let it be for one more day.

Soon, before he realized how long he'd been standing there, mindlessly staring at her, Marla was done with her smoke and they were headed back inside.

Cat lifted her chin. He gave it back. It was all he could do. Frustration filled him as he had to watch her walk away, knowing it was best for her, knowing he should let her go. But everything warred inside him. It felt so wrong. He'd never been a man to deny himself anything, least of all a woman. But at the same time, he wanted her safe, he wanted to do what was right for her, what was best for her, even if she couldn't see it. He had to take care of her, protect her. He owed her that, at least. She deserved no less. It was the best gift he could give her—she'd have his protection. Not just now, but for life. That he swore to himself.

None of that made watching her walk across that lot any easier.

He'd been with a lot of women in his life, but he knew this one was going to haunt him till the day he died.

CHAPTER TWENTY-NINE

The MC waited, hidden around the building at the meeting place. Several unmanned fishing boats floated, moored at the docks. The moon shone down on the slow moving water of Sugar Lake Bayou.

Blood glanced at his watch. One-forty-five a.m.

The sound of tires on pavement reached him, and he peered toward the only road in or out.

A black limousine rolled slowly up and turned into the gravel lot. It parked and waited. The driver and another one of Black Jack's men got out of the front. One lit up a cigarette, blowing the smoke toward the sky.

The MC quietly waited, their hands tightening on their weapons. When no one else got out of the vehicle, Undertaker gave a hand signal to his men.

Mooch took out the driver and the second man with two pinpoint sniper shots. They dropped like stones. Next, Ghost flattened both front tires of the vehicle.

Blood stepped into view. "Come on out, Black Jack."

The rear door opened, and he climbed out with his hands in the air. He glanced, not at the dead men, but at the damaged tires. "Was that necessary?"

Undertaker signaled for the men to check the vehicle, and they moved forward, searching it. Shades popped the trunk and pulled out a duffel bag. Unzipping it, he looked up at Undertaker. "Full of cash."

"Well, that's kind of you, Black Jack," Undertaker said as he came forward. He and Black Jack eyed each other as Blood watched the two most influential men in his life face-off.

Undertaker eyed Black Jack with a smirk. "Rules for a gunfight. Bring a gun." He leveled one at the man. "Preferably two." He lifted a second pistol in his other hand. "And bring all your friends who have guns."

The MC all stepped forward, leveling their weapons toward Black Jack.

"You!" Black Jack bit out. "If it wasn't for you, Etienne would never have left me. He'd be running my business now."

"Too bad. Instead, he's running mine." Undertaker couldn't help rubbing it in with a grin.

Black Jack huffed out a laugh, his eyes moving to Blood's. "You left home for this…this two-bit hoodlum? What could he give you that I couldn't?"

"Respect!" Blood snarled. "Something you'll never understand. Something you've never given me."

"We are blood, you and I. Family. That means something."

Blood spit at his feet. "We ain't shit."

Black Jack jerked his hand up, a natural inborn instinct to strike his son.

In a split second, Undertaker's Glock was pressed to Black Jack's forehead. "Consider your next move very carefully."

"He's mine," Blood bit out.

"By all means, *Son*, you do the honors." Undertaker used the term of endearment on purpose—one Blood knew would drive his father crazy. And it did its job. The man's eyes blazed with fury as Undertaker stepped back.

Blood raised his gun, pointing it at his father's head.

Black Jack's eyes shifted from Undertaker to Blood. "You wouldn't kill your own father."

"Wouldn't I? How is it any different from you killing my mother?"

Black Jack stared him down, showing not one iota of remorse.

"Yeah, I know what really happened. You know Big John didn't follow *all* your orders. He buried her." Blood raised his brows. "Your body won't get the same respect. Gator bait is what you're gonna be."

Black Jack's face tightened.

"Startin' to sink in yet? It finally caught up with you— the lies, the secrets, the manipulations. Your reign as King is over. You went too far, and now you're going down."

Black Jack narrowed his eyes. "The night you were shot in that alley—don't you wonder why they didn't let you die? Take a good look at who saved you."

NICOLE JAMES

"You?"

"My name. You being my son is the only thing that kept the Death Heads from finishing the job that night."

His words mean nothing. Remember what he did. Remember what he is. You owe him no gratitude.

Undertaker spoke low in his ear as if he could read Blood's mind, and reinforced his very thoughts. "Don't let him get under your skin. You don't owe this piece of garbage a thing."

Black Jack stepped closer, and all Blood wanted was to blow a hole through his smug face. Even now, his old man thought he'd won. The vision of Blood's mother lying in that bed flashed through his brain, and he couldn't think straight. A blood red rage took over him. *Breathe. In, out.* The gun bucked in his hand, and life left his father's eyes as he crumpled to the ground.

His hand shook as he lowered his weapon and blew out another breath.

Undertaker looked over at him. "You okay?"

"Yeah."

Undertaker nodded, patted him on the shoulder, and looked down at Black Jack's body. He shook his head. "Fathers and sons. What is it about fathers and sons?"

Blood shook his head, with no explanation to give on the subject.

Undertaker barked out orders to the rest of the men. "Prop them back up in the car. Gotta make this look like nothing's wrong."

They hustled to get the job done.

Ghost looked over at Shades, and they both moved to pat Blood on the shoulder, knowing that hadn't been easy for him to do. He acknowledged their gesture with a nod. He was good, but it was bolstering to know he had brothers at his back—ones who would drive across two states at the drop of a hat to help him. He watched as the two bent to the body at his feet and hefted his father into the back of the limo. Then they moved on to the driver.

"This one's a fat boy, isn't he?" Ghost groaned under the man's weight.

Shades chuckled. "Guess he ate his Wheaties."

Blood stood frozen in place, aware of what was happening but somehow removed from it all. Thankfully, he had brothers to take up the slack while he dealt with what he'd just done.

A few minutes later, a panel van crept up the road, slowly breaking Blood from his spell. The men melted back into the shadows.

Undertaker radioed Easy and Sandman who waited upstream in the boat. "Get ready. They're coming up the road. Radio silence."

"Roger that, boss."

Undertaker glanced over at Blood. "You good? Ready to take care of business?"

He nodded. "Absolutely. I've got some payback coming for what these assholes did to me."

Undertaker grinned. "Yeah, you do."

The van rolled to a stop ten yards from the limousine.

Blood's eyes cut to the bayou. It was only twenty yards

from where the vehicles were parked—a clear shot for the machine gun Sandman had mounted on the boat.

Nothing moved as the van sat idling. Finally, the side cargo door slid open. Four men got out. One approached the limousine and tapped on the window.

At that point the MC opened fire. The sound of automatic weapons reverberated through the quiet night as Blood and his brothers sprayed the crowd of Death Heads, catching them completely by surprise.

They killed the driver instantly, making sure none of them had a fast getaway.

The boat came roaring up, and Sandman lit up the 240 SAW, its muzzle spitting fire and mowing down the Death Heads as they attempted to run for cover.

When the gunfire was over and there were nothing but dead bodies, the quiet was deafening. Soon the muffled barking of a dog began and the sound of sirens whining in the distance carried to them.

"We need to get the fuck out of here," Shades told his father-in-law.

Undertaker nodded.

Mooch, who was listening in on the police bands, announced, "Got the whole alphabet comin' boys. FBI, DEA, ATF."

"Tsk, tsk. Sounds like somebody was under investigation," Ghost teased.

"You know what to do," Undertaker snapped.

The men dragged the dead bodies toward the edge of the Bayou and rolled them into the water. There were three from the limousine and six from the van, but they made quick work of it, working in pairs.

"Let's move!" Undertaker snapped when they were all through, and Blood stood watching his father's lifeless body submerging.

They jumped in the boat and turned it upriver to where Sugar Lake Bayou flowed into the Mississippi River. Easy's cousin's Navy salvage boat raced up the murky dark water carrying them all away in the dark of night like some Special Ops hit squad.

In their wake, several gators slipped under the water from off the bank on the other side of the bayou, heading for the blood soaked waters on the other side. A meal well deserved.

Blood grinned.

There may not be much left to find when the alphabet arrived.

He was good with that.

Cat was wrong about the guilt. He wouldn't think of his father again. The man was no more to him than just another roach under his boot.

He had one stop to make, then he could put it all behind him.

Blood turned his face toward the bow of the boat, the wind washing over him. He was headed home—back to see what awaited him.

He suddenly realized that when he thought of home now, it wasn't the clubhouse he thought of. It was Cat. *When had she become home?*

CHAPTER THIRTY

Cat and Holly sat outside the clubhouse at a picnic table, drinking their early morning coffee. It had taken Cat a while to coax her sister out of her room, but it was such a nice morning, and she knew the fresh air would be good for her.

Blood had given her a lot of needed space to spend with her sister, and Cat appreciated it, but she knew he—along with all the men—had gone out last night and hadn't come back. The only thing Cat had been able to discover was that it was club business, and now she was worried. She hadn't heard from him—not that she should expect to, but still, it was the not knowing that put her nerves on edge.

She was afraid for Blood; she could admit it. Not that he couldn't take care of himself, because the man definitely could, but that didn't mean things couldn't go wrong. Sometimes things don't go as planned. Mistakes get made, luck runs out. She just didn't want to think what her life would be like without him in it. And maybe she didn't know exactly what life *with* him would look like, but she knew if he weren't a part of it, there would be a giant hole in her life.

The new girl—the one who had accompanied the two men with the Alabama bottom rockers on their cuts—came outside with her baby.

Cat hadn't been introduced to her yet, but Blood had told her briefly that she was Undertaker's daughter. She approached the picnic table with a big smile on her face, a coffee mug in one hand, and the tiny infant tucked over her opposite shoulder.

"Good morning."

"Good morning," Cat greeted her with a returning smile, noting the girl's long dark hair and sky-blue eyes.

"You ladies are up early this morning. I thought I'd be the only person awake. This little one has had me up since dawn. I'm Skylar by the way." She set her mug down and joined them.

"I'm Cat Randall. This is my sister, Holly." She shook Skylar's hand. "It's cooler this time of the morning, isn't it?"

Skylar grinned. "Yes, it is. But you can't fool me; you're no more a morning person than I am. You're worried about the boys."

"I suppose so. Are you?"

"I try not to be. I know it bothers Shades for me to worry, but sometimes a girl can't help it, you know?"

Cat nodded. "I heard your father is the President here."
Skylar grinned. "He is."

Cat's eyes moved over her. She sure didn't look like some hardened biker chick. No tattoos, minimal jewelry, a pair of jeans, and a white peasant top. Still, Cat had to ask.

"Was it hard growing up in an MC?"

Skylar chuckled. "Unfortunately or luckily, depending on how you want to look at it, I didn't. You see, I didn't know Undertaker was my father until just a couple of years ago."

"Oh? But…you're married to a club member, right?"

"I am, but I grew up in Birmingham. My best friend had a brother who was in the MC. She and I started hanging out at club parties when we were barely out of high school. I met Shades at one of those parties."

"So you've been together a long time then."

"Not exactly. We started seeing each other, but, well, things happened, and I left town. It wasn't until much later that he and I got back together. It was just before I found out Undertaker was my father."

"Sounds like quite a story." Cat nodded to the baby. "Is she your first?"

"Yes, little Rebel is just four weeks old. I thought it was time she got to meet her grandfather."

"She's precious. Can I hold her?"

"Fair warning, she might spit up on you."

"I'm a nurse. A little spit up doesn't scare me."

Skylar passed her the baby. "I have to admit, I've heard a bit about you from my father. He's impressed by you."

Cat couldn't help the look of surprise on her face. "Really?"

"Blood is like a son to him." Skylar gave her a knowing look. "He thinks you're good for him."

"You know Blood?"

Skylar nodded. "Blood and I, let's just say we didn't exactly hit it off when we first met."

Cat grinned. "Imagine that."

Skylar giggled. "I know, right? He can be a bit overbearing."

"A *bit*?"

"But if you're in trouble, he's a good man to have around. He helped me through some stuff. It surprised me, but he turned out to be someone I could kind of lean on, you know?"

Yes, she definitely knew what Skylar meant. "I've leaned on him, too. Pretty much since I met him."

"And what do you think of him?"

"Um, well…" Cat glanced at Holly. She wasn't sure if her sister was ready to hear any of that. Other than Undertaker, Holly really didn't seem to care for the rest of the MC.

Skylar's eyes shifted to Holly. "I'm very sorry for what you went through."

Her sister nodded, then looked off toward the road. "Do you know when he'll be back?"

"Who?"

"Undertaker."

Skylar and Cat exchanged a look. Cat slid her hand over, covered Holly's, and squeezed. "He'll be back soon, honey. Don't worry."

"He promised."

"I know. And we're both here. Do you want to hold this precious little baby?" Cat offered, dropping her hand to coo and tickle the baby's cheek. The tiny thing grinned back at her, her toothless pink gums showing.

Holly stared at the baby and then rubbed her hands on her jean-covered thighs. "I better not."

Cat looked at her, but before she could respond, the three of them heard the distant roar of motorcycles.

Skylar stood with her arms extended. "Here, I better take her inside. Those precious ears aren't ready for all the thunderous noise that's about to descend."

Cat handed her over.

"If you see my husband—he's the blond one—tell him I'm waiting upstairs."

"Of course."

Skylar headed inside, but paused at the door and looked back to give Cat a parting bit of advice. "Don't be too mad at him."

Cat frowned. "Who?"

"Blood." Then she grinned and disappeared inside.

Holly tensed beside her as the sound of a dozen bikes rode up and came through the stockade gate that two Prospects ran to open wide. Cat put her arm around her, but she was too busy searching the bikes for Blood.

Two-dozen tires kicked up quite a bit of dust as the bikes parked in two rows.

The men dismounted and pulled their helmets off.

And then Blood was walking toward her and the tension in her body fell away. He stopped next to the table, and she jumped up and threw herself into his arms. He caught her to him, holding her tight.

"You didn't come back. I thought something happened," she whispered, her voice breaking.

His deep voice was low and reassuring. "Easy, pretty girl. I'm fine."

She pushed out of his arms, embarrassed by her reaction. He was looking at her in a strange way, almost as if he was uncomfortable with her response to his return. Then he stepped back, and she felt like he was trying to put distance between them emotionally. She frowned. *What had happened?*

Undertaker walked up and looked down at Holly. "Hey, kiddo. You made it out of that room."

She nodded, but gave him a look. "You promised. You promised you wouldn't leave."

"I had some business I had to take care of, darlin'. But I'm here now."

She turned her head away, staring off into space and effectively giving him the cold shoulder.

Undertaker and Blood exchanged a look, and then Undertaker moved toward her, took her chin in his hand, and gently turned her head back. "Hey, little one. Look at me."

She finally met his eyes.

"I've got to go talk to the boys for a few minutes, then I'll come see you, okay?"

"Whatever." She pulled her chin out of his hand, and Undertaker dropped his arm.

Blood looked at Cat. "You don't have to worry about that other problem anymore. It's taken care of. I can take you both back home whenever you're ready."

Cat was taken back by his words. *Was it that easy for him to walk away from her? From everything they'd shared? His debt was paid, and he was done? Was that all she'd been to him?*

Undertaker glanced between them, seeming equally as surprised by Blood's attitude. If he was, he didn't comment, just jerked his chin for Blood to follow him.

Blood nodded and both men headed into the clubhouse without another word.

***

The rest of the crew were already inside; most were at the bar having a drink. Blood followed his President, who paused to speak to Mooch.

"Let 'em have a drink, give me a few minutes, then we'll hold a meeting."

"You got it, boss."

Blood followed Undertaker up to his office, where his President poured them both a drink. Blood took a seat in front of the desk, and Undertaker sat on the edge.

They both downed the contents.

Undertaker dropped the glass in his hand to his thigh and studied Blood. "You okay?"

"You already asked me that, and I already answered."

"Don't be a smartass."

"I'm fine."

"Then what was that about?"

"What was what about?"

"Seriously? We're gonna play this fuckin' game?"

"What do you fucking want from me?"

Undertaker shook his head. "Blood, I know you better than anyone, don't I?"

"Maybe."

"Your family was fucked, we both know that, but your mother was a good woman. She loved you. I think you know that now. Maybe subconsciously you always knew that. She tried to protect you. But you perceived betrayal by her—the most influential molding female in your life—and that warped your view of all women. You couldn't trust any of them."

"There a point to this story?"

"I think when you first started to question that view was when you met my daughter, Skylar. If Shades hadn't been in the picture, I think you two would have been quite a pair."

"Think so?" Blood shook his head. "I never had a shot. Her heart was already given away."

"My point is… I think she opened your eyes to the possibilities.

Blood shook his head again. "I was interested in her for one reason—she was your daughter."

"Bullshit."

Blood grinned. "Okay, that and she has a great ass."

"Hey, that's my daughter." Undertaker punched him in the chest.

"And she's married. Why are we talking about this, ol' man?"

"The one thing that's been missing in your life is a

strong female influence. Every man needs that."

"Even you?"

"Even me."

"Again, what's your point?"

"You got your revenge. That's done. But if you let Cat walk out that door, what does any of this matter?"

"We through here?"

Undertaker grinned. "Guess so. We've got a meeting."

"I've got somewhere I need to go first."

"Where's that?"

"Metairie Cemetery."

Undertaker slowly nodded. "Go ahead. You can miss this meeting."

Blood got up and headed toward the door.

"Blood."

He turned back.

"Just think about what I said."

Blood turned the doorknob and walked out. He wasn't halfway down the hall before he ran into Ghost who stood outside the chapel, smoking a joint.

"Are you smoking pot in the clubhouse? Undertaker's gonna kill you."

He held it out to Blood. "Shh, there's not enough for everybody."

Blood accepted it, took a toke, and blew the smoke at the ceiling. "Thanks for your help last night."

Ghost yawned. "I don't know about you, but I'm beat. Probably gonna fall asleep in this meeting. How about you?"

"I'm gonna miss this one. Got somewhere I have to go."

Ghost nodded and changed the subject. "I like her."

"Who?"

"Come on, dude. You know I'm talking about the hot nurse." He took the joint back and drew some into his lungs. Holding it, he asked, "She sticking around?"

"Doubt it."

Ghost exhaled. "You ask her?"

"Who the fuck are you? Dear Abby?"

Ghost chuckled and passed him the joint. "What's the matter, she getting on your nerves?"

"Please, for the love of God, don't try to psychoanalyze me."

Ghost tried to smother his laughter. "You think you're perfect? You think there are things about you that don't irritate her?"

Blood took a toke. "Like what?"

"Your table manners, your swearing, the paint job on your bike…"

"The paint job on my bike?"

"Well, that's actually from my list."

"Douchebag."

Ghost took the joint back from Blood, grinning. "Getting high and talking about women, that's starting to be our thing."

Blood chuckled. "No shit."

"So, what's the deal with her? You gonna make her your ol' lady?"

"I don't know," Blood answered honestly.

"Hey, she took the fall for you on that gun charge. That's

ol' lady material in my book, Bro. By any brother's standards."

"Bein' my ol' lady... Not sure it's what she wants."

"Well, you are kinda homely," Ghost teased.

Blood rolled his eyes and started to walk away, but Ghost stopped him. "Hey? You know I'll always have your back, right?"

"And I'll always have yours." Blood hit him in the chest with a fist. "Brother, I don't want to lose your friendship."

"And I don't want to lose yours."

Blood arched a brow at him. "So, let's stop talking about women."

They both laughed.

"Agreed," Ghost conceded.

Blood headed downstairs. Shades and Skylar were sitting at a table off in the corner, cooing over their baby.

Skylar looked up and saw Blood. When she did, she pushed the baby into Shades' arms and moved toward him. "Blood, wait."

He paused looking over toward her. *Goddamn it.* He knew what was coming. Seems the whole club had an opinion on his love life.

She moved toward him, looped an arm through his, and walked him toward a quiet corner. When they reached it, he tried to distract her from the lecture he was pretty sure was pending. "So, how's the little mama?"

"Happy. Serene. Tired."

They smiled at each other. Blood tucked a strand of hair behind her ear. "Motherhood looks good on you."

"I met your girl."

"She's not my girl."

"Why not?"

"Skylar, don't start."

"I like her."

He nodded. "I like her, too."

"And?"

"And what?"

"Do you more than like her?"

Blood chuckled. "You just don't quit, do you?"

"Don't fuck this up."

He ruffled the hair on the top of her head, then pulled her close and kissed her forehead. "Love you, too, kid."

Then he walked away.

"Blood! Get back here."

He kept walking. "Shades!"

"Yeah, bro?"

"Go take your ol' lady to bed."

"Six week rule, dude. But thanks for rubbing it in."

"Good to know both of us are in hell."

"Yours is gonna last longer than mine, asshole."

Blood flipped him off over his shoulder as he headed out the door.

He found Mama Ray sitting with Holly at one of the picnic tables, talking to her in a quiet, motherly way. Cat was there, too. When she saw him, she got up and walked over to him. His eyes moved to Holly. "Your sister okay?"

Cat glanced back. "She's fragile, but she's starting to talk more. Everyone's been really sweet to her." She turned back to meet his eyes. "I appreciate the way Undertaker has spent time with her. He's been really gentle with her."

"Imagine that? Maybe us bikers aren't so bad after all," he teased.

"He's hardly left her side."

"Way I hear it, that's her idea."

"Pretty strange, huh?"

"Not so strange." He lifted his chin toward Holly. "She good with Mama Ray for an hour?"

"I suppose. Why?"

"I've got somewhere to go. You want to come with me?"

Cat nodded. "All right."

CHAPTER THIRTY-ONE

Cat stood with Blood at the grave of his mother. They'd had to go to the cemetery's office and ask where her plot was. The stone was plain—her name, date of birth and death, and a two-word inscription. *Loving Mother.*

Cat's eyes moved to Blood. He seemed stoic; the only giveaway that the emotions coursing through him ran deep was the tick in his jaw. He stepped forward, pulled something from his pocket, and set it on top of the stone.

It was the tiny statue of the Virgin Mary—the one he'd taken from the dash of her car. He laid his hand on the granite and bowed his head in silent prayer.

Cat watched, her heart breaking for him and for that little boy who lost his mother so long ago.

After a few minutes, he turned and they both headed back to his bike.

"I'll take you home when you're ready," Blood said as they walked.

She stopped and turned to him. "What if that's not what I want?"

"I'm not having this conversation. You don't want this life. This was nice while it lasted, but it's over now. You're going home, back to your life." He started walking away from her.

"You think you get to call the shots? You decide when we're over? You decide how I feel? You decide what we talk about, when we talk about it?" Her words stopped him, and he turned back to her.

"You know my life. I've laid it all out for you. Never lied about what I am. I'm a biker, Cat. So where does that leave us?"

"I know what you are, Blood. You're a good man."

"No, I'm not."

She walked toward him until she was standing in front of him. "You kept your promise to me. You kept your word. I have no regrets. No regrets for anything."

Blood looked off at the horizon.

"Look at me." She put her hand on his sleeve, and he brought his gaze back to her. "Do you want me to leave? Is that what you want?"

He searched her eyes. "I've got shit to offer you."

She smiled. "I've got a good job, Blood. I don't need a man to support me."

***

Blood stared down at her and thought about

Undertaker's words, and Ghost's, and Skylar's. He'd gotten his revenge. But if he let Cat walk away, what did it matter? What did any of it matter? So he took a chance, and he asked, "How about one to warm your bed. You need one of those?"

She gave him a cocky smile. "Maybe. You applying for the job, handsome?"

"Maybe." He pulled her flush against his body and stared deep into her eyes. "You take me on, you take the club on. You ready for that, Little Miss I Hate Bikers?"

She cocked a brow. "I don't know. *Am* I ready for that?"

"The club might not know how strong you are, but I do."

"You do?"

He nodded. "You'll be fine. You've already won over Sandman, Undertaker, Skylar, Ghost, Mama Ray…"

"And Tante Marie. Don't forget about her."

"Never. Do you know what she told me?"

"What?"

"She told me she prayed to St. Jude and you showed up. A gift from God."

"Oh, did she? Well, she told *me* you weren't the wrong man, you were the right man, and I just needed to figure that out."

His face turned serious. "And did you figure it out? Am I the right man?"

She pulled his face down to hers and kissed him long and deep. When she pulled back, she asked, "What do you think?"

He grinned. "I think that's a big yes."

"Do you want me, Blood?"

"Babe, I look in your eyes… and the decision is very clear. Yes, I want you. Always."

"Then why did you try to run me off?"

"I was offering you the chance to go home. If that's where you feel you belong."

"I belong here. I belong with you."

"I've never had a woman in my life I could trust. But I want that, Cat, I do. And I believe I can have it with you."

"Since I proved myself loyal to the club, you mean?" she teased.

"I'm not gonna deny that what you did the other day, taking the fall like you did, it helped gain my trust. But even before that I knew… I knew how lucky I was to find someone so beautiful, so kind, so loyal, strong, and independent."

"Maybe too independent?"

"I wouldn't have it any other way, Cat."

She smiled at him.

"You're the only thing good and clean and right that I've ever had in my life. That I've ever been able to call mine, all mine—that I've ever *wanted* to call mine. You bring out the good in me."

She studied his eyes. "I'll always worry about you."

He took her face in his hands and tilted her head up, his mouth hovering an inch above hers. "I will always be okay. And I will always come back to you. Baby, you've got to know that by now. Right?"

A smile tugged at the corner of her mouth. "I should know that by now, shouldn't I?"

He hefted her up in his arms, grinning as he smacked her ass. "Yeah, babe, you should." He kissed her, then pulled back to ask, "Who's your man?"

She grinned down at him, her arms wrapped around his neck. "You are."

"I'm gonna remind you of that every day until you know it, until you feel it in your bones."

She cocked her head at him and pretended to consider it. "I could get used to that, I suppose."

He chuckled. "Smartass. Let's go home."

She nodded. "Home. And where's that?"

"Anywhere you are, babe. Anywhere you are."

EPILOGUE

Blood—

I rested my hands on the wrought iron railing of my balcony and looked out over the courtyard and the rooftops of the Quarter beyond. The scent of bougainvillea carried to me and I breathed it in. I loved this place. The Quarter had always had a rich history of music, food, architecture, and an atmosphere all its own. It was home—always had been, always would be.

The rumble of a motorcycle echoed up through the surrounding brick buildings as a Prospect for the club rode past. The club patrolled this part of town now. Black Jack was dead, his compound burned to the ground, and his stranglehold on this Parish broken.

Drugs and prostitution weren't completely eliminated from the area, and probably never would be, but a dark, dirty part of it was gone for good. The club had kicked up their presence, intent on not letting another dirty player step up and fill Black Jack's void. Not today. Not ever, if I had my way.

The Death Heads were long gone, too. Word was the national officers had believed Black Jack had turned on them, not realizing we'd had any involvement. There would still be turf wars to deal with in the future, clubs always wanting to push out their territories, but not today.

"Blood, you're missing the game!" Ghost called from the living room where a bunch of my club—correction, *my family*—were gathered to watch the first Saints game of the season.

Skylar stepped out on the balcony with me, her infant snuggled against her chest. "You okay, Blood?"

I gave her a smile, my finger reaching up to tickle the tiny baby's cheek. She clutched onto it with a tight grip, and Skylar and I exchanged a laugh. "Little Bit has a strong grip."

"Her name's not Little Bit, Blood. It's Rebel."

"Well, Miss Rebel, you keeping mama up at night?"

"She's having a hard time getting her days and nights straight, that's for sure." Skylar yawned.

"Here, let me hold her." I reached for the baby, and Skylar gladly passed her over to me. I cuddled her against my chest, her little butt supported with my forearm while I cradled her back with my big hand.

Dipping my nose to the top of her downy head, I breathed in that new baby smell. It was even sweeter than the bougainvillea.

"You look good with a baby in your arms." Skylar

smiled up at me. "Maybe you should get one of your own."

My eyes lifted to hers. It wasn't something I'd let myself consider until now. "Think so?"

She nodded. "I do."

"Don't know what kind of a father I'd make." Not two weeks ago, the idea would have been preposterous, unthinkable. Now, not so much.

"If you have love to give, that's all you need."

I huffed out a laugh and teased her, something I was good at. "Yeah, babe. Think the Beatles wrote a song about that."

She punched my shoulder. "Shut up."

I smiled down at her, and she smiled back. The baby clutched my soft black t-shirt, her toothless gums gnawing on it and leaving a wet spot. As her tiny fist found her mouth, and she suckled on it, her tiny jaw working, I thought about how life sure could change on a dime. It hadn't been long ago that I'd sat on this very balcony and thought about how something was missing from my life, how there was a part I thought would never be filled, how I thought I'd never get beyond the pain and damage of a tortured past I thought would haunt me forever. Somehow I was starting to put it behind me with the help of a good woman—a woman who was filling that gaping hole in my life and my heart.

I glanced down and saw a car rolling into the courtyard. *Cat.*

She climbed from the vehicle and glanced up, spotting us. I could see her face soften with love as she took in the scene on the balcony—me holding a baby to my chest.

She smiled up at me, her face bright as the sun, and my heart flooded with warmth.

And for the first time ever I could see a future that contained more than just the club—a future with this woman. A future that looked bright as that smile she gave me.

Cat—

I climbed from the car after just having come from the clubhouse. My sister was still staying there, refusing to be far from Undertaker. It was the only place she felt safe. He was kind, patient, and wonderful with her, and I was so grateful to him, but I knew this couldn't go on much longer. I'd already made plans to get her counseling, I was just going to have to take it slow. Undertaker had graciously agreed to let her stay as long as she needed.

He really was sweet with her, and it was a sight to see.

I closed the car door and looked up.

Blood stood on the balcony with Skylar. They both smiled down at me. I was glad the boys had come over to spend some time before some of them would be leaving town, heading back home. Blood needed it. He'd never admit that everything that had transpired had rocked him. But I knew better.

Everything he knew to be true had been shaken, turned on its head, and that took some time to adjust to. That was okay. I'd make sure he had that time.

Now, seeing him with that baby cuddled to his chest, so

tiny that his hand covered her entire back from cute little tush to the base of her wobbly neck—it did something to me. A feeling like warm honey spread through my chest and melted my heart.

I wanted to give him that—a family of his own. Maybe one day he'd be ready. Maybe, judging by the way he grinned down at me, a look of contentment on his face, it would be soon.

I know it had all happened fast, a matter of weeks really, but I also knew, rock solid and true, down to the essence of my being that I loved that man. Already I couldn't imagine a life without him, and I hoped I never would have to. He took care of me, watched out for me, protected me, and made me feel safe in a way I knew he always would.

That was just his way, and I loved that about him. I knew I could count on him to always be there when life went sideways and things went wrong. That moment we'd shared in the shower the first time I was in his place—he'd told me to hold on to the moment, to remember it when times got rough. And I would, but I also knew there would be many more precious moments to share, other moments I could remember and take out and hold onto when times got bad.

Life held promise now—the promise I'd hoped it would hold when I'd first moved to New Orleans. I'd wanted color in my life, and now I had it. I just hadn't expected it would come with a man who wore colors of his own on the back of his leather.

I smiled. I was good with that... *more* than good.

I headed inside to drink a beer and watch the Saints

game with my man and the people he loved and thought of as family—people who were fast becoming family to me as well.

As I walked toward the stairs I looked up at Blood and lifted my chin to him. It was kind of our thing. He winked at me and lifted his chin in return.

And that was all I needed.

The End

PREVIEW OF
UNDERTAKER

When Undertaker saved an innocent young girl from the clutches of a rival MC, he never expected she'd form an attachment to him, refusing to leave the safety of his clubhouse.

But the President of the Evil Dead MC had a club to run. What he didn't have was the time or the experience to help Holly get past the traumatic experience she'd been through. Counseling was what she needed, and he would see she gets it.

The last thing Undertaker expected when that therapist walked through his clubhouse doors was a face from his past.

They'd met years ago when he'd been ordered into counseling as part of his parole. Eleven years locked in a cell does things to a man, but back then Undertaker hadn't had time to deal with all his demons. He had a motorcycle club he needed to get back to, and an untimely death in the ranks had him stepping up to fill the spot of President and fulfill his destiny—one that didn't include the fresh-out-of-college psychology intern who'd been put in charge of his case. She'd known nothing of his problems. How could she?

Besides, he'd scared her to death.

Now, a dozen years later, fate was coming around again, throwing them back together. But Allison Carter wasn't that naïve girl anymore; she was all woman now.

And the President of the Evil Dead's New Orleans Chapter was about to make her his.

Only problem was, he had to let one sweet girl down easy before he could pursue her hot-as-sin therapist.

It wouldn't be so simple when trouble from his past threatened everything.

When an ex-con biker sets his sight on you, do you run? No?

Not even if he comes with more trouble than you can handle?

If you enjoyed Blood, please post a review on Amazon.

Also by Nicole James:

OUTLAW: An Evil Dead MC Story (Book 1)

CRASH: An Evil Dead MC Story (Book 2)

SHADES: An Evil Dead MC Story (Book 3)

WOLF: An Evil Dead MC Story (Book 4)

GHOST: An Evil Dead MC Story (Book 5)

RED DOG: An Evil Dead MC Novella (Book 6)

JAMESON: Brothers Ink Series (Book 1)

RUBY FALLS – Romantic Suspense

Join my newsletter
http://eepurl.com/biN_p5
Connect with me on Facebook
https://www.facebook.com/Nicole-James-533220360061689
Website
www.nicolejames.net

Made in the USA
Coppell, TX
22 February 2023

13282743R00218